GREAT FRENCH SHORT STORIES

Andre Laurent is a literary enthusiast whose passion for English literature has transcended borders and captivated audiences around the world. Born and raised in the enchanting streets of Paris, France, Pierre's love for the written word ignited at an early age. Drawn to the eloquence and intricacy of the English language, he embarked on a remarkable journey to unravel the beauty of literature beyond his native tongue. Throughout his career, Laurent's unique perspective as a Frenchman with an ardent passion for English literature has lent a distinctive flavour to his writing. His ability to seamlessly blend the poetic sensibilities of French literature with the narrative prowess of English storytelling has earned him a dedicated following of readers from diverse cultural backgrounds.

GREAT FRENCH SHORT STORIES

Compiled by **ANDRE LAURENT**

Published by
Rupa Publications India Pvt. Ltd 2023
7/16, Ansari Road, Daryaganj
New Delhi 110002

Sales centres:
Bengaluru Chennai
Hyderabad Jaipur Kathmandu
Kolkata Mumbai Prayagraj

Copyright © Rupa Publications India Pvt. Ltd 2023

All rights reserved.
No part of this publication may be reproduced, transmitted,
or stored in a retrieval system, in any form or by any means,
electronic, mechanical, photocopying, recording or otherwise,
without the prior permission of the publisher.

P-ISBN: 978-93-5702-545-4
E-ISBN: 978-93-5702-546-1

Second impression 2024

10 9 8 7 6 5 4 3 2

Printed in India

This book is sold subject to the condition that it shall not,
by way of trade or otherwise, be lent, resold, hired out, or otherwise
circulated, without the publisher's prior consent, in any form of binding
or cover other than that in which it is published.

CONTENTS

1. The Mirror — Catulle Mendès … 1
2. The Blind of One Eye — François-Marie Arouet de Voltaire … 6
3. The Nose — Voltaire … 10
4. The Envious Man — Voltaire … 16
5. The Minister — Voltaire … 21
6. The Disputes and the Audiences — Voltaire … 23
7. Jealousy — Voltaire … 26
8. The Woman Beaten — Voltaire … 31
9. The Stone — Voltaire … 34
10. The Funeral Pile — Voltaire … 36
11. The Supper — Voltaire … 39
12. The Robber — Voltaire … 41

13. The Fisherman 45
    Voltaire

14. The Guilty Secret 48
    Paul de Kock

15. The Birds in the Letter-Box 56
    René Bazin

16. The Passage of the Red Sea 63
    Henri Murger

17. The Woman and the Cat 70
    Marcel Prévost

18. Tonton 79
    Adolphe Chenevière

19. Father Milon 85
    Guy de Maupassant

20. The Colonel's Ideas 92
    Guy de Maupassant

21. The Moustache 98
    Guy de Maupassant

22. The Blind Man 102
    Guy de Maupassant

23. Indiscretion 107
    Guy de Maupassant

24. Beside Schopenhauer's Corpse 112
    Guy de Maupassant

25. The Door 117
    Guy de Maupassant

26. The Marquis de Fumerol 123
    Guy de Maupassant

27. The Thief *Guy de Maupassant*	131
28. A Vendetta *Guy de Maupassant*	136
29. Legend of Mont St. Michel *Guy de Maupassant*	141
30. My Wife *Guy de Maupassant*	146
31. Clochette *Guy de Maupassant*	153
32. The Beggar *Guy de Maupassant*	159
33. In the Woods *Guy de Maupassant*	165
34. Moonlight *Guy de Maupassant*	171
35. The Love of Long Ago *Guy de Maupassant*	176
36. Friend Joseph *Guy de Maupassant*	181
37. The Effeminates *Guy de Maupassant*	187
38. Rosalie Prudent *Guy de Maupassant*	192
39. The Grave *Guy de Maupassant*	197
40. The Englishman of Étretat *Guy de Maupassant*	201

41.	An Uncomfortable Bed Guy de Maupassant	205
42.	A Portrait Guy de Maupassant	208
43.	The Maid of Thilouse Honore de Balzac	212
44.	How the Pretty Maid of Portillon Convinced Her Judge Honore de Balzac	219
45.	Odd Sayings of Three Pilgrims Honore de Balzac	226
46.	Innocence Honore de Balzac	232
47.	Amycus and Célestine Anatole France	235
48.	The Mass of Shadows Anatole France	240
49.	The Boon of Death Bestowed Anatole France	246
50.	The Last Lesson Alphonse Daudet	250

THE MIRROR

Catulle Mendès

There was once a kingdom where mirrors were unknown. They had all been broken and reduced to fragments by order of the queen, and if the tiniest bit of looking-glass had been found in any house, she would not have hesitated to put all the inmates to death with the most frightful tortures.

Now for the secret of this extraordinary caprice. The queen was dreadfully ugly, and she did not wish to be exposed to the risk of meeting her own image; and, knowing herself to be hideous, it was a consolation to know that other women at least could not see that they were pretty.

You may imagine that the young girls of the country were not at all satisfied. What was the use of being beautiful if you could not admire yourself?

They might have used the brooks and lakes for mirrors; but the queen had foreseen that, and had hidden all of them under closely joined flagstones. Water was drawn from wells so deep that it was impossible to see the liquid surface, and shallow basins were used instead of buckets, because in the latter, there might be reflections.

Such a dismal state of affairs, especially for the pretty coquettes, who were no rarer in this country than in others.

The queen had no compassion, being well content that her subjects should suffer as much annoyance from the lack of a mirror as she felt at the sight of one.

However, in a suburb of the city, there lived a young girl called Jacinta, who was a little better-off than the rest, thanks to her sweetheart, Valentin. For if someone thinks you are beautiful, and loses no chance to tell you so, he is almost as good as a mirror.

'Tell me the truth,' she would say; 'what is the colour of my eyes?'

'They are like dewy forget-me-nots.'

'And my skin is not quite black?'

'You know that your forehead is whiter than freshly fallen snow, and your cheeks are like blush roses.'

'How about my lips?'

'Cherries are pale beside them.'

'And my teeth, if you please?'

'Grains of rice are not as white.'

'But my ears, should I be ashamed of them?'

'Yes, if you would be ashamed of two little pink shells among your pretty curls.'

And so on endlessly; she was delighted, he still charmed more, for his words came from the depth of his heart, and she had the pleasure of hearing herself praised, and he had the delight of seeing her. So, their love grew deeper and more tender every hour, and the day he asked her to marry him, she blushed certainly, but it was not with anger. But, unluckily, the news of their happiness reached the wicked queen, whose only pleasure was to torment others, and Jacinta more than anyone else, on account of her beauty.

A little while before the marriage, Jacinta was walking in the orchard one evening, when an old crone approached, asking for alms, but suddenly jumped back with a shriek as if she had stepped on a toad, crying, 'Heavens, what do I see?'

'What is the matter, my good woman? What is it you see? Tell me.'

'The ugliest creature I ever beheld.'

'Then you are not looking at me,' said Jacinta, with innocent vanity.

'Alas! Yes, my poor child, it is you. I have been on this earth for a long time, but never have I met anyone so hideous as you!'

'What! Am I ugly?'

'A hundred times uglier than I can tell you.'

'But my eyes—'

'They are a sort of dirty grey; but that would be nothing if you had not such an outrageous squint!'

'My complexion—'

'It looks as if you had rubbed coal-dust on your forehead and cheeks.'

'My mouth—'

'It is pale and withered, like a faded flower.'

'My teeth—'

'If the beauty of teeth is to be large and yellow, I never saw any so beautiful as yours.'

'But, at least, my ears—'

'They are so big, so red, and so misshapen, under your coarse elf-locks, that they are revolting. I am not pretty myself, but I should die of shame if mine were like them.' After this last blow, the old witch, having repeated what the queen had taught her, hobbled off, with a harsh croak of laughter, leaving poor Jacinta dissolved in tears, prone on the ground beneath the apple-trees.

Nothing could divert her mind from her grief. 'I am ugly—I am ugly,' she repeated constantly. It was in vain that Valentin assured and reassured her with the most solemn oaths. 'Let me alone; you are lying out of pity. I understand it all now; you never loved me; you are only sorry for me. The beggar woman had no interest in deceiving me. It is only too true—I am ugly. I do not see how you can endure the sight of me.'

To undeceive her, he brought people from far and near; every man declared that Jacinta was created to delight the eyes; even the women said as much, though they were less enthusiastic. But the poor child persisted in her conviction that she was a repulsive object, and when Valentin pressed her to name their wedding-day—'I, your wife!' cried she, 'Never! I love you too dearly to burden you with a being so hideous as I am.' You can fancy the despair of the poor fellow so sincerely in love. He threw himself on his knees; he prayed; he supplicated; she answered still that she was too ugly to marry him.

What was he to do? The only way to give the lie to the old woman and prove the truth to Jacinta was to put a mirror before her. But there was no such thing in the kingdom, and so great was the terror inspired by the queen that no workman dared make one.

'Well, I shall go to Court,' said the lover, in despair. 'Harsh as our mistress is, she cannot fail to be moved by the tears and the beauty of Jacinta. She will retract, for a few hours at least, this cruel edict which has caused our trouble.'

It was not without difficulty that he persuaded the young girl to let him take her to the palace. She did not like to show herself, and asked of what use would be a mirror, only to impress her more deeply with her misfortune; but when he wept, her heart was moved, and she consented, to please him.

'What is all this?' said the wicked queen, 'Who are these people? And what do they want?'

'Your Majesty, you have before you the most unfortunate lover on the face of the earth.'

'Do you consider that a good reason for coming here to annoy me?'

'Have pity on me.'

'What have I to do with your love affairs?'

'If you would permit a mirror——'

The queen rose to her feet, trembling with rage. 'Who dares to speak to me of a mirror?' she said, grinding her teeth.

'Do not be angry, Your Majesty, I beg of you, and deign to hear me. This young girl whom you see before you, so fresh and pretty, is the victim of a strange delusion. She imagines that she is ugly.'

'Well,' said the queen, with a malicious grin, 'she is right. I never saw a more hideous object.'

Jacinta, at these cruel words, thought she would die of mortification. Doubt was no longer possible, she must be ugly. Her eyes closed, she fell on the steps of the throne in a deadly swoon.

But Valentin was affected very differently. He cried out loudly that Her Majesty must be mad to tell such a lie. He had no time to say more. The guards seized him, and at a sign from the queen, the headsman came forward. He was always beside the throne, for she might need his services at any moment.

'Do your duty,' said the queen, pointing out the man who had insulted her. The executioner raised his gleaming axe just as Jacinta came to herself and opened her eyes. Then two shrieks pierced the air. One was a cry of joy, for in the glittering steel Jacinta saw herself, so charmingly pretty—and the other a scream of anguish, as the wicked soul of the queen took flight, unable to bear the sight of her face in the impromptu mirror.

THE BLIND OF ONE EYE

François-Marie Arouet de Voltaire

There lived at Babylon, in the reign of King Moabdar, a young man named Zadig, of a good natural disposition, strengthened and improved by education. Though rich and young, he had learned to moderate his passions; he had nothing stiff or affected in his behaviour, he did not pretend to examine every action by the strict rules of reason, but was always ready to make proper allowances for the weakness of mankind.

It was a matter of surprise that, notwithstanding his sprightly wit, he never exposed by his raillery those vague, incoherent, and noisy discourses, those rash censures, ignorant decisions, coarse jests, and all that empty jingle of words which at Babylon went by the name of conversation. He had learned, in the first book of Zoroaster, that self-love is a football swelled with wind, from which, when pierced, the most terrible tempests issue forth.

Above all, Zadig never boasted of his conquests among the women, nor affected to entertain a contemptible opinion of the fair sex. He was generous, and was never afraid of obliging the ungrateful; remembering the grand precept of Zoroaster, 'When thou eatest, give to the dogs, should they even bite thee.' He was as wise as it is possible for man to be, for he sought to live with the wise.

Instructed in the sciences of the ancient Chaldeans, he understood the principles of natural philosophy, such as they were then supposed to be; and knew as much of metaphysics as hath ever been known in any age, that is, little or nothing at all. He was firmly persuaded, notwithstanding the new philosophy of the times, that the year consisted of three hundred and sixty-five days and six hours, and that the sun was in the centre of the world. But when the principal magi told him, with a haughty and contemptuous air, that his sentiments were of a dangerous tendency, and that it was to be an enemy to the state to believe that the sun revolved round its own axis, and that the year had twelve months, he held his tongue with great modesty and meekness.

Possessed as he was of great riches, and consequently of many friends, blessed with a good constitution, a handsome figure, a mind just and moderate, and a heart noble and sincere, he fondly imagined that he might easily be happy. He was going to be married to Semira, who, in point of beauty, birth, and fortune, was the first match in Babylon. He had a real and virtuous affection for this lady, and she loved him with the most passionate fondness.

The happy moment was almost arrived that was to unite them forever in the bands of wedlock, when happening to take a walk together toward one of the gates of Babylon, under the palm trees that adorn the banks of the Euphrates, they saw some men approaching, armed with sabres and arrows. These were the attendants of young Orcan, the minister's nephew, whom his uncle's creatures had flattered into an opinion that he might do everything with impunity. He had none of the graces nor virtues of Zadig; but thinking himself a much more accomplished man, he was enraged to find that the other was preferred before him. This jealousy, which was merely the effect of his vanity, made him imagine that he was desperately in love with Semira; and accordingly he resolved to carry her off. The ravishers seized her; in the violence of the outrage they wounded her, and made the blood flow from her person, the sight of which would have softened the tigers of Mount Imaus. She pierced the heavens with her complaints. She cried out, 'My dear husband! They tear me from the man I adore.' Regardless of her own danger, she was only concerned for the fate of her dear Zadig, who, in the meantime, defended himself with all the strength that courage and love could inspire. Assisted only by two slaves, he put the ravishers to flight and carried home Semira, insensible and bloody as she was.

On opening her eyes and beholding her deliverer, 'O Zadig!' said she, 'I loved thee formerly as my intended husband; I now love thee as the preserver of my honour and my life.' Never was a heart more deeply affected than that of Semira. Never did a more charming mouth express more moving sentiments, in those glowing words inspired by a sense of the greatest of all favours, and by the most tender transports of a lawful passion.

Her wound was slight and was soon cured. Zadig was more dangerously wounded; an arrow had pierced him near his eye, and penetrated to a considerable depth. Semira wearied Heaven with her prayers for the recovery of her lover. Her eyes were constantly bathed in tears; she anxiously awaited the happy moment when those of Zadig should be able to meet hers; but an abscess growing on the wounded eye gave everything to fear. A messenger was immediately dispatched to Memphis for the great physician Hermes, who came with a numerous retinue. He visited the patient and declared that he would lose his eye. He even foretold the day and hour when this fatal event would happen. 'Had it been the right eye,' said he, 'I could easily have cured it; but the wounds of the left eye are incurable.' All of Babylon lamented the fate of Zadig, and admired the profound knowledge of Hermes.

In two days the abscess broke of its own accord and Zadig was perfectly cured. Hermes wrote a book to prove that it ought not to have been cured. Zadig did not read it; but, as soon as he was able to go abroad, he went to pay a visit to her in whom all his hopes of happiness were centred, and for whose sake alone he wished to have eyes. Semira had been in the country for three days past. He learned on the road that that fine lady, having openly declared that she had an unconquerable aversion to one-eyed men, had the night before given her hand to Orcan. At this news he fell speechless to the ground. His sorrow brought him almost to the brink of the grave. He was long indisposed; but reason at last got the better of his affliction, and the severity of his fate served to console him.

'Since,' said he, 'I have suffered so much from the cruel caprice of a woman educated at court, I must now think of marrying the daughter of a citizen.' He pitched upon Azora, a lady of the greatest prudence, and of the best family in town. He married her and lived with her for three months in all the delights of the most tender union. He only observed that she had a little levity; and was too apt to find that those young men who had the most handsome persons were likewise possessed of most wit and virtue.

Note: This story has been taken from *Zadig the Babylonian*, a novella by Voltaire. Please keep in mind that its context might not be fully conveyed when read independently due to the overarching structure of the larger tale.

THE NOSE

Voltaire

One morning Azora returned from a walk in a terrible passion, uttering the most violent exclamations. 'What aileth thee,' said he, 'my dear spouse? What is it that can thus have discomposed thee?'

'Alas,' said she, 'thou wouldst be as much enraged as I am hadst thou seen what I have just beheld. I have been to comfort the young widow Cosrou, who, within these two days, hath raised a tomb to her young husband, near the rivulet that washes the skirts of this meadow. She vowed to heaven, in the bitterness of her grief, to remain at this tomb while the water of the rivulet should continue to run near it.' 'Well,' said Zadig, 'she is an excellent woman, and loved her husband with the most sincere affection.'

'Ah,' replied Azora, 'didst thou but know in what she was employed when I went to wait upon her!'

'In what, pray, beautiful Azora? Was she turning the course of the rivulet?'

Azora broke out into such long invectives and loaded the young widow with such bitter reproaches, that Zadig was far from being pleased with this ostentation of virtue.

Zadig had a friend named Cador, one of those young men in whom his wife discovered more probity and merit than in others. He made him his confidant, and secured his fidelity as much as possible by a considerable present. Azora, having passed two days with a friend in the country, returned home on the third. The servants told her, with tears in their eyes, that her husband died suddenly the night before; that they were afraid to send her an account of this mournful event; and that they had just been depositing his corpse in the tomb of his ancestors, at the end of the garden.

She wept, she tore her hair, and swore she would follow him to the grave.

In the evening Cador begged leave to wait upon her, and joined his tears with hers. Next day they wept less, and dined together. Cador told her that his friend had left him the greatest part of his estate; and that he should think himself extremely happy in sharing his fortune with her. The lady wept, fell into a passion, and at last became more mild and gentle. They sat longer at supper than at dinner. They now talked with greater confidence. Azora praised the deceased; but owned that he had many failings from which Cador was free.

During supper Cador complained of a violent pain in his side. The lady, greatly concerned, and eager to serve him, caused all kinds of essences to be brought, with which she anointed him, to try if some of them might not possibly ease him of his pain. She lamented that the great Hermes was not still in Babylon. She even condescended to touch the side in which Cador felt such exquisite pain.

'Art thou subject to this cruel disorder?' said she to him with a compassionate air.

'It sometimes brings me,' replied Cador, 'to the brink of the grave; and there is but one remedy that can give me relief, and that is to apply to my side the nose of a man who is lately dead.'

'A strange remedy, indeed!' said Azora.

'Not more strange,' replied he, 'than the sachels of Arnon against the apoplexy.' This reason, added to the great merit of the young man, at last determined the lady.

'After all,' said she, 'when my husband shall cross the bridge Tchinavar, in his journey to the other world, the angel Asrael will not refuse him a passage because his nose is a little shorter in the second life than it was in the first.' She then took a razor, went to her husband's tomb, bedewed it with her tears, and drew near to cut off the nose of Zadig, whom she found extended at full length in the tomb. Zadig arose, holding his nose with one hand, and, putting back the razor with the other, 'Madam,' said he, 'don't exclaim so violently against young Cosrou; the project of cutting off my nose is equal to that of turning the course of a rivulet.' Zadig found by experience that the first month of marriage, as it is written in the book of Zend, is the moon of honey, and that the second is the moon of wormwood. He was some time after obliged to repudiate Azora, who became too difficult to be pleased; and he then sought for happiness in the study of nature. 'No man,' said he, 'can be happier than a philosopher who reads in this great book which God hath placed before our eyes. The truths he discovers are his own; he nourishes and exalts his soul; he lives in peace; he fears nothing from men; and his tender spouse will not come to cut off his nose.'

Possessed of these ideas, he retired to a country house on the banks of the Euphrates. There he did not employ himself in calculating how many inches of water flow in a second of time under the arches of a bridge, or whether there fell a cube line of rain in the month of the Mouse more than in the month of the Sheep. He never dreamed of making silk of cobwebs, or porcelain of broken bottles; but he chiefly studied the properties of plants and animals; and soon acquired a sagacity that made him discover a thousand differences where other men see nothing but uniformity.

One day, as he was walking near a little wood, he saw one of the queen's eunuchs running toward him, followed by several officers, who appeared to be in great perplexity, and who ran to and fro like men distracted, eagerly searching for something they had lost of great value. 'Young man,' said the first eunuch, 'hast thou seen the queen's dog?' 'It is a female,' replied Zadig. 'Thou art in the right,' returned the first eunuch. 'It is a very small she-spaniel,' added Zadig; 'She has lately whelped; she limps on the left forefoot, and has very long ears.' 'Thou hast seen her,' said the first eunuch, quite out of breath. 'No,' replied Zadig, 'I have not seen her, nor did I so much as know that the queen had a dog.'

Exactly at the same time, by one of the common freaks of fortune, the finest horse in the king's stable had escaped from the jockey in the plains of Babylon. The principal huntsman and all the other officers ran after him with as much eagerness and anxiety as the first eunuch had done after the spaniel. The principal huntsman addressed himself to Zadig, and asked him if he had not seen the king's horse passing by. 'He is the fleetest horse in the king's stable,' replied Zadig; 'he is five feet high, with very small hoofs, and a tail three feet and a half in length; the studs on his bit are gold of twenty-three carats, and his shoes are silver of eleven pennyweights.' 'What way did he take? Where is he?' demanded the chief huntsman. 'I have not seen him,' replied Zadig, 'and never heard talk of him before.'

The principal huntsman and the first eunuch never doubted but that Zadig had stolen the king's horse and the queen's spaniel. They therefore had him conducted before the assembly of the grand Desterham, who condemned him to the knout, and to spend the rest of his days in Siberia. Hardly was the sentence passed when the horse and the spaniel were both found. The judges were reduced to the disagreeable necessity of reversing their sentence; but they condemned Zadig to pay four hundred ounces of gold for having said that he had not seen what he had seen. This fine he was obliged to pay; after which he was permitted to plead his cause before the counsel of the grand Desterham, when he spoke to the following effect:

'Ye stars of justice, abyss of sciences, mirrors of truth, who have the weight of lead, the hardness of iron, the splendour of the diamond, and many properties of gold: Since I am permitted to speak before this august assembly, I swear to you by Oramades that I have never seen the queen's respectable spaniel, nor the sacred horse of the king of kings. The truth of the matter was as follows: I was walking toward the little wood, where I afterwards met the venerable eunuch, and the most illustrious chief huntsman. I observed on the sand the traces of an animal, and could easily perceive them to be those of a little dog. The light and long furrows impressed on little eminences of sand between the marks of the paws plainly discovered that it was a female, whose dugs were hanging down, and that therefore she must have whelped a few days before. Other traces of a different kind, that always appeared to have gently brushed the surface of the sand near the marks of the forefeet, showed me that she had very long ears; and as I remarked that there was always a slighter impression made on the sand by one foot than the other three, I found that the spaniel of our august queen was a little lame, if I may be allowed the expression.

'With regard to the horse of the king of kings, you will be pleased to know that, walking in the lanes of this wood, I observed the marks of a horse's shoes, all at equal distances. This must be a horse, said I to myself, that gallops excellently. The dust on the trees in the road that was but seven feet wide was a little brushed off, at the distance of three feet and a half from the middle of the road. This horse, said I, has a tail three feet and a half long, which being whisked to the right and left, has swept away the dust. I observed under the trees that formed an arbour five feet in height, that the leaves of the branches were newly fallen; from whence I inferred that the horse had touched them, and that he must therefore be five feet high. As to his bit, it must be gold of twenty-three carats, for he had rubbed its bosses against a stone which I knew to be a touchstone, and which I had tried. In a word, from the marks made by his shoes on flints of another kind, I concluded that he was shod with silver eleven deniers fine.'

All the judges admired Zadig for his acute and profound discernment. The news of this speech was carried even to the king and queen. Nothing was talked of but Zadig in the antechambers, the chambers, and the cabinet; and though many of the magi were of opinion that he ought to be burned as a sorcerer, the king ordered his officers to restore him the four hundred ounces of gold which he had been obliged to pay. The register, the attorneys, and bailiffs went to his house with great formality, to carry him back his four hundred ounces. They only retained three hundred and ninety-eight of them to defray the expenses of justice; and their servants demanded their fees.

Zadig saw how extremely dangerous it sometimes is to appear too knowing, and therefore resolved that on the next occasion of the like nature, he would not tell what he had seen.

Such an opportunity soon offered. A prisoner of state made his escape, and passed under the window of Zadig's house. Zadig was examined and made no answer. But it was proved that he had looked at the prisoner from this window. For this crime, he was condemned to pay five hundred ounces of gold; and, according to the polite custom of Babylon, he thanked his judges for their indulgence.

'Great God!' said he to himself, 'What a misfortune it is to walk in a wood through which the queen's spaniel or the king's horse has passed! How dangerous to look out of a window! And how difficult to be happy in this life!'

Note: This story has been taken from *Zadig the Babylonian*, a novella by Voltaire. Please keep in mind that its context might not be fully conveyed when read independently due to the overarching structure of the larger tale.

THE ENVIOUS MAN

Voltaire

Zadig resolved to comfort himself by philosophy and friendship for the evils he had suffered from fortune. He had in the suburbs of Babylon a house elegantly furnished, in which he assembled all the arts and all the pleasures worthy of the pursuit of a gentleman. In the morning his library was open to the learned. In the evening his table was surrounded by good company. But he soon found what very dangerous guests these men of letters are. A heated dispute arose over one of Zoroaster's laws, which forbids the eating of a gryphon. 'Why,' said some of them, 'prohibit the eating of a gryphon, if there is no such an animal in nature?' 'There must necessarily be such an animal,' said the others, 'since Zoroaster forbids us to eat it.' Zadig would fain have reconciled them by saying, 'If there are no gryphons, we cannot possibly eat them; and thus either way we shall obey Zoroaster.'

A learned man, who had composed thirteen volumes on the properties of the gryphon, and was besides the chief théurgite, hastened away to accuse Zadig before one of the principal magi, named Yebor, the greatest blockhead and therefore the greatest fanatic among the Chaldeans. This man would have impaled Zadig to do honours to the sun, and would then have recited the breviary of Zoroaster with greater satisfaction. The friend Cador (a friend is better than a hundred priests) went to Yebor, and said to him, 'Long live the sun and the gryphons; beware of punishing Zadig; he is a saint; he has gryphons in his inner court and does not eat them; and his accuser is an heretic, who dares to maintain that rabbits have cloven feet and are not unclean.'

'Well,' said Yebor, shaking his bald pate, 'we must impale Zadig for having thought contemptuously of gryphons, and the other for having spoken disrespectfully of rabbits.' Cador hushed up the affair by means of a maid of honour with whom he had a love affair, and who had great interest in the College of the Magi. Nobody was impaled.

This levity occasioned a great murmuring among some of the doctors, who from thence predicted the fall of Babylon. 'Upon what does happiness depend?' said Zadig. 'I am persecuted by everything in the world, even on account of beings that have no existence.' He cursed those men of learning, and resolved for the future to live with none but good company.

He assembled at his house the most worthy men and the most beautiful ladies of Babylon. He gave them delicious suppers, often preceded by concerts of music, and always animated by polite conversation, from which he knew how to banish that affectation of wit which is the surest method of preventing it entirely, and of spoiling the pleasure of the most agreeable society. Neither the choice of his friends nor that of the dishes was made by vanity; for in everything he preferred the substance to the shadow; and by these means he procured that real respect to which he did not aspire.

Opposite to his house lived one Arimazes, a man whose deformed countenance was but a faint picture of his still more deformed mind. His heart was a mixture of malice, pride, and envy. Having never been able to succeed in any of his undertakings, he revenged himself on all around him by loading them with the blackest calumnies. Rich as he was, he found it difficult to procure a set of flatterers. The rattling of the chariots that entered Zadig's court in the evening filled him with uneasiness; the sound of his praises enraged him still more. He sometimes went to Zadig's house, and sat down at table without being desired; where he spoiled all the pleasure of the company, as the harpies are said to infect the viands they touch. It happened that one day he took it in his head to give entertainment to a lady, who, instead of accepting it, went to sup with Zadig. At another time, as he was talking with Zadig at court, a minister of state came up to them, and invited Zadig to supper without inviting Arimazes. The most implacable hatred has seldom a more solid foundation. This man, who in Babylon was called the Envious, resolved to ruin Zadig because he was called the Happy. 'The opportunity of doing mischief occurs a hundred times in a day, and that of doing good but once a year,' as sayeth the wise Zoroaster.

The envious man went to see Zadig, who was walking in his garden with two friends and a lady, to whom he said many gallant things, without any other intention than that of saying them. The conversation turned upon a war which the king had just brought to a happy conclusion against the prince of Hircania, his vassal. Zadig, who had signalized his courage in this short war, bestowed great praises on the king, but greater still on the lady. He took out his pocket-book, and wrote four lines extempore, which he gave to this amiable person to read. His friends begged they might see them; but modesty, or rather a well-regulated self-love, would not allow him to grant their request. He knew that extemporary verses are never approved of by any but by the person in whose honour they are written. He therefore tore in two the leaf on which he had written them, and threw both the pieces into a thicket of rose-bushes, where the rest of the company sought for them in vain. A slight shower falling soon after obliged them to return to the house. The envious man, who stayed in the garden, continued the search till at last he found a piece of the leaf. It had been torn in such a manner that each half of a line formed a complete sense, and even a verse of a shorter measure; but what was still more surprising, these short verses were found to contain the most injurious reflections on the king. They ran thus:

To flagrant crimes
His crown he owes,

To peaceful times
The worst of foes.

The envious man was now happy for the first time of his life. He had it in his power to ruin a person of virtue and merit. Filled with this fiendlike joy, he found means to convey to the king the satire written by the hand of Zadig, who, together with the lady and his two friends, was thrown into prison.

His trial was soon finished, without his being permitted to speak for himself. As he was going to receive his sentence, the envious man threw himself in his way and told him with a loud voice that his verses were good for nothing. Zadig did not value himself on being a good poet; but it filled him with inexpressible concern to find that he was condemned for high treason; and that the fair lady and his two friends were confined in prison for a crime of which they were not guilty. He was not allowed to speak because his writing spoke for him. Such was the law of Babylon. Accordingly he was conducted to the place of execution, through an immense crowd of spectators, who durst not venture to express their pity for him, but who carefully examined his countenance to see if he died with a good grace. His relations alone were inconsolable, for they could not succeed to his estate. Three-fourths of his wealth were confiscated into the king's treasury, and the other fourth was given to the envious man.

Just as he was preparing for death, the king's parrot flew from its cage and alighted on a rosebush in Zadig's garden. A peach had been driven thither by the wind from a neighbouring tree, and had fallen on a piece of the written leaf of the pocketbook to which it stuck. The bird carried off the peach and the paper and laid them on the king's knee. The king took up the paper with great eagerness and read the words, which formed no sense, and seemed to be the endings of verses. He loved poetry; and there is always some mercy to be expected from a prince of that disposition. The adventure of the parrot set him a-thinking.

The queen, who remembered what had been written on the piece of Zadig's pocketbook, caused it to be brought. They compared the two pieces together and found them to tally exactly; they then read the verses as Zadig had written them.

> TYRANTS ARE PRONE TO FLAGRANT CRIMES.
> TO CLEMENCY HIS CROWN HE OWES.
> TO CONCORD AND TO PEACEFUL TIMES.
> LOVE ONLY IS THE WORST OF FOES

The king gave immediate orders that Zadig should be brought before him, and that his two friends and the lady should be set at liberty. Zadig fell prostrate on the ground before the king and queen; he humbly begged their pardon for having made such bad verses and spoke with so much propriety, wit, and good sense, that Their Majesties desired they might see him again. He did himself that honour, and insinuated himself still farther into their good graces. They gave him all the wealth of the envious man; but Zadig restored him back the whole of it. And this instance of generosity gave no other pleasure to the envious man than that of having preserved his estate.

The king's esteem for Zadig increased every day. He admitted him into all his parties of pleasure, and consulted him in all affairs of state. From that time, the queen began to regard him with an eye of tenderness that might one day prove dangerous to herself, to the king, her august comfort, to Zadig, and to the kingdom in general. Zadig now began to think that happiness was not so unattainable as he had formerly imagined.

Note: This story has been taken from *Zadig the Babylonian*, a novella by Voltaire. Please keep in mind that its context might not be fully conveyed when read independently due to the overarching structure of the larger tale.

THE MINISTER

Voltaire

The king had lost his first minister and chose Zadig to supply his place. All the ladies in Babylon applauded the choice; for, since the foundation of the empire, there had never been such a young minister. But all the courtiers were filled with jealousy and vexation. The envious man in particular was troubled with a spitting of blood and a prodigious inflammation in his nose. Zadig, having thanked the king and queen for their goodness, went likewise to thank the parrot. 'Beautiful bird,' said he, ''tis thou that hast saved my life and made me first minister. The queen's spaniel and the king's horse did me a great deal of mischief; but thou hast done me much good. Upon such slender threads as these do the fates of mortals hang! But,' added he, 'this happiness perhaps will vanish very soon.'

'Soon,' replied the parrot.

Zadig was somewhat startled at this word. But as he was a good natural philosopher and did not believe parrots to be prophets, he quickly recovered his spirits and resolved to execute his duty to the best of his power.

He made everyone feel the sacred authority of the laws, but no one felt the weight of his dignity. He never checked the deliberation of the diran; and every vizier might give his opinion without the fear of incurring the minister's displeasure. When he gave judgement, it was not he that gave it, it was the law; the rigour of which, however, whenever it was too severe, he always took care to soften; and when laws were wanting, the equity of his decisions was such as might easily have made them pass for those of

Zoroaster. It is to him that the nations are indebted for this grand principle, to wit, that it is better to run the risk of sparing the guilty than to condemn the innocent. He imagined that laws were made as well to secure the people from the suffering of injuries as to restrain them from the commission of crimes. His chief talent consisted in discovering the truth, which all men seek to obscure.

This great talent he put into practice from the very beginning of his administration. A famous merchant of Babylon, who died in the Indies, divided his estate equally between his two sons, after having disposed of their sister in marriage, and left a present of thirty thousand pieces of gold to that son who should be found to have loved him best. The eldest raised a tomb to his memory; the youngest increased his sister's portion, by giving her part of his inheritance. Everyone said that the eldest son loved his father best, and the youngest his sister; and that the thirty thousand pieces belonged to the eldest.

Zadig sent for both of them, one after the other. To the eldest he said: 'Thy father is not dead; he is recovered of his last illness, and is returning to Babylon.' 'God be praised,' replied the young man; 'but his tomb cost me a considerable sum.' Zadig afterwards said the same to the youngest. 'God be praised,' said he, 'I will go and restore to my father all that I have; but I could wish that he would leave my sister what I have given her.' 'Thou shalt restore nothing,' replied Zadig, 'and thou shalt have the thirty thousand pieces, for thou art the son who loves his father best.'

Note: This story has been taken from *Zadig the Babylonian*, a novella by Voltaire. Please keep in mind that its context might not be fully conveyed when read independently due to the overarching structure of the larger tale.

THE DISPUTES AND THE AUDIENCES

Voltaire

In this manner he daily discovered the subtilty of his genius and the goodness of his heart. The people at once admired and loved him. He passed for the happiest man in the world. The whole empire resounded with his name. All the ladies ogled him. All the men praised him for his justice. The learned regarded him as an oracle; and even the priests confessed that he knew more than the old archmage Yebor. They were now so far from prosecuting him on account of the gryphon, that they believed nothing but what he thought credible.

There had reigned in Babylon, for the space of fifteen hundred years, a violent contest that had divided the empire into two sects. The one pretended that they ought to enter the temple of Mitra with the left foot foremost; the other held this custom in detestation and always entered with the right foot first. The people waited with great impatience for the day on which the solemn feast of the sacred fire was to be celebrated, to see which sect Zadig would favour. All the world had their eyes fixed on his two feet, and the whole city was in the utmost suspense and perturbation. Zadig jumped into the temple with his feet joined together, and afterwards proved, in an eloquent discourse, that the Sovereign of heaven and earth, who accepted not the persons of men, makes no distinction between the right and left foot. The envious man and his wife alleged that his discourse was not figurative enough, and that he did not make the rocks and mountains to dance with sufficient agility.

'He is dry,' said they, 'and void of genius: he does not make the fleas to fly, and stars to fall, nor the sun to melt wax; he has not the true Oriental style.' Zadig contented himself with having the style of reason. All the world favoured him, not because he was on the right road or followed the dictates of reason, or was a man of real merit, but because he was the prime vizier.

He terminated, with the same happy address, the grand difference between the white and the black magi. The former maintained that it was the height of impiety to pray to God with the face turned toward the east in winter; the latter asserted that God abhorred the prayers of those who turned toward the west in summer. Zadig decreed that every man should be allowed to turn as he pleased.

Thus he found out the happy secret of finishing all affairs, whether of a private or a public nature, in the morning. The rest of the day he was employed in superintending and promoting the embellishments of Babylon. He exhibited tragedies that drew tears from the eyes of the spectators, and comedies that shook their sides with laughter; a custom which had long been disused, and which his good taste now induced him to revive. He never affected to be more knowing in the polite arts than the artists themselves; he encouraged them by rewards and honours, and was never jealous of their talents. In the evening, the king was highly entertained with his conversation, and the queen still more. 'Great minister!' said the king. 'Amiable minister!' said the queen; and both of them added, 'It would have been a great loss to the state had such a man been hanged.'

Never was a man in power obliged to give so many audiences to the ladies. Most of them came to consult him about no business at all, that so they might have some business with him. But none of them won his attention.

Meanwhile Zadig perceived that his thoughts were always distracted, as well when he gave audience as when he sat in judgement. He did not know to what to attribute this absence of mind; and that was his only sorrow.

He had a dream in which he imagined that he laid himself

down upon a heap of dry herbs, among which there were many prickly ones that gave him great uneasiness, and that he afterwards reposed himself on a soft bed of roses, from which there sprung a serpent that wounded him to the heart with its sharp and venomed tongue. 'Alas,' said he, 'I have long lain on these dry and prickly herbs, I am now on the bed of roses; but what shall be the serpent?'

Note: This story has been taken from *Zadig the Babylonian*, a novella by Voltaire. Please keep in mind that its context might not be fully conveyed when read independently due to the overarching structure of the larger tale.

JEALOUSY

Voltaire

Zadig's calamities sprung even from his happiness and especially from his merit. He conversed every day with the king and Astarte, his august comfort. The charms of his conversation were greatly heightened by that desire of pleasing, which is to the mind what dress is to beauty. His youth and graceful appearance insensibly made an impression on Astarte, which she did not at first perceive. Her passion grew and flourished in the bosom of innocence. Without fear or scruple, she indulged the pleasing satisfaction of seeing and hearing a man who was so dear to her husband and to the empire in general. She was continually praising him to the king. She talked of him to her women, who were always sure to improve on her praises. And thus everything contributed to pierce her heart with a dart, of which she did not seem to be sensible. She made several presents to Zadig, which discovered a greater spirit of gallantry than she imagined. She intended to speak to him only as a queen satisfied with his services and her expressions were sometimes those of a woman in love.

Astarte was much more beautiful than that Semira who had such a strong aversion to one-eyed men, or that other woman who had resolved to cut off her husband's nose. Her unreserved familiarity, her tender expressions, at which she began to blush; and her eyes, which, though she endeavoured to divert them to other objects, were always fixed upon his, inspired Zadig with a passion that filled him with astonishment. He struggled hard to get the better of it. He called to his aid the precepts of philosophy, which had always stood him in stead; but from thence, though he could derive the light of knowledge, he could procure no remedy to cure the disorders of his lovesick heart. Duty, gratitude, and violated majesty presented themselves to his mind as so many avenging gods. He struggled; he conquered; but this victory, which he was obliged to purchase afresh every moment, cost him many sighs and tears. He no longer dared to speak to the queen with that sweet and charming familiarity which had been so agreeable to them both. His countenance was covered with a cloud. His conversation was constrained and incoherent. His eyes were fixed on the ground; and when, in spite of all his endeavours to the contrary, they encountered those of the queen, they found them bathed in tears and darting arrows of flame. They seemed to say, 'We adore each other and yet are afraid to love; we both burn with a fire which we both condemn.'

Zadig left the royal presence full of perplexity and despair, having his heart oppressed with a burden which he was no longer able to bear. In the violence of his perturbation, he involuntarily betrayed the secret to his friend Cador, in the same manner as a man who, having long supported the fits of a cruel disease, discovers his pain by a cry extorted from him by a more severe fit and by the cold sweat that covers his brow.

'I have already discovered,' said Cador, 'the sentiments which thou wouldst fain conceal from thyself. The symptoms by which the passions show themselves are certain and infallible. Judge, my dear Zadig, since I have read thy heart, whether the king will not discover something in it that may give him offence. He has no other fault but that of being the most jealous man in the world. Thou canst resist the violence of thy passion with greater fortitude than the queen because thou art a philosopher, and because thou art Zadig. Astarte is a woman: she suffers her eyes to speak with so much imprudence, as she does not as yet think herself guilty. Conscious of her innocence, she unhappily neglects those external appearances which are so necessary. I shall tremble for her so long as she has nothing wherewithal to reproach herself. Were ye both of one mind, ye might easily deceive the whole world. A growing passion, which we endeavour to suppress, discovers itself in spite of all our efforts to the contrary; but love, when gratified, is easily concealed.'

Zadig trembled at the proposal of betraying the king, his benefactor; and never was he more faithful to his prince than when guilty of an involuntary crime against him.

Meanwhile the queen mentioned the name of Zadig so frequently and with such a blushing and downcast look; she was sometimes so lively and sometimes so perplexed when she spoke to him in the king's presence, and was seized with such deep thoughtfulness at his going away, that the king began to be troubled. He believed all that he saw and imagined all that he did not see. He particularly remarked that his wife's shoes were blue and that Zadig's shoes were blue; that his wife's ribbons were yellow and that Zadig's bonnet was yellow; and these were terrible symptoms to a prince of so much delicacy. In his jealous mind, suspicions were turned into certainty.

All the slaves of kings and queens are so many spies over their hearts. They soon observed that Astarte was tender and that Moabdar was jealous. The envious man brought false reports to the king. The monarch now thought of nothing but in what manner he might best execute his vengeance. He at one night resolved to poison the queen, and in the morning to put Zadig to death by the bowstring. The orders were given to a merciless eunuch, who commonly executed his acts of vengeance. There happened at that time to be in the king's chamber a little dwarf, who, though dumb, was not deaf. He was allowed, on account of his insignificance, to go wherever he pleased, and, as a domestic animal, was a witness of what passed in the most profound secrecy. This little mute was strongly attached to the queen and Zadig. With equal horror and surprise, he heard the cruel orders given. But how to prevent the fatal sentence that, in a few hours, was to be carried into execution! He could not write, but he could paint; and excelled particularly in drawing a striking resemblance. He employed a part of the night in sketching out with his pencil what he meant to impart to the queen. The piece represented the king in one corner, boiling with rage, and giving orders to the eunuch; a bowstring, and a bowl on a table; the queen in the middle of the picture, expiring in the arms of her woman, and Zadig strangled at her feet. The horizon, represented a rising sun, to express that this shocking execution was to be performed in the morning. As soon as he had finished the picture he ran to one of Astarte's women, awakened her, and made her understand that she must immediately carry it to the queen.

At midnight, a messenger knocks at Zadig's door, awakes him, and gives him a note from the queen. He doubts whether it is a dream; and opens the letter with a trembling hand. But how great was his surprise! And who can express the consternation and despair into which he was thrown upon reading these words: 'Fly this instant, or thou art a dead man. Fly, Zadig, I conjure thee by our mutual love and my yellow ribbons. I have not been guilty, but I find I must die like a criminal.'

Zadig was hardly able to speak. He sent for Cador, and, without uttering a word, gave him the note. Cador forced him to obey, and forthwith to take the road to Memphis. 'Shouldst thou dare,' said he, 'to go in search of the queen, thou wilt hasten her death. Shouldst thou speak to the king, thou wilt infallibly ruin her. I will take upon me the charge of her destiny; follow thy own. I will spread a report that thou hast taken the road to India. I will soon follow thee, and inform thee of all that shall have passed in Babylon.' At that instant, Cador caused two of the swiftest dromedaries to be brought to a private gate of the palace. Upon one of these he mounted Zadig, whom he was obliged to carry to the door, and who was ready to expire with grief. He was accompanied by a single domestic; and Cador, plunged in sorrow and astonishment, soon lost sight of his friend.

This illustrious fugitive arriving on the side of a hill, from whence he could take a view of Babylon, turned his eyes toward the queen's palace, and fainted away at the sight; nor did he recover his senses but to shed a torrent of tears and to wish for death. At length, after his thoughts had been long engrossed in lamenting the unhappy fate of the loveliest woman and the greatest queen in the world, he for a moment turned his views on himself and cried: 'What then is human life? O virtue, how hast thou served me! Two women have basely deceived me, and now a third, who is innocent, and more beautiful than both the others, is going to be put to death! Whatever good I have done hath been to me a continual source of calamity and affliction; and I have only been raised to the height of grandeur, to be tumbled down the most horrid precipice of misfortune.' Filled with these gloomy reflections, his eyes overspread with the veil of grief, his countenance covered with the paleness of death, and his soul plunged in an abyss of the blackest despair, he continued his journey toward Egypt.

Note: This story has been taken from *Zadig the Babylonian*, a novella by Voltaire. Please keep in mind that its context might not be fully conveyed when read independently due to the overarching structure of the larger tale.

THE WOMAN BEATEN

Voltaire

Zadig directed his course by the stars. The constellation of Orion and the splendid Dog Star guided his steps toward the pole of Cassiopeia. He admired those vast globes of light, which appear to our eyes but as so many little sparks, while the earth, which in reality is only an imperceptible point in nature, appears to our fond imaginations as something so grand and noble.

He then represented to himself the human species as it really is, as a parcel of insects devouring one another on a little atom of clay. This true image seemed to annihilate his misfortunes, by making him sensible of the nothingness of his own being, and of that of Babylon. His soul launched out into infinity, and, detached from the senses, contemplated the immutable order of the universe. But when returning to himself, and entering into his own heart, he considered that Astarte had perhaps died for him, the universe vanished from his sight, and he beheld nothing in the whole compass of nature but Astarte expiring and Zadig unhappy. While he thus alternately gave up his mind to this flux and reflux of sublime philosophy and intolerable grief, he advanced toward the frontiers of Egypt; and his faithful domestic was already in the first village, in search of lodging.

Upon reaching the village, Zadig generously took the part of a woman attacked by her jealous lover. The combat grew so fierce that Zadig slew the lover. The Egyptians were then just and humane. The people conducted Zadig to the town house. They first of all ordered his wounds to be dressed and then examined him and his servant apart, in order to discover the truth. They found that Zadig was not an assassin; but as he was guilty of having killed a man, the law condemned him to be a slave. His two camels were sold for the benefit of the town; all the gold he had brought with him was distributed among the inhabitants; and his person, as well as that of the companion of his journey, was exposed to sale in the marketplace.

An Arabian merchant, named Setoc, made the purchase; but as the servant was fitter for labour than the master, he was sold at a higher price. There was no comparison between the two men. Thus Zadig became a slave subordinate to his own servant. They were linked together by a chain fastened to their feet, and in this condition, they followed the Arabian merchant to his house. By the way Zadig comforted his servant, and exhorted him to patience; he could not help making, according to his usual custom, some reflections on human life. 'I see,' said he, 'that the unhappiness of my fate hath an influence on thine. Hitherto everything has turned out to me in a most unaccountable manner. I have been condemned to pay a fine for having seen the marks of a spaniel's feet. I thought that I should once have been impaled on account of a gryphon. I have been sent to execution for having made some verses in praise of the king. I have been upon the point of being strangled because the queen had yellow ribbons; and now I am a slave with thee, because a brutal wretch beat his mistress. Come, let us keep a good heart; all this perhaps will have an end. The Arabian merchants must necessarily have slaves; and why not me as well as another, since, as well as another, I am a man? This merchant will not be cruel; he must treat his slaves well, if he expects any advantage from them.' But while he spoke thus, his heart was entirely engrossed by the fate of the Queen of Babylon.

Two days after, the merchant Setoc set out for Arabia Deserta, with his slaves and his camels. His tribe dwelt near the Desert of Oreb. The journey was long and painful. Setoc set a much greater value on the servant than the master, because the former was more expert in loading the camels; and all the little marks of distinction were shown to him. A camel having died within two days' journey of Oreb, his burden was divided and laid on the backs of the servants; and Zadig had his share among the rest.

Setoc laughed to see all his slaves walking with their bodies inclined. Zadig took the liberty to explain to him the cause, and inform him of the laws of the balance. The merchant was astonished, and began to regard him with other eyes. Zadig, finding he had raised his curiosity, increased it still further by acquainting him with many things that related to commerce, the specific gravity of metals, and commodities under an equal bulk; the properties of several useful animals; and the means of rendering those useful that are not naturally so. At last Setoc began to consider Zadig as a sage, and preferred him to his companion, whom he had formerly so much esteemed. He treated him well and had no cause to repent of his kindness.

Note: This story has been taken from *Zadig the Babylonian*, a novella by Voltaire. Please keep in mind that its context might not be fully conveyed when read independently due to the overarching structure of the larger tale.

THE STONE

Voltaire

As soon as Setoc arrived among his own tribe, he demanded the payment of five hundred ounces of silver, which he had lent to a Jew in presence of two witnesses; but as the witnesses were dead, and the debt could not be proved, the Hebrew appropriated the merchant's money to himself, and piously thanked God for putting it in his power to cheat an Arabian. Setoc imparted this troublesome affair to Zadig, who was now his counsel.

'In what place,' said Zadig, 'didst thou lend the five hundred ounces to this infidel?'

'Upon a large stone,' replied the merchant, 'that lies near Mount Oreb.'

'What is the character of thy debtor?' said Zadig.

'That of a knave,' returned Setoc.

'But I ask thee whether he is lively or phlegmatic, cautious or imprudent?'

'He is, of all bad payers,' said Setoc, 'the most lively fellow I ever knew.'

'Well,' resumed Zadig, 'allow me to plead thy cause.' In effect, Zadig, having summoned the Jew to the tribunal, addressed the judge in the following terms: 'Pillar of the throne of equity, I come to demand of this man, in the name of my master, five hundred ounces of silver, which he refuses to pay.'

'Hast thou any witnesses?' said the judge.

'No, they are dead; but there remains a large stone upon which the money was counted; and if it pleases thy grandeur to order the stone to be sought for, I hope that it will bear witness. The

Hebrew and I will tarry here till the stone arrives; I will send for it at my master's expense.'

'With all my heart,' replied the judge, and immediately applied himself to the discussion of other affairs.

When the court was going to break up, the judge said to Zadig. 'Well, friend, hast not thy stone come yet?'

The Hebrew replied with a smile, 'Thy grandeur may stay here till the morrow, and after all not see the stone. It is more than six miles from hence; and it would require fifteen men to move it.'

'Well,' cried Zadig, 'did not I say that the stone would bear witness? Since this man knows where it is, he thereby confesses that it was upon it that the money was counted.' The Hebrew was disconcerted, and was soon after obliged to confess the truth. The judge ordered him to be fastened to the stone, without meat or drink, till he should restore the five hundred ounces, which were soon after paid.

The slave Zadig and the stone were held in great repute in Arabia.

Note: This story has been taken from *Zadig the Babylonian*, a novella by Voltaire. Please keep in mind that its context might not be fully conveyed when read independently due to the overarching structure of the larger tale.

THE FUNERAL PILE

Voltaire

Setoc, charmed with the happy issue of this affair, made his slave his intimate friend. He had now conceived as great esteem for him as ever the King of Babylon had done; and Zadig was glad that Setoc had no wife. He discovered in his master a good natural disposition, much probity of heart, and a great share of good sense; but he was sorry to see that, according to the ancient custom of Arabia, he adored the host of heaven; that is, the sun, moon, and stars. He sometimes spoke to him on this subject with great prudence and discretion. At last he told him that these bodies were like all other bodies in the universe, and no more deserving of our homage than a tree or a rock.

'But,' said Setoc, 'they are eternal beings; and it is from them we derive all we enjoy. They animate nature; they regulate the seasons; and, besides, are removed at such an immense distance from us that we cannot help revering them.'

'Thou receivest more advantage,' replied Zadig, 'from the waters of the Red Sea, which carry thy merchandise to the Indies. Why may it not be as ancient as the stars? And if thou adorest what is placed at a distance from thee, thou oughtest to adore the land of the Gangarides, which lies at the extremity of the earth.'

'No,' said Setoc, 'the brightness of the stars commands my adoration.'

At night, Zadig lit a great number of candles in the tent where he was to sup with Setoc; and the moment his patron appeared, he fell on his knees before these lighted tapers, and said, 'Eternal and shining luminaries! be ye always propitious to me.' Having thus said, he sat down at the table, without taking the least notice of Setoc.

'What art thou doing?' said Setoc to him in amazement.

'I act like thee,' replied Zadig, 'I adore these candles, and neglect their master and mine.' Setoc comprehended the profound sense of this apologue. The wisdom of his slave sunk deep into his soul; he no longer offered incense to the creatures, but adored the eternal Being who made them.

There prevailed at that time in Arabia a shocking custom, sprung originally from Leythia, and which, being established in the Indies by the credit of the Brahmans, threatened to overrun all the East. When a married man died, and his beloved wife aspired to the character of a saint, she burned herself publicly on the body of her husband. This was a solemn feast and was called the Funeral Pile of Widowhood, and that tribe in which most women had been burned was the most respected.

An Arabian of Setoc's tribe being dead, his widow, whose name was Almona, and who was very devout, published the day and hour when she intended to throw herself into the fire, amidst the sound of drums and trumpets. Zadig remonstrated against this horrible custom; he showed Setoc how inconsistent it was with the happiness of mankind to suffer young widows to burn themselves every other day, widows who were capable of giving children to the state, or at least of educating those they already had; and he convinced him that it was his duty to do all that lay in his power to abolish such a barbarous practice.

'The women,' said Setoc, 'have possessed the right of burning themselves for more than a thousand years; and who shall dare to abrogate a law which time hath rendered sacred? Is there anything more respectable than ancient abuses?'

'Reason is more ancient,' replied Zadig; 'Meanwhile, speak thou to the chiefs of the tribes and I will go to wait on the young widow.'

Accordingly he was introduced to her; and, after having insinuated himself into her good graces by some compliments on her beauty and told her what a pity it was to commit so many charms to the flames, he at last praised her for her constancy and courage. 'Thou must surely have loved thy husband,' said he to her, 'with the most passionate fondness.'

'Who, I?' replied the lady. 'I loved him not at all. He was a brutal, jealous, insupportable wretch; but I am firmly resolved to throw myself on his funeral pile.'

'It would appear then,' said Zadig, 'that there must be a very delicious pleasure in being burned alive.'

'Oh! it makes nature shudder,' replied the lady, 'but that must be overlooked. I am a devotee, and I should lose my reputation and all the world would despise me if I did not burn myself.'

Zadig, having made her acknowledge that she burned herself to gain the good opinion of others and to gratify her own vanity, entertained her with a long discourse, calculated to make her a little in love with life, and even went so far as to inspire her with some degree of goodwill for the person who spoke to her.

'Alas!' said the lady, 'I believe I should desire thee to marry me.'

Zadig's mind was too much engrossed with the idea of Astarte not to elude this declaration; but he instantly went to the chiefs of the tribes, told them what had passed, and advised them to make a law, by which a widow should not be permitted to burn herself till she had conversed privately with a young man for the space of an hour. Since that time not a single woman hath burned herself in Arabia. They were indebted to Zadig alone for destroying in one day a cruel custom that had lasted for so many ages and thus, he became the benefactor of Arabia.

Note: This story has been taken from *Zadig the Babylonian*, a novella by Voltaire. Please keep in mind that its context might not be fully conveyed when read independently due to the overarching structure of the larger tale.

THE SUPPER

Voltaire

Setoc, who could not separate himself from this man, in whom dwelt wisdom, carried him to the great fair of Balzora, whither the richest merchants in the earth resorted. Zadig was highly pleased to see so many men of different countries united in the same place. He considered the whole universe as one large family assembled at Balzora.

Setoc, after having sold his commodities at a very high price, returned to his own tribe with his friend Zadig; who learned upon his arrival that he had been tried in his absence and was now going to be burned by a slow fire. Only the friendship of Almona saved his life. Like so many pretty women she possessed great influence with the priesthood. Zadig thought it best to leave Arabia.

Setoc was so charmed with the ingenuity and address of Almona that he made her his wife. Zadig departed, after having thrown himself at the feet of his fair deliverer. Setoc and he took leave of each other with tears in their eyes, swearing an eternal friendship, and promising that the first of them that should acquire a large fortune should share it with the other.

Zadig directed his course along the frontiers of Assyria, still musing on the unhappy Astarte, and reflecting on the severity of fortune which seemed determined to make him the sport of her cruelty and the object of her persecution.

'What,' said he to himself, 'four hundred ounces of gold for having seen a spaniel! Condemned to lose my head for four bad verses in praise of the king! Ready to be strangled because the queen had shoes of the colour of my bonnet! Reduced to slavery for having succoured a woman who was beat! And on the point of being burned for having saved the lives of all the young widows of Arabia!'

Note: This story has been taken from *Zadig the Babylonian*, a novella by Voltaire. Please keep in mind that its context might not be fully conveyed when read independently due to the overarching structure of the larger tale.

THE ROBBER

Voltaire

Arriving on the frontiers which divide Arabia Petraea from Syria, he passed by a pretty strong castle, from which a party of armed Arabians sallied forth. They instantly surrounded him and cried, 'All thou hast belongs to us, and thy person is the property of our master.' Zadig replied by drawing his sword; his servant, who was a man of courage, did the same. They killed the first Arabians that presumed to lay hands on them; and, though the number was redoubled, they were not dismayed, but resolved to perish in the conflict. Two men defended themselves against a multitude; and such a combat could not last long.

The master of the castle, whose name was Arbogad, having observed from a window the prodigies of valour performed by Zadig, conceived a high esteem for this heroic stranger. He descended in haste and went in person to call off his men and deliver the two travellers.

'All that passes over my lands,' said he, 'belongs to me, as well as what I find upon the lands of others; but thou seemest to be a man of such undaunted courage that I will exempt thee from the common law.' He then conducted him to his castle, ordering his men to treat him well; and in the evening, Arbogad supped with Zadig.

The lord of the castle was one of those Arabians who are commonly called robbers; but he now and then performed some good actions amid a multitude of bad ones. He robbed with a furious rapacity, and granted favours with great generosity; he was intrepid in action; affable in company; a debauchee at table, but gay in debauchery; and particularly remarkable for his frank and open behaviour. He was highly pleased with Zadig, whose lively conversation lengthened the repast.

At last Arbogad said to him; 'I advise thee to enrol thy name in my catalogue; thou canst not do better; this is not a bad trade; and thou mayest one day become what I am at present.'

'May I take the liberty of asking thee,' said Zadig, 'how long thou hast followed this noble profession?'

'From my most tender youth,' replied the lord. 'I was a servant to a pretty good-natured Arabian, but could not endure the hardships of my situation. I was vexed to find that fate had given me no share of the earth, which equally belongs to all men. I imparted the cause of my uneasiness to an old Arabian, who said to me: "My son, do not despair; there was once a grain of sand that lamented that it was no more than a neglected atom in the desert; at the end of a few years it became a diamond; and is now the brightest ornament in the crown of the king of the Indies." This discourse made a deep impression on my mind. I was the grain of sand, and I resolved to become the diamond. I began by stealing two horses; I soon got a party of companions; I put myself in a condition to rob small caravans; and thus, by degrees, I destroyed the difference which had formerly subsisted between me and other men. I had my share of the good things of this world; and was even recompensed with usury for the hardships I had suffered. I was greatly respected, and became the captain of a band of robbers. I seized this castle by force. The Satrap of Syria had a mind to dispossess me of it; but I was too rich to have anything to fear. I gave the Satrap a handsome present, by which means I preserved my castle and increased my possessions. He even appointed me treasurer of the tributes which Arabia Petraea pays to the king of kings. I perform my office of receiver with great punctuality; but take the freedom to dispense with that of paymaster.

'The grand Desterham of Babylon sent hither a pretty Satrap in the name of King Moabdar, to have me strangled. This man arrived with his orders: I was apprised of all; I caused to be strangled in his presence the four persons he had brought with him to draw the noose; after which I asked him how much his commission of strangling me might be worth. He replied that his fees would amount to about three hundred pieces of gold. I then convinced him that he might gain more by staying with me. I made him an inferior robber; and he is now one of my best and richest officers. If thou wilt take my advice thy success may be equal to his; never was there a better season for plunder, since King Moabdar is killed, and all Babylon thrown into confusion.'

'Moabdar killed!' said Zadig, 'And what has become of Queen Astarte?'

'I know not,' replied Arbogad. 'All I know is, that Moabdar lost his senses and was killed; that Babylon is a scene of disorder and bloodshed; that all the empire is desolated; that there are some fine strokes to be struck yet; and that, for my own part, I have struck some that are admirable.'

'But the queen,' said Zadig; 'for heaven's sake, knowest thou nothing of the queen's fate?'

'Yes,' replied he, 'I have heard something of a prince of Hircania; if she was not killed in the tumult, she is probably one of his concubines; but I am much fonder of booty than news. I have taken several women in my excursions; but I keep none of them. I sell them at a high price, when they are beautiful, without inquiring who they are. In commodities of this kind rank makes no difference, and a queen that is ugly will never find a merchant. Perhaps I may have sold Queen Astarte; perhaps she is dead; but, be it as it will, it is of little consequence to me, and I should imagine as little to thee.' So saying, he drank a large draught which threw all his ideas into such confusion that Zadig could obtain no further information.

Zadig remained for some time without speech, sense, or motion. Arbogad continued drinking; told stories; constantly repeated that he was the happiest man in the world; and exhorted Zadig to put himself in the same condition. At last, the soporiferous fumes of the wine lulled him into a gentle repose.

Zadig passed the night in the most violent perturbation. 'What,' said he, 'did the king lose his senses? And is he killed? I cannot help lamenting his fate. The empire is rent in pieces; and this robber is happy. O fortune! O destiny! A robber is happy, and the most beautiful of nature's works hath perhaps perished in a barbarous manner or lives in a state worse than death. O Astarte! What has become of thee?'

At daybreak, he questioned all those he met in the castle; but they were all busy, and he received no answer. During the night, they had made a new capture, and they were now employed in dividing the spoils. All he could obtain in this hurry and confusion was an opportunity of departing, which he immediately embraced, plunged deeper than ever in the most gloomy and mournful reflections.

Zadig proceeded on his journey with a mind full of disquiet and perplexity, and wholly employed on the unhappy Astarte, on the King of Babylon, on his faithful friend Cador, on the happy robber Arbogad; in a word, on all the misfortunes and disappointments he had hitherto suffered.

Note: This story has been taken from *Zadig the Babylonian*, a novella by Voltaire. Please keep in mind that its context might not be fully conveyed when read independently due to the overarching structure of the larger tale.

THE FISHERMAN

Voltaire

At a few leagues' distance from Arbogad's castle, he came to the banks of a small river, still deploring his fate, and considering himself as the most wretched of mankind. He saw a fisherman lying on the brink of the river, scarcely holding, in his weak and feeble hand, a net which he seemed ready to drop, and lifting up his eyes to Heaven.

'I am certainly,' said the fisherman, 'the most unhappy man in the world. I was universally allowed to be the most famous dealer in cream cheese in Babylon, and yet I am ruined. I had the most handsome wife that any man in my station could have; and by her I have been betrayed. I had still left a paltry house, and that I have seen pillaged and destroyed. At last I took refuge in this cottage, where I have no other resource than fishing, and yet I cannot catch a single fish. Oh, my net! no more will I throw thee into the water; I will throw myself in thy place.' So saying, he arose and advanced forward, in the attitude of a man ready to throw himself into the river, and thus to finish his life.

'What!' said Zadig to himself, 'are there men as wretched as I?' His eagerness to save the fisherman's life was as this reflection. He ran to him, stopped him, and spoke to him with a tender and compassionate air. It is commonly supposed that we are less miserable when we have companions in our misery. This, according to Zoroaster, does not proceed from malice, but necessity. We feel ourselves insensibly drawn to an unhappy person as to one like ourselves. The joy of the happy would be an insult; but two men in distress are like two slender trees, which, mutually supporting each other, fortify themselves against the storm.

'Why,' said Zadig to the fisherman, 'dost thou sink under thy misfortunes?'

'Because,' replied he, 'I see no means of relief. I was the most considerable man in the village of Derlback, near Babylon, and with the assistance of my wife I made the best cream cheese in the empire. Queen Astarte and the famous minister Zadig were extremely fond of them.'

Zadig, transported, said, 'What, knowest thou nothing of the queen's fate?'

'No, my lord,' replied the fisherman; 'but I know that neither the queen nor Zadig has paid me for my cream cheeses; that I have lost my wife, and am now reduced to despair.'

'I flatter myself,' said Zadig, 'that thou wilt not lose all thy money. I have heard of this Zadig; he is an honest man; and if he returns to Babylon, as he expects, he will give thee more than he owes thee. Believe me, go to Babylon. I shall be there before thee, because I am on horseback, and thou art on foot. Apply to the illustrious Cador; tell him thou hast met his friend; wait for me at his house; go, perhaps thou wilt not always be unhappy.'

'Oh, powerful Oromazes!' continued he, 'thou employest me to comfort this man; whom wilt thou employ to give me consolation?' So saying, he gave the fisherman half the money he had brought from Arabia. The fisherman, struck with surprise and ravished with joy, kissed the feet of the friend of Cador, and said, 'Thou art surely an angel sent from Heaven to save me!'

Meanwhile, Zadig continued to make fresh inquiries, and to shed tears. 'What, my lord!' cried the fisherman, 'art thou then so unhappy, thou who bestowest favours?'

'Am a hundred times more unhappy than thou art,' replied Zadig.

'But how is it possible,' said the good man, 'that the giver can be more wretched than the receiver?'

'Because,' replied Zadig, 'thy greatest misery arose from poverty, and mine is seated in the heart.'

'Did Orcan take thy wife from thee?' said the fisherman.

This word recalled to Zadig's mind the whole of his adventures.

He repeated the catalogue of his misfortunes, beginning with the queen's spaniel, and ending with his arrival at the castle of the robber Arbogad. 'Ah!' said he to the fisherman, 'Orcan deserves to be punished; but it is commonly such men as those that are the favourites of fortune. However, go thou to the house of Lord Cador, and there wait for my arrival.' They then parted, the fisherman walked, thanking Heaven for the happiness of his condition; and Zadig rode, accusing fortune for the hardness of his lot.

Note: This story has been taken from *Zadig the Babylonian*, a novella by Voltaire. Please keep in mind that its context might not be fully conveyed when read independently due to the overarching structure of the larger tale.

THE GUILTY SECRET

Paul de Kock

Nathalie de Hauteville was twenty-two years old, and had been a widow for three years. She was one of the prettiest women in Paris; her large dark eyes shone with remarkable brilliancy, and she united the sparkling vivacity of an Italian and the depth of feeling of a Spaniard to the grace which always distinguishes a Parisian born and bred. Considering herself too young to be entirely alone, she had long ago invited M. d'Ablaincourt, an old uncle of hers, to come and live with her.

M. d'Ablaincourt was an old bachelor; he had never loved anything in this world but himself. He was an egotist, too lazy to do any one an ill turn, but at the same time too selfish to do any one a kindness, unless it would tend directly to his own advantage. And yet, with an air of complaisance, as if he desired nothing so much as the comfort of those around him, he consented to his niece's proposal, in the hope that she would do many little kind offices for him, which would add materially to his comfort.

M. d'Ablaincourt accompanied his niece when she resumed her place in society; but sometimes, when he felt inclined to stay at home, he would say to her: 'My dear Nathalie, I am afraid you will not be much amused this evening. They will only play cards; besides, I don't think any of your friends will be there. Of course, I am ready to take you, if you wish to go.'

And Nathalie, who had great confidence in all her uncle said, would stay at home.

In the same manner, M. d'Ablaincourt, who was a great gourmand, said to his niece: 'My dear, you know that I am not at all fond of eating, and am satisfied with the simplest fare; but I must tell you that your cook puts too much salt in everything! It is very unwholesome.'

So they changed the cook.

Again, the garden was out of order; the trees before the old gentleman's window must be cut down, because their shade would doubtless cause a dampness in the house prejudicial to Nathalie's health; or the surrey was to be changed for a landau.

Nathalie was a coquette. Accustomed to charm, she listened with smiles to the numerous protestations of admiration which she received. She sent all who aspired to her hand to her uncle, saying: 'Before I give you any hope, I must know my uncle's opinion.'

It is likely that Nathalie would have answered differently if she had ever felt a real preference for any one; but heretofore she seemed to have preferred her liberty.

The old uncle, for his part, being now master in his niece's house, was very anxious for her to remain as she was. A nephew might be somewhat less submissive than Nathalie. Therefore, he never failed to discover some great fault in each of those who sought an alliance with the pretty widow.

Besides his egotism and his epicureanism, the dear uncle had another passion—to play backgammon. The game amused him very much; but the difficulty was to find any one to play with. If, by accident, any of Nathalie's visitors understood it, there was no escape from a long siege with the old gentleman; but most people preferred cards.

In order to please her uncle, Nathalie tried to learn this game; but it was almost impossible. She could not give her attention to one thing for so long a time. Her uncle scolded. Nathalie gave up in despair.

'It was only for your own amusement that I wished to teach it to you,' said the good M. d'Ablaincourt.

Things were at this crisis when, at a ball one evening, Nathalie was introduced to a M. d'Apremont, a captain in the navy.

Nathalie raised her eyes, expecting to see a great sailor, with a wooden leg and a bandage over one eye; when to her great surprise, she beheld a man of about thirty, tall and finely formed, with two sound legs and two good eyes.

Armand d'Apremont had entered the navy at a very early age, and had arrived, although very young, to the dignity of a captain. He had amassed a large fortune, in addition to his patrimonial estates, and he had now come home to rest after his labours. As yet, however, he was a single man, and, moreover, had always laughed at love.

But when he saw Nathalie, his opinions underwent a change. For the first time in his life, he regretted that he had never learned to dance, and he kept his eyes fixed on her constantly.

His attention to the young widow soon became a subject of general conversation, and, at last, the report reached the ears of M. d'Ablaincourt. When Nathalie mentioned, one evening, that she expected the captain to spend the evening with her, the old man grew almost angry.

'Nathalie,' said he, 'you act entirely without consulting me. I have heard that the captain is very rude and unpolished in his manners. To be sure, I have only seen him standing behind your chair; but he has never even asked after my health. I only speak for your interest, as you are so giddy.'

Nathalie begged her uncle's pardon, and even offered not to receive the captain's visit; but this he forbore to require—secretly resolving not to allow these visits to become too frequent.

But how frail are all human resolutions—overturned by the merest trifle! In this case, the game of backgammon was the unconscious cause of Nathalie's becoming Mme. d'Apremont. The captain was an excellent hand at backgammon. When the uncle heard this, he proposed a game; and the captain, who understood that it was important to gain the uncle's favour, readily acceded.

This did not please Nathalie. She preferred that he should be occupied with herself. When all the company was gone, she turned to her uncle, saying: 'You were right, uncle, after all. I do not admire the captain's manners; I see now that I should not have invited him.'

'On the contrary, Niece, he is a very well-behaved man. I have invited him to come here very often, and play backgammon with me—that is, to pay his addresses to you.'

Nathalie saw that the captain had gained her uncle's heart, and she forgave him for having been less attentive to her. He soon came again, and, thanks to the backgammon, increased in favour with the uncle.

He soon captivated the heart of the pretty widow, also. One morning, Nathalie came blushing to her uncle.

'The captain has asked me to marry him. What do you advise me to do?'

He reflected for a few moments. 'If she refuses him, d'Apremont will come here no longer, and then no more backgammon. But if she marries him, he will always be here, and I shall have my games.' And the answer was: 'You had better marry him.'

Nathalie loved Armand; but she would not yield too easily. She sent for the captain.

'If you really love me—'

'Ah, can you doubt it?'

'Hush! do not interrupt me. If you really love me, you will give me one proof of it.'

'Anything you ask. I swear—'

'No, you must never swear any more; and, one thing more, you must never smoke. I detest the smell of tobacco, and I will not have a husband who smokes.'

Armand sighed, and promised.

The first months of their marriage passed smoothly, but sometimes Armand became thoughtful, restless, and grave. After some time, these fits of sadness became more frequent.

'What is the matter?' asked Nathalie one day, on seeing him stamp with impatience. 'Why are you so irritable?'

'Nothing—nothing at all!' replied the captain, as if ashamed of his ill humour.

'Tell me,' Nathalie insisted, 'have I displeased you in anything?'

The captain assured her that he had no reason to be anything but delighted with her conduct on all occasions, and for a time he was all right. Then soon, he was worse than before.

Nathalie was distressed beyond measure. She imparted her anxiety to her uncle, who replied: 'Yes, my dear, I know what you mean; I have often remarked it myself, at backgammon. He is very inattentive, and often passes his hand over his forehead, and starts up as if something agitated him.'

And one day, when his old habits of impatience and irritability reappeared, more marked than ever, the captain said to his wife: 'My dear, an evening walk will do me a world of good; an old sailor like myself cannot bear to sit around the house after dinner. Nevertheless, if you have any objection—'

'Oh, no! What objection can I have?'

He went out, and continued to do so, day after day, at the same hour. Invariably he returned in the best of good humour.

Nathalie was now unhappy indeed. 'He loves some other woman, perhaps,' she thought, 'and he must see her every day. Oh, how wretched I am! But I must let him know that his perfidy is discovered. No, I will wait until I have some certain proof wherewith to confront him.'

And she went to seek her uncle. 'Ah, I am the most unhappy creature in the world!' she sobbed.

'What is the matter?' cried the old man, leaning back in his armchair.

'Armand leaves the house for two hours every evening, after dinner, and comes back in high spirits and as anxious to please me as on the day of our marriage. Oh, uncle, I cannot bear it any longer! If you do not assist me to discover where he goes, I will seek a separation.'

'But, my dear niece—'

'My dear uncle, you, who are so good and obliging, grant me this one favour. I am sure there is some woman in the secret.'

M. d'Ablaincourt wished to prevent a rupture between his niece and nephew, which would interfere very much with the quiet, peaceable life which he led at their house. He pretended to follow Armand; but came back very soon, saying he had lost sight of him.

'But in what direction does he go?'

'Sometimes one way, and sometimes another, but always alone; so your suspicions are unfounded. Be assured, he only walks for exercise.'

But Nathalie was not to be duped in this way. She sent for a little errand boy, of whose intelligence she had heard a great deal.

'M. d'Apremont goes out every evening.'

'Yes, Madame.'

'To-morrow, you will follow him; observe where he goes, and come and tell me privately. Do you understand?'

'Yes, Madame.'

Nathalie waited impatiently for the next day, and for the hour of her husband's departure. At last, the time came—the pursuit is going on—Nathalie counted the moments. After three-quarters of an hour, the messenger arrived, covered with dust.

'Well,' exclaimed Nathalie, 'speak! Tell me everything that you have seen!'

'Madame, I followed M. d'Apremont, at a distance, as far as the Rue Vieille du Temple, where he entered a small house, in an alley. There was no servant to let him in.'

'An alley! No servant! Dreadful!'

'I went in directly after him, and heard him go up-stairs and unlock a door.'

'Open the door himself, without knocking! Are you sure of that?'

'Yes, Madame.'

'The wretch! So he has a key! But, go on.'

'When the door shut after him, I stole softly up-stairs, and peeped through the keyhole.'

'You shall have twenty francs more.'

'I peeped through the keyhole, and saw him drag a trunk along the floor.'

'A trunk?'

'Then he undressed himself, and—'

'Undressed himself!'

'Then, for a few seconds, I could not see him, and directly he appeared again, in a sort of grey blouse, and a cap on his head.'

'A blouse! What in the world does he want with a blouse? What next?'

'I came away, then, Madame, and made haste to tell you; but he is there still.'

'Well, now run to the corner and get me a cab, and direct the coachman to the house where you have been.'

While the messenger went for the cab, Nathalie hurried on her hat and cloak, and ran into her uncle's room.

'I have found him out—he loves another. He's at her house now, in a grey blouse. But I will go and confront him, and then you will see me no more.'

The old man had no time to reply. She was gone, with her messenger, in the cab. They stopped at last.

'Here is the house.'

Nathalie got out, pale and trembling.

'Shall I go up-stairs with you, Madame?' asked the boy.

'No, I will go alone. The third story, isn't it?'

'Yes, Madame; the left-hand door, at the head of the stairs.'

It seemed that now, indeed, the end of all things was at hand.

Nathalie mounted the dark, narrow stairs, and arrived at the door, and, almost fainting, she cried: 'Open the door, or I shall die!'

The door was opened, and Nathalie fell into her husband's arms. He was alone in the room, clad in a grey blouse, and—smoking a Turkish pipe.

'My wife!' exclaimed Armand, in surprise.

'Your wife—who, suspecting your perfidy, has followed you, to discover the cause of your mysterious conduct!'

'How, Nathalie, my mysterious conduct? Look, here it is!' (Showing his pipe.) 'Before our marriage, you forbade me to smoke, and I promised to obey you. For some months I kept my promise; but you know what it cost me; you remember how irritable and sad I became. It was my pipe, my beloved pipe, that I regretted. One day, in the country, I discovered a little cottage, where a peasant was smoking. I asked him if he could lend me a blouse and cap; for I should like to smoke with him, but it was necessary to conceal it from you, as the smell of smoke, remaining in my clothes, would have betrayed me. It was soon settled between us. I returned thither every afternoon, to indulge in my favourite occupation; and, with the precaution of a cap to keep the smoke from remaining in my hair, I contrived to deceive you. This is all the mystery. Forgive me.'

Nathalie kissed him, crying: 'I might have known it could not be! I am happy now, and you shall smoke as much as you please, at home.'

And Nathalie returned to her uncle, saying: 'Uncle, he loves me! He was only smoking, but hereafter he is to smoke at home.'

'I can arrange it all,' said d'Ablaincourt; 'he shall smoke while he plays backgammon.'

'In that way,' thought the old man, 'I shall be sure of my game.'

THE BIRDS IN THE LETTER-BOX

René Bazin

Nothing can describe the peace that surrounded the country parsonage. The parish was small, moderately honest, prosperous, and was used to the old priest, who had ruled it for thirty years. The town ended at the parsonage, and there began meadows which sloped down to the river and were filled in summer with the perfume of flowers and all the music of the earth. Behind the great house, a kitchen-garden encroached on the meadow. The first ray of the sun was for it, and so was the last. Here the cherries ripened in May, and the currants often earlier, and a week before Assumption, usually, you could not pass within a hundred feet without breathing among the hedges the heavy odour of the melons.

But you must not think that the abbé of St. Philémon was a gourmand. He had reached the age when appetite is only a memory. His shoulders were bent, his face was wrinkled, he had two little grey eyes, one of which could not see any longer, and he was so deaf in one ear that if you happened to be on that side you just had to get round on the other.

Mercy, no! He did not eat all the fruits in his orchard. The boys got their share—and a big share—but the biggest share, by all odds, was eaten by the birds—the blackbirds, who lived there very comfortably all the year, and sang in return the best they could; the orioles, pretty birds of passage, who helped them in summer, and the sparrows, and the warblers of every variety; and the tomtits, swarms of them, with feathers as thick as your fingers, and they hung on the branches and pecked at a grape or scratched a pear—veritable little beasts of prey, whose only 'thank you' was a shrill cry like a saw.

Even to them, old age had made the abbé of St. Philémon indulgent. 'The beasts cannot correct their faults,' he used to say; 'if I got angry at them for not changing I'd have to get angry with a good many of my parishioners!'

And he contented himself with clapping his hands together loud when he went into his orchard, so he should not see too much stealing.

Then there was a spreading of wings, as if all the silly flowers cut off by a great wind were flying away; grey, and white, and yellow, and mottled, a short flight, a rustling of leaves, and then quiet for five minutes. But what minutes! Fancy, if you can, that there was not one factory in the village, not a weaver or a blacksmith, and that the noise of men with their horses and cattle, spreading over the wide, distant plains, melted into the whispering of the breeze and was lost. Mills were unknown, the roads were little frequented, the railroads were very far away. Indeed, if the ravagers of his garden had repented for long, the abbé would have fallen asleep of the silence over his breviary.

Fortunately, their return was prompt; a sparrow led the way, a jay followed, and then the whole swarm was back at work. And the abbé could walk up and down, close his book or open it, and murmur: 'They'll not leave me a berry this year!'

It made no difference; not a bird left his prey, any more than if the good abbé had been a cone-shaped pear-tree, with thick leaves, balancing himself on the gravel of the walk.

The birds know that those who complain take no action. Every year they built their nests around the parsonage of St. Philémon in greater numbers than anywhere else. The best places were quickly taken, the hollows in the trees, the holes in the walls, the forks of the apple-trees and the elms, and you could see a brown beak, like the point of a sword, sticking out of a wisp of straw between all the rafters of the roof. One year, when all the places were taken,

I suppose, a tomtit, in her embarrassment, spied the slit of the letter-box protected by its little roof, at the right of the parsonage gate. She slipped in, was satisfied with the result of her explorations, and brought the materials to build a nest. There was nothing she neglected that would make it warm, neither the feathers, nor the horsehair, nor the wool, nor even the scales of lichens that cover old wood.

One morning the housekeeper came in perfectly furious, carrying a paper. She had found it under the laurel bush, at the foot of the garden.

'Look, sir, a paper, and dirty, too! They are up to fine doings!'

'Who, Philomène?'

'Your miserable birds; all the birds that you let stay here! Pretty soon they'll be building their nests in your soup-tureens!'

'I haven't but one.'

'Haven't they got the idea of laying their eggs in your letter-box! I opened it because the postman rang and that doesn't happen every day. It was full of straw and horsehair and spiders' webs, with enough feathers to make a quilt, and, in the midst of all that, a beast that I didn't see hissed at me like a viper!'

The abbé of St. Philémon began to laugh like a grandfather when he hears of a baby's pranks.

'That must be a tomtit,' said he, 'they are the only birds clever enough to think of it. Be careful not to touch it, Philomène.'

'No fear of that; it is not nice enough!'

The abbé went hastily through the garden, the house, the court planted with asparagus, till he came to the wall which separated the parsonage from the public road, and there he carefully opened the letter-box, in which there would have been room enough for all the mail received in a year by all the inhabitants of the village.

Sure enough, he was not mistaken. The shape of the nest, like a pine-cone, its colour and texture, and the lining, which showed through, made him smile. He heard the hiss of the brooding bird inside and replied:

'Rest easy, little one, I know you. Twenty-one days to hatch your eggs and three weeks to raise your family; that is what you want? You shall have it. I'll take away the key.'

He did take away the key, and when he had finished the morning's duties—visits to his parishioners who were ill or in trouble; instructions to a boy who was to pick him out some fruit at the village: a climb up the steeple because a storm had loosened some stones, he remembered the tomtit and began to be afraid she would be troubled by the arrival of a letter while she was hatching her eggs.

The fear was almost groundless, because the people of St. Philémon did not receive any more letters than they sent. The postman had little to do on his rounds but to eat soup at one house, to have a drink at another and, once in a long while, to leave a letter from some conscript, or a bill for taxes at some distant farm. Nevertheless, since St. Robert's Day was near, which, as you know, comes on the 29th of April, the abbé thought it wise to write to the only three friends worthy of that name, whom death had left him, a layman and two priests: 'My friend, do not congratulate me on my Saint's Day this year, if you please. It would inconvenience me to receive a letter at this time. Later I shall explain, and you will appreciate my reasons.'

They thought that his eye was worse and did not write.

The abbé of St. Philémon was delighted. For three weeks he never entered his gate one time without thinking of the eggs, speckled with pink, that were lying in the letter-box, and when the twenty-first day came round he bent down and listened with his ear close to the slit of the box. Then he stood up beaming:

'I hear them chirp, Philomène; I hear them chirp. They owe their lives to me, sure enough, and they'll not be the ones to regret it any more than I.'

He had in his bosom the heart of a child that had never grown old.

Now, at the same time, in the green room of the palace, at

the chief town of the department, the bishop was deliberating over the appointments to be made with his regular councillors, his two grand vicars, the dean of the chapter, the secretary-general of the palace, and the director of the great academy. After he had appointed several vicars and priests, he made this suggestion:

'Gentlemen of the council, I have in mind a candidate suitable in all respects for the parish of X———; but I think it would be well, at least, to offer that charge and that honour to one of our oldest priests, the abbé of St. Philémon. He will undoubtedly refuse it, and his modesty, no less than his age, will be the cause; but we shall have shown, as far as we could, our appreciation of his virtues.'

The five councillors approved unanimously, and that very evening a letter was sent from the palace, signed by the bishop, and which contained in a postscript: 'Answer at once, my dear abbé; or, better, come to see me, because I must submit my appointments to the government within three days.'

The letter arrived at St. Philémon the very day the tomtits were hatched. The postman had difficulty in slipping it into the slit of the box, but it disappeared inside and lay touching the base of the nest, like a white pavement at the bottom of the dark chamber.

The time came when the tiny points on the wings of the little tomtits began to be covered with down. There were fourteen of them, and they twittered and staggered on their little feet, with their beaks open up to their eyes, never ceasing, from morning till night, to wait for food, eat it, digest it, and demand more. That was the first period, when the baby birds hadn't any sense. But in birds it doesn't last long. Very soon they quarrelled in the nest, which began to break with the fluttering of their wings, then they tumbled out of it and walked along the side of the box, peeped through the slit at the big world outside, and at last they ventured out.

The abbé of St. Philémon, with a neighbouring priest, attended this pleasant garden party. When the little ones appeared beneath the roof of the box—two, three—together and took their flight, came back, started again, like bees at the door of a hive, he said:

'Behold, a babyhood ended and a good work accomplished. They are hardy and strong, everyone.'

The next day, during his hour of leisure after dinner, the abbé came to the box with the key in his hand. 'Tap, tap,' he went. There was no answer. 'I thought so,' said he. Then he opened the box and, mingled with the débris of the nest, the letter fell into his hands.

'Good Heavens!' said he, recognizing the writing. 'A letter from the bishop; and in what state! How long has it been here?'

His cheek grew pale as he read.

'Philomène, harness Robin quickly.'

She came to see what was the matter before obeying.

'What have you there, sir?'

'The bishop has been waiting for me for three weeks!'

'You've missed your chance,' said the old woman.

The abbé was away until the next evening. When he came back he had a peaceful air, but sometimes peace is not attained without effort and we have to struggle to keep it. When he had helped to unharness Robin and had given him some hay, had changed his cassock and unpacked his box, from which he took a dozen little packages of things bought on his visit to the city, it was the very time that the birds assembled in the branches to tell each other about the day. There had been a shower and the drops still fell from the leaves as they were shaken by these bohemian couples looking for a good place to spend the night.

Recognizing their friend and master as he walked up and down the gravel path, they came down, fluttered about him, making an unusually loud noise, and the tomtits, the fourteen of the nest, whose feathers were still not quite grown, essayed their first spirals about the pear-trees and their first cries in the open air.

The abbé of St. Philémon watched them with a fatherly eye, but his tenderness was sad, as we look at things that have cost us dear.

'Well, my little ones, without me you would not be here, and without you I would be dead. I do not regret it at all, but don't insist. Your thanks are too noisy.'

He clapped his hands impatiently.

He had never been ambitious, that is very sure, and, even at that moment, he told the truth. Nevertheless, the next day, after a night spent in talking to Philomène, he said to her:

'Next year, Philomène, if the tomtit comes back, let me know. It is decidedly inconvenient.'

But the tomtit never came again—and neither did the letter from the bishop!

THE PASSAGE OF THE RED SEA

Henri Murger

For five or six years, Marcel had been engaged upon the famous painting which he said was meant to represent the Passage of the Red Sea; and for five or six years, this masterpiece in colour had been obstinately refused by the jury. Indeed, from its constant journeying back and forth, from the artist's studio to the Musée, and from the Musée to the studio, the painting knew the road so well that one needed only to set it on rollers and it would have been quite capable of reaching the Louvre alone. Marcel, who had repainted the picture ten times, and minutely gone over it from top to bottom, vowed that only a personal hostility on the part of the members of the jury could account for the ostracism which annually turned him away from the Salon, and in his idle moments he had composed, in honour of those watch-dogs of the Institut, a little dictionary of insults, with illustrations of a savage irony. This collection gained celebrity and enjoyed, among the studios and in the École des Beaux-Arts, the same sort of popular success as that achieved by the immortal complaint of Giovanni Bellini, painter by appointment to the Grand Sultan of the Turks; every dauber in Paris had a copy stored away in his memory.

For a long time, Marcel had not allowed himself to be discouraged by the emphatic refusal which greeted him at each exposition. He was comfortably settled in his opinion that his picture was, in a modest way, the companion piece long awaited by the 'Wedding of Cana,' that gigantic masterpiece whose dazzling splendour the dust of three centuries has not dimmed. Accordingly, each year, at the time of the Salon, Marcel sent his picture to be examined by the jury. Only, in order to throw the examiners off the track and, if possible, to make them abandon the policy of exclusion which they seemed to have adopted toward the 'Passage of the Red Sea,' Marcel, without in any way disturbing the general scheme of his picture, modified certain details and changed its title.

For instance, on one occasion, it arrived before the jury under the name of the 'Passage of the Rubicon!' but Pharaoh, poorly disguised under Caesar's mantle, was recognized and repulsed with all the honours that were his due.

The following year, Marcel spread over the level plane of his picture a layer of white representing snow, planted a pine-tree in one corner, and, dressing an Egyptian as a grenadier of the Imperial Guard, rechristened the painting the 'Passage of the Beresina.'

The jury, which on that very day had polished its spectacles on the lining of its illustrious coat, was not in any way taken in by this new ruse. It recognized perfectly well the persistent painting, above all by a big brute of a horse of many colours, which was rearing out of one of the waves of the Red Sea. The coat of that horse had served Marcel for all his experiments in colour, and in private conversation he called it his synoptic table of fine tones, because he had reproduced, in their play of light and shade, all possible combinations of colour. But once again, insensible to this detail, the jury seemed scarcely able to find blackballs enough to emphasise their refusal of the 'Passage of the Beresina.'

'Very well,' said Marcel; 'no more than I expected. Next year I shall send it back under the title of "Passage des Panoramas."'

'That will be one on them—on them—on them, them, them,' sang the musician, Schaunard, fitting the words to a new air he had been composing—a terrible air, noisy as a gamut of thunderclaps, and the accompaniment to which was a terror to every piano in the neighbourhood.

'How could they refuse that picture without having every drop of the vermilion in my Red Sea rise up in their faces and cover them with shame?' murmured Marcel, as he gazed at the painting.

'When one thinks that it contains a good hundred crowns' worth of paint, and a million of genius, not to speak of the fair days of my youth, fast growing bald as my hat! But they shall never have the last word; until my dying breath I shall keep on sending them my painting. I want to have it engraved upon their memory.'

'That is certainly the surest way of ever getting it engraved,' said Gustave Colline, in a plaintive voice, adding to himself: 'That was a good one, that was—really a good one; I must get that off the next time I am asked out.'

Marcel continued his imprecations, which Schaunard continued to set to music.

'Oh, they won't accept me,' said Marcel. 'Ah! the government pays them, boards them, gives them the Cross, solely for the one purpose of refusing me once a year, on the 1st of March. I see their idea clearly now—I see it perfectly clearly; they are trying to drive me to break my brushes. They hope, perhaps, by refusing my Red Sea, to make me throw myself out of the window in despair. But they know very little of the human heart if they expect to catch me with such a clumsy trick. I shall no longer wait for the time of the annual Salon. Beginning with to-day, my work becomes the canvas of Damocles, eternally suspended over their existence. From now on, I am going to send it once a week to each one of them, at their homes, in the bosom of their families, in the full heart of their private life. It shall trouble their domestic joy, it shall make them think that their wine is sour, their dinner burned, their wives bad-tempered. They will very soon become insane, and will have to be put in strait-jackets when they go to the Institut, on the days when there are meetings. That idea pleases me.'

A few days later, when Marcel had already forgotten his terrible plans for vengeance upon his persecutors, he received a visit from Father Medicis. For that was the name by which the brotherhood called a certain Jew, whose real name was Soloman, and who at that time was well known throughout the bohemia of art and literature, with which he constantly had dealings. Father Medicis dealt in all sorts of bric-à-brac. He sold complete house-furnishings for from twelve francs up to a thousand crowns. He would buy anything, and knew how to sell it again at a profit. His shop, situated in the Place du Carrousel, was a fairy spot where one could find everything that one might wish. All the products of nature, all the creations of art, all that comes forth from the bowels of the earth or from the genius of man, Medicis found it profitable to trade in. His dealings included everything, absolutely everything that exists; he even put a price upon the Ideal. Medicis would even buy ideas, to use himself or to sell again. Known to all writers and artists, intimate friend of the palette, familiar spirit of the writing-desk, he was the Asmodeus of the arts. He would sell you cigars in exchange for the plot of a dime novel, slippers for a sonnet, a fresh catch of fish for a paradox; he would talk at so much an hour with newspaper reporters whose duty was to record the lively capers of the smart set. He would get you passes to the parliament buildings, or invitations to private parties; he gave lodgings by the night, the week, or the month to homeless artists, who paid him by making copies of old masters in the Louvre. The greenroom had no secrets for him; he could place your plays for you with some manager; he could obtain for you all sorts of favours. He carried in his head a copy of the almanack of twenty-five thousand addresses, and knew the residence, the name, and the secrets of all the celebrities, even the obscure ones.

In entering the abode of the bohemians, with that knowing air which characterised him, the Jew divined that he had arrived at a propitious moment. As a matter of fact, the four friends were at that moment gathered in council, and under the domination of a ferocious appetite were discussing the grave question of bread and meat. It was Sunday, the last day of the month. Fatal day, sinister date!

The entrance of Medicis was accordingly greeted with a joyous chorus, for they knew that the Jew was too avaricious of his time to waste it in mere visits of civility; accordingly his presence always announced that he was open to a bargain.

'Good evening, gentlemen,' said the Jew; 'how are you?'

'Colline,' said Rodolphe from where he lay upon the bed, sunk in the delights of maintaining a horizontal line, 'practise the duties of hospitality and offer our guest a chair; a guest is sacred. I salute you, Abraham,' added the poet.

Colline drew forward a chair which had about as much elasticity as a piece of bronze and offered it to the Jew, Medicis let himself fall into the chair, and started to complain of its hardness, when he remembered that he himself had once traded it off to Colline in exchange for a profession of faith, which he afterward sold to a deputy. As he sat down, the pockets of the Jew gave forth a silvery sound, and this melodious symphony threw the four bohemians into a reverie that was full of sweetness.

'Now,' said Rodolphe, in a low tone, to Marcel, 'let us hear the song. The accompaniment sounds all right.'

'Monsieur Marcel,' said Medicis. 'I have simply come to make your fortune. That is to say, I have come to offer you a superb opportunity to enter into the world of art. Art, as you very well know, Monsieur Marcel, is an arid road, in which glory is the oasis.'

'Father Medicis,' said Marcel, who was on coals of impatience, 'in the name of fifty per cent, your revered patron saint, be brief.'

'Here is the offer,' replied Medicis. 'A wealthy amateur, who is collecting a picture-gallery destined to make the tour of Europe, has commissioned me to procure for him a series of remarkable works. I have come to give you a chance to be included in this collection. In one word, I have come to purchase your "Passage of the Red Sea."'

'Money down?' asked Marcel.

'Money down,' answered the Jew, sounding forth the full orchestra of his pockets.

'Go on, Medicis,' said Marcel, pointing to his painting. 'I wish to leave to you the honour of fixing for yourself the price of that work of art which is priceless.'

The Jew laid upon the table fifty crowns in bright new silver.

'Keep them going,' said Marcel; 'that is a good beginning.'

'Monsieur Marcel,' said Medicis, 'you know very well that my first word is always my last word. I shall add nothing more. But think; fifty crowns; that makes one hundred and fifty francs. That is quite a sum.'

'A paltry sum,' answered the artist; 'just in the robe of my Pharaoh there are fifty crowns' worth of cobalt. Pay me at least something for my work.'

'Hear my last word,' replied Medicis. 'I will not add a penny more; but, I offer dinner for the crowd, wines included, and after dessert I will pay in gold.'

'Do I hear any one object?' howled Colline, striking three blows of his fist upon the table. 'It is a bargain.'

'Come on,' said Marcel. 'I agree.'

'I will send for the picture to-morrow,' said the Jew. 'Come, gentlemen, let us start. Your places are all set.'

The four friends descended the stairs, singing the chorus from 'The Huguenots', 'to the table, to the table.'

Medicis treated the bohemians in a fashion altogether sumptuous. He offered them a lot of things which, up to now. had remained for them a mystery. Dating from this dinner, lobster ceased to be a myth to Schaunard, and he acquired a passion for that amphibian which was destined to increase to the verge of delirium.

The four friends went forth from this splendid feast as intoxicated as on a day of vintage. Their inebriety came near bearing deplorable fruits for Marcel, because as he passed the shop of his tailor, at two o'clock in the morning, he absolutely insisted upon awakening his creditor in order to give him, on account, the one hundred and fifty francs that he had just received. But a gleam of reason still awake in the brain of Colline held back the artist from the brink of this precipice.

A week after this festivity Marcel learned in what gallery his picture had found a place. Passing along the Faubourg Saint-Honoré, he stopped in the midst of a crowd that seemed to be staring at a sign newly placed above a shop. This sign was none other than Marcel's painting, which had been sold by Medicis to a dealer in provisions. Only the 'Passage of the Red Sea' had once again undergone a modification and bore a new title. A steamboat had been added to it, and it was now called 'In the Port of Marseille.' A flattering ovation arose among the crowd when they discovered the picture. And Marcel turned away delighted with this triumph, and murmured softly: 'The voice of the people is the voice of God!'

THE WOMAN AND THE CAT

Marcel Prévost

'Yes,' said our old friend Tribourdeaux, a man of culture and a philosopher, which is a combination rarely found among army surgeons; 'yes, the supernatural is everywhere; it surrounds us and hems us in and permeates us. If science pursues it, it takes flight and cannot be grasped. Our intellect resembles those ancestors of ours who cleared a few acres of forest; whenever they approached the limits of their clearing, they heard low growls and saw gleaming eyes everywhere circling them about. I myself have had the sensation of having approached the limits of the unknown several times in my life, and on one occasion in particular.'

A young lady present interrupted him:

'Doctor, you are evidently dying to tell us a story. Come now, begin!'

The doctor bowed.

'No, I am not in the least anxious, I assure you. I tell this story as seldom as possible, for it disturbs those who hear it, and it disturbs me also. However, if you wish it, here it is:

'In 1863 I was a young physician stationed at Orléans. In that patrician city, full of aristocratic old residences, it is difficult to find bachelor apartments; and, as I like both plenty of air and plenty of room, I took up my lodging on the first floor of a large building situated just outside the city, near Saint-Euverte. It had been originally constructed to serve as the warehouse and also as the dwelling of a manufacturer of rugs. In course of time, the manufacturer had failed, and this big barrack that he had built, falling out of repair through lack of tenants, had been sold for a song with all its furnishings. The purchaser hoped to make a future profit out of his purchase, for the city was growing in that direction; and, as a matter of fact, I believe that at the present time the house is included within the city limits. When I took up my quarters there, however, the mansion stood alone on the verge of the open country, at the end of a straggling street on which a few stray houses produced at dusk the impression of a jaw from which most of the teeth have fallen out.

'I leased one-half of the first floor, an apartment of four rooms. For my bedroom and my study, I took the two that fronted on the street; in the third room, I set up some shelves for my wardrobe, and the other room I left empty. This made a very comfortable lodging for me, and I had, for a sort of promenade, a broad balcony that ran along the entire front of the building, or rather one-half of the balcony, since it was divided into two parts (please note this carefully) by a fan of ironwork, over which, however, one could easily climb.

'I had been living there for about two months when, one night in July on returning to my rooms, I saw with a good deal of surprise a light shining through the windows of the other apartment on the same floor, which I had supposed to be uninhabited. The effect of this light was extraordinary. It lit up with a pale, yet perfectly distinct, reflection, parts of the balcony, the street below, and a bit of the neighbouring fields.

'I thought to myself, "Aha! I have a neighbour."

'The idea indeed was not altogether agreeable, for I had been rather proud of my exclusive proprietorship. On reaching my bedroom, I passed noiselessly out upon the balcony, but already the light had been extinguished. So I went back into my room, and sat down to read for an hour or two. From time to time I seemed to hear about me, as though within the walls, light footsteps; but after finishing my book, I went to bed, and speedily fell asleep.

'About midnight, I suddenly awoke with a curious feeling that something was standing beside me. I raised myself in bed, lit a candle, and this is what I saw. In the middle of the room stood an immense cat gazing upon me with phosphorescent eyes, and with its back slightly arched. It was a magnificent Angora, with long fur and a fluffy tail, and of a remarkable colour—exactly like that of the yellow silk that one sees in cocoons—so that, as the light gleamed upon its coat, the animal seemed to be made of gold.

'It slowly moved toward me on its velvety paws, softly rubbing its sinuous body against my legs. I leaned over to stroke it, and it permitted my caress, purring, and finally leaping upon my knees. I noticed then that it was a female cat, quite young, and that she seemed disposed to permit me to pet her as long as I would. Finally, however, I put her down upon the floor, and tried to induce her to leave the room; but she leaped away from me and hid herself somewhere among the furniture, though as soon as I had blown out my candle, she jumped upon my bed. Being sleepy, however, I didn't molest her, but dropped off into a doze, and the next morning when I awoke in broad daylight I could find no sign of the animal at all.

'Truly, the human brain is a very delicate instrument, and one that is easily thrown out of gear. Before I proceed, just sum up for yourselves the facts that I have mentioned: a light seen and presently extinguished in an apartment supposed to be uninhabited; and a cat of a remarkable colour, which appeared and disappeared in a way that was slightly mysterious. Now there isn't anything very strange about that, is there? Very well. Imagine, now, that these unimportant facts are repeated day after day and under the same conditions throughout a whole week, and then, believe me, they become of importance enough to impress the mind of a man who is living all alone, and to produce in him a slight disquietude such as I spoke of in commencing my story, and such as is always caused when one approaches the sphere of the unknown. The human mind is so formed that it always unconsciously applies the principle of the causa efficiens. For every series of facts that are identical, it demands a cause, a law; and a vague dismay seizes upon it when it is unable to guess this cause and to trace out this law.

'I am no coward, but I have often studied the manifestation of fear in others, from its most puerile form in children up to its most tragic phase in madmen. I know that it is fed and nourished by uncertainties, although when one actually sets himself to investigate the cause, this fear is often transformed into simple curiosity.

'I made up my mind, therefore, to ferret out the truth. I questioned my caretaker, and found that he knew nothing about my neighbours. Every morning an old woman came to look after the neighbouring apartment; my caretaker had tried to question her, but either she was completely deaf or else she was unwilling to give him any information, for she had refused to answer a single word. Nevertheless, I was able to satisfactorily explain the first thing that I had noted—that is to say, the sudden extinction of the light at the moment when I entered the house. I had observed that the windows next to mine were covered only by long lace curtains; and as the two balconies were connected, my neighbour, whether man or woman, had no doubt a wish to prevent any indiscreet inquisitiveness on my part, and therefore had always put out the light on hearing me come in. To verify this supposition, I tried a very simple experiment, which succeeded perfectly. I had a cold supper brought in one day about noon by my servant, and that evening I did not go out. When darkness came on, I took my station near the window. Presently, I saw the balcony shining with the light that streamed through the windows of the neighbouring apartment. At once, I slipped quietly out upon my balcony, and stepped softly over the ironwork that separated the two parts. Although I knew that I was exposing myself to a positive danger, either of falling and breaking my neck, or of finding myself face to face with a man, I experienced no perturbation. Reaching the lighted window without having made the slightest noise, I found it partly open; its curtains, which for me were quite transparent since I was on the dark side of the window, made me wholly invisible to anyone who should look toward the window from the interior of the room.

'I saw a vast chamber furnished quite elegantly, though it was obviously out of repair, and lighted by a lamp suspended from the ceiling. At the end of the room was a low sofa upon which was reclining a woman who seemed to me to be both young and pretty. Her loosened hair fell over her shoulders in a rain of gold. She was looking at herself in a hand mirror, patting herself, passing her arms over her lips, and twisting about her supple body with a curiously feline grace. Every movement that she made caused her long hair to ripple in glistening undulations.

'As I gazed upon her I confess that I felt a little troubled, especially when all of a sudden the young girl's eyes were fixed upon me—strange eyes, eyes of a phosphorescent green that gleamed like the flame of a lamp. I was sure that I was invisible, being on the dark side of a curtained window. That was simple enough, yet nevertheless I felt that I was seen. The girl, in fact, uttered a cry, and then turned and buried her face in the sofa-pillows.

'I raised the window, rushed into the room toward the sofa, and leaned over the face that she was hiding. As I did so, being really very remorseful, I began to excuse and to accuse myself, calling myself all sorts of names, and begging pardon for my indiscretion. I said that I deserved to be driven from her presence, but begged not to be sent away without at least a word of pardon. For a long time, I pleaded thus without success, but at last she slowly turned, and I saw that her fair young face was stirred with just the faintest suggestion of a smile. When she caught a glimpse of me, she murmured something of which I did not then quite get the meaning.

'"It is you," she cried out; "it is you!"

'As she said this, and as I looked at her, not knowing yet exactly what to answer, I was harassed by the thought: Where on earth have I already seen this face, this look, this very gesture? Little by little, however, I found my tongue, and after saying a few more words in apology for my unpardonable curiosity, and getting brief but not offended answers, I took leave of her, and, retiring through the window by which I had come, went back to my own room. Arriving there, I sat a long time by the window in the darkness, charmed by the face that I had seen, and yet singularly disquieted. This woman, so beautiful, so amiable, living so near to me, who said to me, "It is you," exactly as though she had already known me, who spoke so little, who answered all my questions with evasion, excited in me a feeling of fear. She had, indeed, told me her name—Linda—and that was all. I tried in vain to drive away the remembrance of her greenish eyes, which in the darkness seemed still to gleam upon me, and of those glints which, like electric sparks, shone in her long hair whenever she stroked it with her hand. Finally, however, I retired for the night; but scarcely was my head upon the pillow when I felt some moving body descend upon my feet. The cat had appeared again. I tried to chase her away, but she kept returning again and again, until I ended by resigning myself to her presence; and, just as before, I went to sleep with this strange companion near me. Yet my rest was this time a troubled one, and broken by strange and fitful dreams.

'Have you ever experienced the sort of mental obsession which gradually causes the brain to be mastered by some single absurd idea—an idea almost insane, and one which your reason and your will alike repel, but which nevertheless gradually blends itself with your thought, fastens itself upon your mind, and grows and grows? I suffered cruelly in this way on the days that followed my strange adventure. Nothing new occurred, but in the evening, going out onto the balcony, I found Linda standing upon her side of the iron fan. We chatted together for a while in the half darkness, and, as before, I returned to my room to find that in a few moments the golden cat appeared, leaped upon my bed, made a nest for herself there, and remained until the morning. I knew now to whom the cat belonged, for Linda had answered that very same evening, on my speaking of it, 'Oh, yes, my cat; doesn't she look exactly as though she were made of gold?' As I said, nothing new had occurred, yet nevertheless a vague sort of terror began little by little to master me and to develop itself in my mind, at first merely as a bit of foolish fancy, and then as a haunting belief that dominated my entire thought, so that I perpetually seemed to see a thing which it was in reality quite impossible to see.'

'Why, it's easy enough to guess,' interrupted the young lady who had spoken at the beginning of his story.

'Linda and the cat were the same thing.'

Tribourdeaux smiled.

'I should not have been quite so positive as that,' he said, 'even then; but I cannot deny that this ridiculous fancy haunted me for many hours when I was endeavouring to snatch a little sleep amid the insomnia that a too active brain produced. Yes, there were moments when these two beings with greenish eyes, sinuous movements, golden hair, and mysterious ways, seemed to me to be blended into one, and to be merely the double manifestation of a single entity. As I said, I saw Linda again and again, but in spite of all my efforts to come upon her unexpectedly, I never was able to see them both at the same time. I tried to reason with myself, to convince myself that there was nothing really inexplicable in all of this, and I ridiculed myself for being afraid both of a woman and of a harmless cat. In truth, at the end of all my reasoning, I found that I was not so much afraid of the animal alone or of the woman alone, but rather of a sort of quality which existed in my fancy and inspired me with a fear of something that was incorporeal—fear of a manifestation of my own spirit, fear of a vague thought, which is, indeed, the very worst of fears.

'I began to be mentally disturbed. After long evenings spent in confidential and very unconventional chats with Linda, in which little by little my feelings took on the colour of love, I passed long days of secret torment, such as incipient maniacs must experience. Gradually, a resolve began to grow up in my mind, a desire that became more and more importunate in demanding a solution to this unceasing and tormenting doubt; and the more I cared for

Linda, the more it seemed absolutely necessary to push this resolve to its fulfilment. I decided to kill the cat.

'One evening before meeting Linda on the balcony, I took out of my medical cabinet a jar of glycerin and a small bottle of hydrocyanic acid, together with one of those little pencils of glass which chemists use in mixing certain corrosive substances. That evening, for the first time, Linda allowed me to caress her. I held her in my arms and passed my hand over her long hair, which snapped and cracked under my touch in a succession of tiny sparks. As soon as I regained my room, the golden cat, as usual, appeared before me. I called her to me; she rubbed herself against me with arched back and extended tail, purring the while with the greatest amiability. I took the glass pencil in my hand, moistened the point in the glycerin, and held it out to the animal, which licked it with her long red tongue. I did this three or four times, but the next time, I dipped the pencil in the acid. The cat unhesitatingly touched it with her tongue. In an instant she became rigid, and a moment after, a frightful tetanic convulsion caused her to leap thrice into the air, and then to fall upon the floor with a dreadful cry—a cry that was truly human. She was dead!

'With the perspiration starting from my forehead and with trembling hands I threw myself upon the floor beside the body that was not yet cold. The starting eyes had a look that froze me with horror. The blackened tongue was thrust out between the teeth; the limbs exhibited the most remarkable contortions. I mustered all my courage with a violent effort of will, took the animal by the paws, and left the house. Hurrying down the silent street, I proceeded to the quays along the banks of the Loire, and, on reaching them, threw my burden into the river. Until daylight I roamed around the city, just where I know not; and not until the sky began to grow pale and then to be flushed with light did I at last have the courage to return home. As I laid my hand upon the door, I shivered. I had a dread of finding there still living, as in the celebrated tale of Poe, the animal that I had so lately put to death.

But no, my room was empty. I fell half-fainting upon my bed, and for the first time I slept, with a perfect sense of being all alone, a sleep like that of a beast or of an assassin, until evening came.'

Someone here interrupted, breaking in upon the profound silence in which we had been listening.

'I can guess the end. Linda disappeared at the same time as the cat.'

'You see perfectly well,' replied Tribourdeaux, 'that there exists between the facts of this story a curious coincidence, since you are able to guess exactly their relation. Yes, Linda disappeared. They found in her apartment her dresses, her linen, all even to the night-robe that she was to have worn that night, but there was nothing that could give the slightest clue to her identity. The owner of the house had let the apartment to "Mademoiselle Linda, concert-singer." He knew nothing more. I was summoned before the police magistrate. I had been seen on the night of her disappearance roaming about with a distracted air in the vicinity of the river. Luckily the judge knew me; luckily also, he was a man of no ordinary intelligence. I related to him privately the entire story, just as I have been telling it to you. He dismissed the inquiry; yet I may say that very few have ever had so narrow an escape as mine from a criminal trial.'

For several moments, the silence of the company was unbroken. Finally a gentleman, wishing to relieve the tension, cried out:

'Come now, doctor, confess that this is really all fiction; that you merely want to prevent these ladies from getting any sleep to-night.'

Tribourdeaux bowed stiffly, his face unsmiling and a little pale.

'You may take it as you will,' he said.

TONTON

Adolphe Chenevière

There are men who seem born to be soldiers. They have the face, the bearing, the gesture, the quality of mind. But there are others who have been forced to become so, in spite of themselves and of the rebellion of reason and the heart, through a rash deed, a disappointment in love, or simply because their destiny demanded it, being sons of soldiers and gentlemen. Such is the case of my friend Captain Robert de X——. And I said to him one summer evening, under the great trees of his terrace, which is washed by the green and sluggish Marne:

'Yes, old fellow, you are sensitive. What the deuce would you have done on a campaign where you were obliged to shoot, to strike down with a sabre and to kill? And then, too, you have never fought, except against the Arabs, and that is quite another thing.'

He smiled, a little sadly. His handsome mouth, with its blond moustache, was almost like that of a youth. His blue eyes were dreamy for an instant, then little by little he began to confide to me his thoughts, his recollections and all that was mystic and poetic in his soldier heart.

'You know we are soldiers in my family. We have a Marshal of France and two officers who died on the field of honour. I have perhaps obeyed a law of heredity. I believe rather that my imagination has carried me away. I saw war through my reveries of epic poetry. In my fancy, I dwelt only upon the intoxication of victory, the triumphant flourish of trumpets and women throwing flowers to the victor. And then I loved the sonorous words of the great captains, the dramatic representations of martial glory.

My father was in the third regiment of Zouaves, the one which was hewn in pieces at Reichshoffen, in the Niederwald, and which, in 1859 at Palestro, made that famous charge against the Austrians and hurled them into the great canal. It was superb; without them, the Italian divisions would have been lost. Victor Emmanuel marched with the Zouaves. After this affair, while still deeply moved, not by fear but with admiration for this regiment of demons and heroes, he embraced their old colonel and declared that he would be proud, were he not a king, to join the regiment. Then the Zouaves acclaimed him corporal of the Third. And for a long time on the anniversary festival of St. Palestro, when the roll was called, they shouted "Corporal of the First Squad, in the First company of the First Battalion, Victor Emmanuel," and a rough old sergeant solemnly responded: "Sent as long into Italy."

'That is the way my father talked to us, and by these recitals, a soldier was made of a dreamy child. But later, what a disillusion! Where is the poetry of battle? I have never made any campaign except in Africa, but that has been enough for me. And I believe the army surgeon is right, who said to me one day: "If instantaneous photographs could be taken after a battle, and millions of copies made and scattered through the world, there would be no more war. The people would refuse to take part in it."

'Africa, yes, I have suffered there. On one occasion, I was sent to the south, six hundred kilometres from Oran, beyond the oasis of Fignig, to destroy a tribe of rebels... On this expedition, we had a pretty serious affair with a military chief of the great desert, called Bon-Arredji. We killed nearly all of the tribe, and seized nearly fifteen hundred sheep; in short, it was a complete success. We also captured the wives and children of the chief. A dreadful thing happened at that time, under my very eyes! A woman was fleeing, pursued by a black mounted soldier. She turned around and shot at him with a revolver. The horse-soldier was furious, and struck her down with one stroke of his sabre. I did not have the time to interfere. I dismounted from my horse to take the woman up. She was dead, and almost decapitated. I uttered not one word of reproach to the Turkish soldier, who smiled fiercely, and turned back.

'I placed the poor body sadly on the sand, and was going to remount my horse, when I perceived, a few steps back, behind a thicket, a little girl five or six years old. I recognized at once that she was a Touareg, of white race, notwithstanding her tawny colour. I approached her. Perhaps she was not afraid of me, because I was white like herself. I took her on the saddle with me, without resistance on her part, and returned slowly to the place where we were to camp for the night. I expected to place her under the care of the women whom we had taken prisoners, and were carrying away with us. But all refused, saying that she was a vile little Touareg, belonging to a race which carries misfortune with it and brings forth only traitors.

'I was greatly embarrassed. I would not abandon the child… I felt somewhat responsible for the crime, having been one of those who had directed the massacre. I had made an orphan! I must take her part. One of the prisoners of the band had said to me (I understand a little of the gibberish of these people) that if I left the little one to these women they would kill her because she was the daughter of a Touareg, whom the chief had preferred to them, and that they hated the petted, spoiled child, whom he had given rich clothes and jewels. What was to be done?

'I had a wide-awake orderly, a certain Michel of Batignolles. I called him and said to him: "Take care of the little one." "Very well, Captain, I will take her in charge." He then petted the child, made her sociable, and led her away with him, and two hours later, he had manufactured a little cradle for her out of biscuit boxes which are used on the march for making coffins. In the evening, Michel put her to bed in it. He had christened her "Tonton," an abbreviation of Touareg. In the morning the cradle was bound on an ass, and behold Tonton following the column with the baggage, in the convoy of the rear guard, under the indulgent eye of Michel.

'This lasted for days and weeks. In the evening at the halting place, Tonton was brought into my tent, with the goat, which furnished her the greater part of her meals, and her inseparable friend, a large chameleon, captured by Michel, and responding or not responding to the name of Achilles.

'Ah, well! old fellow, you may believe me or not; but it gave me pleasure to see the little one sleeping in her cradle, during the short night full of alarm, when I felt the weariness of living, the dull sadness of seeing my companions dying, one by one, leaving the caravan; the enervation of the perpetual state of alertness, always attacking or being attacked, for weeks and months. I, with the gentle instincts of a civilised man, was forced to order the beheading of spies and traitors, the binding of women in chains and the kidnapping of children, to raid the herds, to make myself an Attila. And this had to be done without a moment of wavering, and I, the cold and gentle Celt, whom you know, remained there, under the scorching African sun. Then what repose of soul, what strange meditations were mine, when free at last, at night, in my sombre tent, around which death might be prowling, I could watch the little Touareg, saved by me, sleeping in her cradle by the side of her chameleon lizard. Ridiculous, is it not? But, go there and lead the life of a brute, of a plunderer and assassin, and you will see how at times your civilised imagination will wander away to take refuge from itself.

'I could have rid myself of Tonton. In an oasis we met some rebels, bearing a flag of truce, and exchanged the women for guns and ammunition. I kept the little one, notwithstanding the five months of march we must make, before returning to Tlemcen. She had grown gentle, was inclined to be mischievous, but was yielding and almost affectionate with me. She ate with the rest, never wanting to sit down, but running from one to another around the table. She had proud little manners, as if she knew herself to be a daughter of the chief's favourite, obeying only the officers and treating Michel with an amusing scorn. All this was to have a sad ending. One day, I did not find the chameleon in the cradle, though I remembered having seen it there the evening before. I had even taken it in my hands and caressed it before Tonton, who had just gone to bed. Then, I gave it back to her and went out. Accordingly, I questioned her. She took me by the hand, and leading me to the campfire, showed me the charred skeleton of the chameleon, explaining to me, the best she could, that she had thrown it in the fire, because I had petted it! Oh! women! women! And she gave a horrible imitation of the lizard, writhing in the midst of the flames, and she smiled with delighted eyes. I was indignant. I seized her by the arm, shook her a little, and finished by boxing her ears.

'My dear fellow, from that day, she appeared not to know me. Tonton and I sulked; we were angry. However, one morning, as I felt the sun was going to be terrible, I went myself to the baggage before the loading for departure, and arranged a sheltering awning over the cradle. Then to make peace, I embraced my little friend. But as soon as we were on the march, she furiously tore off the canvas with which I had covered the cradle. Michel put it all in place again, and there was a new revolt. In short, it was necessary to yield because she wanted to be able to lean outside of her box, under the fiery sun, to look at the head of the column, of which I had the command. I saw this on arriving at the resting place. Then Michel brought her under my tent. She had not yet fallen asleep, but followed with her eyes all of my movements, with a grave air, without a smile, or gleam of mischief.

'She refused to eat and drink; the next day she was ill, with sunken eyes and body burning with fever. When the major wished to give her medicine, she refused to take it, and ground her teeth together to keep from swallowing.

'There remained still six days' march before arriving at Oran. I wanted to give her into the care of the nuns. She died before I could do so, very suddenly, with a severe attack of meningitis. She never wanted to see me again. She was buried under a clump of

African shrubs near Geryville, in her little campaign cradle. And do you know what was found in her cradle? The charred skeleton of the poor chameleon, which had been the indirect cause of her death. Before leaving the bivouac, where she had committed her crime, she had picked it out of the glowing embers, and brought it into the cradle, and that is why her little fingers were burned. Since the beginning of the meningitis, the major had never been able to explain the cause of these burns.'

Robert was silent for an instant, then murmured: 'Poor little one! I feel remorseful. If I had not given her that blow... who knows?... she would perhaps be still living...

'My story is sad, is it not? Ah, well, it is still the sweetest of my African memories. War is beautiful! Eh?'

And Robert shrugged his shoulders...

FATHER MILON

Guy de Maupassant

For a month, the hot sun has been parching the fields. Nature is expanding beneath its rays; the fields are green as far as the eye can see. The big azure dome of the sky is unclouded. The farms of Normandy, scattered over the plains and surrounded by a belt of tall beeches, look, from a distance, like little woods. On closer view, after lowering the worm-eaten wooden bars, you imagine yourself in an immense garden, for all the ancient apple-trees, as gnarled as the peasants themselves, are in bloom. The sweet scent of their blossoms mingles with the heavy smell of the earth and the penetrating odour of the stables. It is noon. The family is eating under the shade of a pear tree planted in front of the door; father, mother, the four children, and the help—two women and three men are all there. All are silent. The soup is eaten, and then a dish of potatoes fried with bacon is brought on.

From time to time, one of the women gets up and takes a pitcher down to the cellar to fetch more cider.

The man, a big fellow about forty years old, is watching a grapevine, still bare, which is winding and twisting like a snake along the side of the house.

At last he says: 'Father's vine is budding early this year. Perhaps we may get something from it.'

The woman then turns round and looks, without saying a word.

This vine is planted on the spot where their father had been shot.

It was during the war of 1870. The Prussians were occupying

the whole country. General Faidherbe, with the Northern Division of the army, was opposing them.

The Prussians had established their headquarters at this farm. The old farmer to whom it belonged, Father Pierre Milon, had received and quartered them to the best of his ability.

For a month, the German vanguard had been in this village. The French remained motionless, ten leagues away; and yet, every night, some of the Uhlans disappeared.

Of all the isolated scouts, of all those who were sent to the outposts, in groups of not more than three, not one ever returned.

They were picked up the next morning in a field or in a ditch. Even their horses were found along the roads with their throats cut.

These murders seemed to be done by the same men, who could never be found.

The country was terrorized. Farmers were shot on suspicion, women were imprisoned; children were being frightened in order to try and obtain information. Nothing could be ascertained.

But, one morning, Father Milon was found stretched out in the barn, with a sword gash across his face.

Two Uhlans were found dead about a mile and a half from the farm. One of them was still holding his bloody sword in his hand. He had fought, tried to defend himself. A court-martial was immediately held in the open air, in front of the farm. The old man was brought before it.

He was sixty-eight years old, small, thin, bent, with two big hands resembling the claws of a crab. His colourless hair was sparse and thin, like the down of a young duck, allowing patches of his scalp to be seen. The brown and wrinkled skin of his neck showed big veins which disappeared behind his jaws and came out again at the temples. He had the reputation of being miserly and hard to deal with.

They stood him up between four soldiers, in front of the kitchen table, which had been dragged outside. Five officers and the colonel seated themselves opposite him.

The colonel spoke in French:

'Father Milon, since we have been here, we have only had praise for you. You have always been obliging and even attentive to us. But to-day a terrible accusation is hanging over you, and you must clear the matter up. How did you receive that wound on your face?'

The peasant answered nothing.

The colonel continued:

'Your silence accuses you, Father Milon. But I want you to answer me! Do you understand? Do you know who killed the two Uhlans who were found this morning near Calvaire?'

The old man answered clearly:

'I did.'

The colonel, surprised, was silent for a minute, looking straight at the prisoner. Father Milon stood impassive, with the stupid look of the peasant, his eyes lowered as though he were talking to the priest. Just one thing betrayed an uneasy mind; he was continually swallowing his saliva, with a visible effort, as though his throat were terribly contracted.

The man's family, his son Jean, his daughter-in-law and his two grandchildren were standing a few feet behind him, bewildered and affrighted.

The colonel went on:

'Do you also know who killed all the scouts who have been found dead, for a month, throughout the country, every morning?'

The old man answered with the same stupid look:

'I did.'

'You killed them all?'

'Uh huh! I did.'

'You alone? All alone?'

'Uh huh!'

'Tell me how you did it.'

This time the man seemed moved; the necessity for talking any length of time annoyed him visibly. He stammered:

'I dunno! I simply did it.'

The colonel continued:

'I warn you that you will have to tell me everything. You might as well make up your mind right away. How did you begin?'

The man cast a troubled look toward his family, standing close behind him. He hesitated a minute longer, and then suddenly made up his mind to obey the order.

'I was coming home one night at about ten o'clock, the night after you got here. You and your soldiers had taken more than fifty ecus' worth of forage from me, as well as a cow and two sheep. I said to myself: "As much as they take from you; just so much will you make them pay back." And then, I had other things on my mind which I will tell you. Just then, I noticed one of your soldiers who was smoking his pipe by the ditch behind the barn. I went and got my scythe, and crept up slowly behind him, so that he couldn't hear me. And I cut his head off with one single blow, just as I would a blade of grass, before he could say 'Booh!' If you look at the bottom of the pond, you will find him tied up in a potato-sack, with a stone fastened to it.

'I got an idea. I took all his clothes, from his boots to his cap, and hid them away in the little wood behind the yard.'

The old man stopped. The officers remained speechless, looking at each other. The questioning began again, and this is what they learned:

Once this murder was committed, the man had lived with this one thought: 'Kill the Prussians!' He hated them with the blind, fierce hate of the greedy yet patriotic peasant. He had his idea, as he said. He waited several days.

He was allowed to go and come as he pleased, because he had shown himself so humble, submissive and obliging to the invaders. Each night, he saw the outposts leave. One night he followed them, having heard the name of the village to which the men were going, and having learned the few words of German which he needed for his plan through associating with the soldiers.

He left through the back yard, slipped into the woods, found the dead man's clothes and put them on. Then he began to crawl through the fields, following along the hedges in order to keep out of sight, listening to the slightest noises, as wary as a poacher.

As soon as he thought the time was ripe, he approached the road and hid behind a bush. He waited for a while. Finally, toward midnight, he heard the sound of a galloping horse. The man put his ear to the ground in order to make sure that only one horseman was approaching, then he got ready.

An Uhlan came galloping along, carrying dispatches. As he went, he was all eyes and ears. When he was only a few feet away, Father Milon dragged himself across the road, moaning: 'Hilfe! Hilfe!' (Help! Help!) The horseman stopped, and recognizing a German, he thought he was wounded and dismounted, coming nearer without any suspicion, and just as he was leaning over the unknown man, he received, in the pit of his stomach, a heavy thrust from the long curved blade of the sabre. He dropped without suffering pain, quivering only in the final throes. Then the farmer, radiant with the silent joy of an old peasant, got up again, and, for his own pleasure, cut the dead man's throat. He then dragged the body to the ditch and threw it in.

The horse quietly awaited its master. Father Milon mounted him and started galloping across the plains.

About an hour later he noticed two more Uhlans who were returning home, side by side. He rode straight for them, once more crying, 'Hilfe! Hilfe!'

The Prussians, recognizing the uniform, let him approach without distrust. The old man passed between them like a cannon-ball, felling them both, one with his sabre and the other with a revolver.

Then he killed the horses, German horses! After that he quickly returned to the woods and hid one of the horses. He left his uniform there and again put on his old clothes; then going back into bed, he slept until morning.

For four days he did not go out, waiting for the inquest to be terminated; but on the fifth day, he went out again and killed two more soldiers by the same stratagem. From that time on, he did not stop. Each night he wandered about in search of adventure, killing Prussians, sometimes here and sometimes there, galloping through deserted fields, in the moonlight, a lost Uhlan, a hunter of men. Then, his task accomplished, leaving behind him the bodies lying along the roads, the old farmer would return and hide his horse and uniform.

He went, toward noon, to carry oats and water quietly to his mount, and he fed it well as he required from it a great amount of work.

But one of those whom he had attacked the night before, in defending himself, slashed the old peasant across the face with his sabre.

However, he had killed them both. He had come back and hidden the horse and put on his ordinary clothes again; but as he reached home he began to feel faint, and had dragged himself as far as the stable, being unable to reach the house.

They had found him there, bleeding, on the straw.

When he had finished his tale, he suddenly lifted up his head and looked proudly at the Prussian officers.

The colonel, who was gnawing at his moustache, asked:

'You have nothing else to say?'

'Nothing more; I have finished my task; I killed sixteen, not one more or less.'

'Do you know that you are going to die?'

'I haven't asked for mercy.'

'Have you been a soldier?'

'Yes, I served my time. And then, you had killed my father, who was a soldier of the First Emperor. And last month you killed my youngest son, François, near Évreux. I owed you one for that; I paid. We are quits.'

The officers were looking at each other.

The old man continued:

'Eight for my father, eight for the boy—we are quits. I did not seek any quarrel with you. I don't know you. I don't even know where you come from. And here you are, ordering me about in my home as though it were your own. I took my revenge upon the others. I'm not sorry.'

And, straightening up his bent back, the old man folded his arms in the attitude of a modest hero.

The Prussians talked in a low tone for a long time. One of them, a captain, who had also lost his son the previous month, was defending the poor wretch. Then the colonel arose and, approaching Father Milon, said in a low voice:

'Listen, old man, there is perhaps a way of saving your life, it is to—'

But the man was not listening, and, his eyes fixed on the hated officer, while the wind played with the downy hair on his head, he distorted his slashed face, giving it a truly terrible expression, and, swelling out his chest, he spat, as hard as he could, right in the Prussian's face.

The colonel, furious, raised his hand, and for the second time, the man spat in his face.

All the officers had jumped up and were shrieking orders at the same time.

In less than a minute, the old man, still impassive, was pushed up against the wall and shot, looking smilingly at Jean, his eldest son, his daughter-in-law and his two grandchildren, who witnessed this scene in dumb terror.

THE COLONEL'S IDEAS

Guy de Maupassant

'Upon my word,' said Colonel Laporte, 'although I am old and gouty, my legs as stiff as two pieces of wood, yet if a pretty woman were to tell me to go through the eye of a needle, I believe I should take a jump at it, like a clown through a hoop. I shall die like that; it is in the blood. I am an old beau, one of the old school, and the sight of a woman, a pretty woman, stirs me to the tips of my toes. There!

'We are all very much alike in France in this respect; we still remain knights, knights of love and fortune, since God has abolished whose bodyguard we really were. But nobody can ever get woman out of our hearts; there she is, and there she will remain, and we love her, and shall continue to love her, and go on committing all kinds of follies on her account, as long as there is a France on the map of Europe; and even if France were to be wiped off the map, there would always be Frenchmen left.

'When I am in the presence of a woman, of a pretty woman, I feel capable of anything. By Jove! when I feel her looks penetrating me, her confounded looks which set your blood on fire, I should like to do I don't know what; to fight a duel, to have a row, to smash the furniture, in order to show that I am the strongest, the bravest, the most daring and the most devoted of men.

'But I am not the only one, certainly not; the whole French army is like me, I swear to you. From the common soldier to the general, we all start out, from the van to the rear guard, when there is a woman in the case, a pretty woman. Do you remember what Joan of Arc made us do formerly? Come. I will make a bet that if a pretty woman had taken command of the army on the eve of Sedan, when Marshal MacMahon was wounded, we should have broken through the Prussian lines, by Jove! and had a drink out of their guns.

'It was not a Trochu, but a Sainte-Genèvieve, who was needed in Paris; and I remember a little anecdote of the war which proves that we are capable of everything in the presence of a woman.

'I was a captain, a simple captain, at the time, and I was in command of a detachment of scouts, who were retreating through a district which was swarmed with Prussians. We were surrounded, pursued, tired out and half dead with fatigue and hunger, but we were bound to reach Bar-sur-Tain before the morrow, otherwise we would be shot, cut down, massacred. I do not know how we managed to escape so far. However, we had ten leagues to go during the night, ten leagues through the night, ten leagues through the snow, and with empty stomachs, and I thought to myself:

'It is all over; my poor devils of fellows will never be able to do it.'

'We had eaten nothing since the day before, and the whole day, we remained hidden in a barn, huddled close together, so as not to feel the cold so much, unable to speak or even move, and sleeping by fits and starts, as one does when worn out with fatigue.

'It was dark by five o'clock, that wan darkness of the snow, and I shook my men. Some of them would not get up; they were almost incapable of moving or of standing upright; their joints were stiff from cold and hunger.

'Before us, there was a large expanse of flat, bare country; the snow was still falling like a curtain, in large, white flakes, which concealed everything under a thick, frozen coverlet, a coverlet of frozen wool. One might have thought that it was the end of the world.

'"Come, my lads, let us start."

'They looked at the thick white flakes that were coming down, and they seemed to think: "We have had enough of this; we may just as well die here!" Then I took out my revolver and said:

"'I will shoot the first man who flinches." And so they set off, but very slowly, like men whose legs were of very little use to them, and I sent four of them three hundred yards ahead to scout, and the others followed pell-mell, walking at random and without any order. I put the strongest in the rear, with orders to quicken the pace of the sluggards with the points of their bayonets in the back.

'The snow seemed as if it were going to bury us alive; it powdered our kepis and cloaks without melting, and made phantoms of us, a kind of spectre of dead, weary soldiers. I said to myself: "We shall never get out of this except by a miracle."

'Sometimes we had to stop for a few minutes, on account of those who could not follow us, and then we heard nothing except the falling snow, that vague, almost indiscernible sound made by the falling flakes. Some of the men shook themselves, others did not move, and so I gave the order to set off again. They shouldered their rifles, and with weary feet we resumed our march, when suddenly the scouts fell back. Something had alarmed them; they had heard voices in front of them. I sent forward six men and a sergeant and waited.

'All at once a shrill cry, a woman's cry, pierced through the heavy silence of the snow, and in a few minutes, they brought back two prisoners, an old man and a girl, whom I questioned in a low voice. They were escaping from the Prussians, who had occupied their house during the evening and had gotten drunk. The father was alarmed on his daughter's account, and, without even telling their servants, they had made their escape in the darkness. I saw immediately that they belonged to the better class. I invited them to accompany us, and we started off again, the old man who knew the road acting as our guide.

'It had ceased snowing, the stars appeared and the cold became intense. The girl, who was leaning on her father's arm, walked unsteadily as though in pain, and several times she murmured:

"'I have no feeling at all in my feet"; and I suffered more than she did to see that poor little woman dragging herself like that through the snow. But suddenly she stopped and said:

'"Father, I am so tired that I cannot go any further."

'The old man wanted to carry her, but he could not even lift her up, and she sank to the ground with a deep sigh. We all gathered round her, and, as for me, I stamped my foot in perplexity, not knowing what to do, and being unwilling to abandon that man and girl like that, when suddenly one of the soldiers, a Parisian whom they had nicknamed Pratique, said:

'"Come, comrades, we must carry the young lady, otherwise we shall not show ourselves Frenchmen, confound it!"

'I really believe that I swore with pleasure. "That is very good of you, my children," I said; "and I will take my share of the burden."

'We could indistinctly see, through the darkness, the trees of a little wood on the left. Several of the men went into it, and soon came back with a bundle of branches made into a litter.

'"Who will lend his cape? It is for a pretty girl, comrades," Pratique said, and ten cloaks were thrown to him. In a moment the girl was lying, warm and comfortable, among them, and was raised upon six shoulders. I placed myself at their head, on the right, well pleased with my position.

'We started off much more briskly, as if we had had a drink of wine, and I even heard some jokes. A woman is quite enough to electrify Frenchmen, you see. The soldiers, who had become cheerful and warm, had almost reformed their ranks, and an old 'franc-tireur' who was following the litter, waiting for his turn to replace the first of his comrades who might give out, said to one of his neighbours, loud enough for me to hear: "I am not a young man now, but by—, there is nothing like the women to put courage into you!"

'We went on, almost without stopping, until three o'clock in the morning, when suddenly our scouts fell back once more, and soon the whole detachment showed nothing but a vague shadow on the ground, as the men lay on the snow. I gave my orders in a low voice, and heard the harsh, metallic sound of the cocking of rifles. There, in the middle of the plain, some strange object was moving about. It looked like some enormous animal running about, now stretching out like a serpent, now coiling itself into a ball, darting to the right, then to the left, then stopping, and presently starting off again. But presently, that wandering shape came nearer, and I saw a dozen lancers at full gallop, one behind the other. They had lost their way and were trying to find it.

'They were so near by that time that I could hear the loud breathing of their horses, the clinking of their swords and the creaking of their saddles, and cried: "Fire!"

'Fifty rifle shots broke the stillness of the night, then there were four or five reports, and at last, one single shot was heard, and when the smoke had cleared away, we saw that the twelve men and nine horses had fallen. Three of the animals were galloping away at a furious pace, and one of them was dragging the dead body of its rider, which rebounded violently from the ground; his foot was caught in the stirrup.

'One of the soldiers behind me gave a terrible laugh and said: "There will be some widows there!"

'Perhaps he was married. A third added: "It did not take long!"

'A head emerged from the litter.

'"What is the matter?" she asked; "are you fighting?"

'"It is nothing, Mademoiselle," I replied; "we have got rid of a dozen Prussians!"

'"Poor fellows!" she said. But as she was cold, she quickly disappeared beneath the cloaks again, and we started off once more. We marched on for a long time, and at last, the sky began to grow lighter. The snow became quite clear, luminous and glistening, and a rosy tint appeared in the east. Suddenly a voice in the distance cried:

'"Who goes there?"

'The whole detachment halted, and I advanced to give the countersign. We had reached the French lines, and, as my men defiled before the outpost, a commandant on horseback, whom I had informed of what had taken place, asked in a sonorous voice, as he saw the litter pass him: "What have you in there?"

'And immediately a small head covered with light hair appeared, dishevelled and smiling, and replied:

"'It is I, Monsieur."

'At this, the men raised a hearty laugh, and we felt quite light-hearted, while Pratique, who was walking by the side of the litter, waved his kepi and shouted:

"'Vive la France!" And I felt really affected. I do not know why, except that I thought it a pretty and gallant thing to say.

'It seemed to me as if we had just saved the whole of France and had done something that other men could not have done, something simple and really patriotic. I shall never forget that little face, you may be sure; and if I had to give my opinion about abolishing drums, trumpets and bugles, I should propose to replace them in every regiment with a pretty girl, and that would be even better than playing "La Marseillaise". By Jove! it would put some spirit into a trooper to have a Madonna like that, a live Madonna, by the colonel's side.'

He was silent for a few moments and then continued, with an air of conviction, and nodding his head:

'All the same, we are very fond of women, we Frenchmen!'

THE MOUSTACHE

Guy de Maupassant

CHÂTEAU DE SOLLES,
July 30, 1883.

My Dear Lucy:

I have no news. We live in the drawing-room, looking out at the rain. We cannot go out in this frightful weather, so we have theatricals. How stupid they are, my dear, these drawing entertainments in the repertory of real life! Everything is forced, coarse, heavy. The jokes are like cannon balls, smashing everything in their passage. No wit, nothing natural, no sprightliness, no elegance. These literary men, in truth, know nothing of society. They are perfectly ignorant of how people think and talk in our set. I do not mind if they despise our customs, our conventionalities, but I do not forgive them for not knowing them. When they want to be humorous, they make puns that would do for a barrack; when they try to be jolly, they give us jokes that they must have picked up on the outer boulevard in those beer houses artists are supposed to frequent, where one has heard the same students' jokes for fifty years.

So we have taken to theatricals. As we are only two women, my husband takes the part of a soubrette, and, in order to do that, he has shaved off his moustache. You cannot imagine, my dear Lucy, how it changes him! I no longer recognize him by day or at night. If he did not let it grow again I think I should no longer love him; he looks so horrid like this.

In fact, a man without a moustache is no longer a man. I do not care much for a beard; it almost always makes a man look untidy. But a moustache, oh, a moustache is indispensable to a manly face. No, you would never believe how these little hair bristles on the upper lip are a relief to the eye and good in other ways. I have thought over the matter a great deal but hardly dare to write my thoughts. Words look so different on paper and the subject is so difficult, so delicate, so dangerous that it requires infinite skill to tackle it.

Well, when my husband appeared, shaven, I understood at once that I never could fall in love with a strolling actor nor a preacher, even if it were Father Didon, the most charming of all! Later, when I was alone with him (my husband), it was worse still. Oh, my dear Lucy, never let yourself be kissed by a man without a moustache; their kisses have no flavour, none whatsoever! They no longer have the charm, the mellowness and the snap—yes, the snap—of a real kiss. The moustache is the spice.

Imagine placing a piece of dry—or moist—parchment on your lips. That is the kiss of the man without a moustache. It is not worthwhile.

Whence comes this charm of the moustache, will you tell me? Do I know myself? It tickles your face, you feel it approaching your mouth and it sends a little shiver through you down to the tips of your toes.

And on your neck! Have you ever felt a moustache on your neck? It intoxicates you, makes you feel creepy, goes to the tips of your fingers. You wriggle, shake your shoulders, toss back your head. You wish to get away and, at the same time, to remain there; it is delightful, but irritating. But how good it is!

A lip without a moustache is like a body without clothing; and one must wear clothes, very few, if you like, but still some clothing.

I recall a sentence (uttered by a politician) which has been running in my mind for three months. My husband, who keeps up with the newspapers, read to me one evening a very singular speech by our Minister of Agriculture, who was called M. Meline. He may have been superseded by this time. I do not know.

I was paying no attention, but the name Meline struck me. It recalled, I do not exactly know why, the 'Scènes de la vie de bohème'. I thought it was about some grisette. That shows how scraps of the speech entered my mind. This M. Meline was making this statement to the people of Amiens, I believe, and I have ever since been trying to understand what he meant: 'There is no patriotism without agriculture!' Well, I have just discovered his meaning, and I affirm in my turn that there is no love without a moustache. When you say it that way it sounds comical, does it not?

There is no love without a moustache!

'There is no patriotism without agriculture,' said M. Meline, and he was right, that minister; I now understand why.

From a very different point of view, the moustache is essential. It gives character to the face. It makes a man look gentle, tender, violent, a monster, a rake, enterprising! The hairy man, who does not shave off his whiskers, never has a refined look, for his features are concealed; and the shape of the jaw and the chin betrays a great deal to those who understand.

The man with a moustache retains his own peculiar expression and his refinement at the same time.

And how many different varieties of moustaches there are! Sometimes they are twisted, curled, coquettish. Those seem to be chiefly devoted to women.

Sometimes they are pointed, sharp as needles, and threatening. That kind prefers wine, horses and war.

Sometimes they are enormous, overhanging, and frightful. These big ones generally conceal a fine disposition, a kindliness that borders on weakness and a gentleness that savours of timidity.

But what I adore above all in the moustache is that it is French, altogether French. It came from our ancestors, the Gauls, and has remained the insignia of our national character.

It is boastful, gallant and brave. It sips wine gracefully and knows how to laugh with refinement, while the broad-bearded jaws are clumsy in everything they do.

I recall something that made me weep all my tears and also—I see it now—made me love a moustache on a man's face.

It was during the war, when I was living with my father. I was a young girl then. One day there was a skirmish near the château. I had heard the firing of the cannon and of the artillery all morning, and that evening, a German colonel came and took up his abode in our house. He left the following day.

My father was informed that there were a number of dead bodies in the fields. He had them brought to our place so that they might be buried together. They were laid all along the great avenue of pines as fast as they brought them in, on both sides of the avenue, and as they began to smell unpleasant, their bodies were covered with earth until the deep trench could be dug. Thus, one saw only their heads which seemed to protrude from the clayey earth and were almost as yellow, with their closed eyes.

I wanted to see them. But when I saw those two rows of frightful faces, I thought I should faint. However, I began to look at them, one by one, trying to guess what kind of men they had been.

The uniforms were concealed beneath the earth, and yet immediately, yes, immediately, my dear, I recognized the Frenchmen by their moustache!

Some of them had shaved on the very day of the battle, as though they wished to be elegant up to the last; others seemed to have a week's growth, but all wore the French moustache, very plain, the proud moustache that seems to say: 'Do not take me for my bearded friend, little one; I am a brother.'

And I cried. Oh, I cried a great deal more than I should have if I had not recognized them, the poor dead fellows.

It was wrong of me to tell you this. Now I am sad and cannot chatter any longer. Well, good-bye, dear Lucy. I send you a hearty kiss. Long live the moustache!

JEANNE

THE BLIND MAN

Guy de Maupassant

How is it that the sunlight gives us such joy? Why does this radiance, when it falls on the earth, fill us with the joy of living? The whole sky is blue, the fields are green, the houses all white, and our enchanted eyes drink in those bright colours which bring delight to our souls. And then there springs up in our hearts a desire to dance, to run, to sing, a happy lightness of thought, a sort of enlarged tenderness; we feel a longing to embrace the sun.

The blind, as they sit in the doorways, impassive in their eternal darkness, remain as calm as ever in the midst of this fresh gaiety, and, not understanding what is taking place around them, they continually check their dogs as they attempt to play.

When, at the close of the day, they are returning home on the arm of a young brother or a little sister, if the child says: 'It was a very fine day!' the other answers: 'I could notice that it was fine. Loulou wouldn't keep quiet.'

I knew one of these men whose life was one of the cruellest martyrdoms that could possibly be conceived.

He was a peasant, the son of a Norman farmer. As long as his father and mother lived, he was more or less taken care of; he suffered little, save for his horrible infirmity; but as soon as the old people were gone, an atrocious life of misery commenced for him. Dependent on a sister of his, everybody in the farmhouse treated him as a beggar who is eating the bread of strangers. At every meal the very food he swallowed was made a subject of reproach against him; he was called a drone, a clown, and although his brother-in-law had taken possession of his portion of the inheritance, he was helped grudgingly to soup, getting just enough to save him from starving.

His face was very pale and his two big white eyes looked like wafers. He remained unmoved at all the insults hurled at him, so reserved that one could not tell whether he felt them.

Moreover, he had never known any tenderness, his mother having always treated him unkindly and caring very little for him; for in country places, useless persons are considered a nuisance, and the peasants would be glad to kill the infirm of their species, as poultry do.

As soon as he finished his soup, he went and sat outside the door in summer, and in winter, beside the fireside, and did not stir again all evening. He made no gesture, no movement; only his eyelids, quivering from some nervous affection, fell down sometimes over his white, sightless orbs. Had he any intellect, any thinking faculty, any consciousness of his own existence? Nobody cared to inquire.

For some years, things went on in this fashion. But his incapacity for work as well as his impassiveness eventually exasperated his relatives, and he became a laughingstock, a sort of butt for merriment, a prey to the inborn ferocity, to the savage gaiety of the brutes who surrounded him.

It is easy to imagine all the cruel practical jokes inspired by his blindness. And, in order to have some fun in return for feeding him, they now converted his meals into hours of pleasure for the neighbours and of punishment for the helpless creature himself.

The peasants from the nearest houses came to watch this entertainment; it was talked about from door to door, and every day the kitchen of the farmhouse was full of people. Sometimes they placed before his plate, when he was beginning to eat his soup, some cat or dog. The animal instinctively perceived the man's infirmity, and, softly approaching, commenced eating noiselessly, lapping up the soup daintily; and, when they lapped the food rather noisily, rousing the poor fellow's attention, they would prudently scamper away to avoid the blow of the spoon directed at random by the blind man!

Then the spectators ranged along the wall would burst out laughing, nudge each other and stamp their feet on the floor. And he, without ever uttering a word, would continue eating with his right hand, while stretching out his left to protect his plate.

Another time they made him chew corks, bits of wood, leaves or even filth, which he was unable to distinguish.

After this they got tired even of these practical jokes, and the brother-in-law, angry at having to support him always, struck him, cuffed him incessantly, laughing at his futile efforts to ward off or return the blows. Then came a new pleasure—the pleasure of smacking his face. And the plough-men, the servant girls and even every passing vagabond were every moment giving him cuffs, which caused his eyelashes to twitch spasmodically. He did not know where to hide himself and remained with his arms always held out to guard against people coming too close to him.

At last, he was forced to beg.

He was placed somewhere on the high-road on market-days, and as soon as he heard the sound of footsteps or the rolling of a vehicle, he reached out his hat, stammering:

'Charity, if you please!'

But the peasant is not lavish, and for whole weeks he did not bring back a sou.

Then he became the victim of furious, pitiless hatred. And this is how he died.

One winter the ground was covered with snow, and it was freezing hard. His brother-in-law led him one morning a great distance along the high road in order that he might solicit alms. The blind man was left there all day; and when night came on, the brother-in-law told the people of his house that he could find no trace of the mendicant. Then he added:

'Pooh! best not bother about him! He was cold and got

someone to take him away. Never fear! He's not lost. He'll turn up soon enough tomorrow to eat the soup.'

Next day he did not come back.

After long hours of waiting, stiffened with the cold, feeling that he was dying, the blind man began to walk. Being unable to find his way along the road, owing to its thick coating of ice, he went on at random, falling into ditches, getting up again, without uttering a sound, his sole object being to find some house where he could take shelter.

But, by degrees, the descending snow made a numbness steal over him, and his feeble limbs being incapable of carrying him farther, he sat down in the middle of an open field. He did not get up again.

The white flakes which fell continuously buried him, so that his body, quite stiff and stark, disappeared under the incessant accumulation of their rapidly thickening mass, and nothing was left to indicate the place where he lay.

His relatives made a pretence of inquiring about him and searching for him for about a week. They even made a show of weeping.

The winter was severe, and the thaw did not set in quickly. Now, one Sunday, on their way to mass, the farmers noticed a great flight of crows, who were whirling incessantly above the open field, and then descending like a shower of black rain at the same spot, ever going and coming.

The following week these gloomy birds were still there. There was a crowd of them up in the air, as if they had gathered from all corners of the horizon, and they swooped down with a great cawing into the shining snow, which they covered like black patches, and in which they kept pecking obstinately. A young fellow went to see what they were doing and discovered the body of the blind man, already half devoured, mangled. His wan eyes had disappeared, pecked out by the long, voracious beaks.

And I can never feel the glad radiance of sunlit days without sadly remembering and pondering over the fate of the beggar, who was such an outcast in life that his horrible death was a relief to all who had known him.

INDISCRETION

Guy de Maupassant

They had loved each other before marriage with a pure and lofty love. They had first met on the sea-shore. He had thought this young girl charming, as she passed by with her light-coloured parasol and her dainty dress amid the marine landscape against the horizon. He had loved her, blonde and slender, in these surroundings of blue oceans and spacious skies. He could not distinguish the tenderness which this budding woman awoke in him from the vague and powerful emotion which the fresh salt air and the grand scenery of surf, sunshine and waves aroused in his soul.

She, on the other hand, had loved him because he courted her, because he was young, rich, kind, and attentive. She had loved him because it is natural for young girls to love men who whisper sweet nothings to them.

So, for three months, they had lived side by side, and hand in hand. The greeting which they exchanged in the morning before the bath, in the freshness of the morning, or in the evening on the sand, under the stars, in the warmth of a calm night, whispered low, very low, already had the flavour of kisses, though their lips had never met.

Each dreamed of the other at night, each thought of the other on awaking, and, without yet having voiced their sentiments, each longing for the other, body and soul.

After marriage their love descended to earth. It was at first a tireless, sensuous passion, then exalted tenderness composed of tangible poetry, more refined caresses, and new and foolish inventions. Every glance and gesture was an expression of passion.

But, little by little, without even noticing it, they began to get tired of each other. Love was still strong, but they had nothing more to reveal to each other, nothing more to learn from each other, no new tale of endearment, no unexpected outburst, no new way of expressing the well-known, oft-repeated verb.

They tried, however, to rekindle the dwindling flame of first love. Every day, they tried some new trick or desperate attempt to bring back to their hearts the uncooled ardour of their first days of married life. They tried moonlight walks under the trees, in the sweet warmth of the summer evenings: the poetry of mist-covered beaches; the excitement of public festivals.

One morning Henriette said to Paul:

'Will you take me to a café for dinner?'

'Certainly, dearie.'

'To some well-known café?'

'Of course!'

He looked at her with a questioning glance, seeing that she was thinking of something which she did not wish to tell.

She went on:

'You know, one of those cafés—oh, how can I explain myself?—a sporty café!'

He smiled: 'Of course, I understand—you mean in one of the cafés which are commonly called Bohemian.'

'Yes, that's it. But take me to one of the big places, one where you are known, one where you have already supped—no—dined—well, you know—I—I—oh! I will never dare say it!'

'Go ahead, dearie. Little secrets should no longer exist between us.'

'No, I dare not.'

'Go on; don't be prudish. Tell me.'

'Well, I—I—I want to be taken for your sweetheart—there! and I want the boys, who do not know that you are married, to take me for such; and you too—I want you to think that I am your sweetheart for one hour, in that place which must hold so many memories for you. There! And I will play that I am your sweetheart. It's awful, I know—I am abominably ashamed, I am as red as a peony. Don't look at me!'

He laughed, greatly amused, and answered:

'All right, we will go to-night to a very swell place where I am well known.'

Toward seven o'clock, they went up the stairs of one of the big cafés on the Boulevard, he, smiling, with the look of a conqueror, she, timid, veiled, delighted. They were immediately shown to one of the luxurious private dining-rooms, furnished with four large arm-chairs and a red plush couch. The head waiter entered and brought them the menu. Paul handed it to his wife.

'What do you want to eat?'

'I don't care; order whatever is good.'

After handing his coat to the waiter, he ordered dinner and champagne. The waiter looked at the young woman and smiled. He took the order and murmured:

'Will Monsieur Paul have his champagne sweet or dry?'

'Dry, very dry.'

Henriette was pleased to hear that this man knew her husband's name. They sat on the couch, side by side, and began to eat.

Ten candles lit the room and were reflected in the mirrors all around them, which seemed to increase the brilliancy a thousandfold. Henriette drank glass after glass in order to keep up her courage, although she felt dizzy after the first few glasses. Paul, excited by the memories which returned to him, kept kissing his wife's hands. His eyes were sparkling.

She was feeling strangely excited in this new place, restless, pleased, a little guilty, but full of life. Two waiters, serious, silent, accustomed to seeing and forgetting everything, to entering the room only when it was necessary and to leaving it when they felt they were intruding, were silently flitting hither and thither.

Toward the middle of the dinner, Henriette was well under

the influence of champagne. She was prattling along fearlessly, her cheeks flushed, her eyes glistening.

'Come, Paul; tell me everything.'

'What, sweetheart?'

'I don't dare tell you.'

'Go on!'

'Have you loved many women before me?'

He hesitated, a little perplexed, not knowing whether he should hide his adventures or boast of them.

She continued:

'Oh! please tell me. How many have you loved?'

'A few.'

'How many?'

'I don't know. How do you expect me to know such things?'

'Haven't you counted them?'

'Of course not.'

'Then you must have loved a good many!'

'Perhaps.'

'About how many? Just tell me about how many.'

'But I don't know, dearest. Some years a good many, and some years only a few.'

'How many a year, did you say?'

'Sometimes twenty or thirty, sometimes only four or five.'

'Oh! that makes more than a hundred in all!'

'Yes, just about.'

'Oh! I think that is dreadful!'

'Why dreadful?'

'Because it's dreadful when you think of it—all those women—and always—always the same thing. Oh! it's dreadful, just the same—more than a hundred women!'

He was surprised that she should think that dreadful, and answered, with the air of superiority which men take with women when they wish to make them understand that they have said something foolish:

'That's funny! If it is dreadful to have a hundred women, it's dreadful to have one.'

'Oh, no, not at all!'

'Why not?'

'Because with one woman you have a real bond of love which attaches you to her, while with a hundred women it's not the same at all. There is no real love. I don't understand how a man can associate with such women.'

'But they are all right.'

'No, they can't be!'

'Yes, they are!'

'Oh, stop; you disgust me!'

'But then, why did you ask me how many sweethearts I had had?'

'Because—'

'That's no reason!'

'What were they—actresses, little shop-girls, or society women?'

'A few of each.'

'It must have been rather monotonous toward the end.'

'Oh, no; it's amusing to change.'

She remained thoughtful, staring at her champagne glass. It was full—she drank it in one gulp; then putting it back on the table, she threw her arms around her husband's neck and murmured in his ear:

'Oh! how I love you, sweetheart! how I love you!'

He threw his arms around her in a passionate embrace. A waiter, who was just entering, backed out, closing the door discreetly. In about five minutes the head waiter came back, solemn and dignified, bringing the fruit for dessert. She was once more holding between her fingers a full glass, and gazing into the amber liquid as though seeking unknown things. She murmured in a dreamy voice:

'Yes, it must be fun!'

BESIDE SCHOPENHAUER'S CORPSE

Guy de Maupassant

He was slowly dying, as consumptives die. I saw him each day, about two o'clock, sitting beneath the hotel windows on a bench in the promenade, looking out on the calm sea. He remained for some time without moving, in the heat of the sun, gazing mournfully at the Mediterranean. Every now and then, he cast a glance at the lofty mountains with beclouded summits that shut in Menton; then, with a very slow movement, he would cross his long legs, so thin that they seemed like two bones, around which fluttered the cloth of his trousers, and he would open a book, always the same book. And then he did not stir any more, but read on, read on with his eye and his mind; all his wasting body seemed to read, all his soul plunged, lost, disappeared, in this book, up to the hour when the cool air made him cough a little. Then, he got up and reentered the hotel.

He was a tall German, with a fair beard, who breakfasted and dined in his own room, and spoke to nobody.

A vague curiosity attracted me to him. One day, I sat down by his side, having taken up a book, too, to keep up appearances, a volume of Musset's poems.

And I began to look through 'Rolla.'

Suddenly, my neighbour said to me, in good French:

'Do you know German, Monsieur?'

'Not at all, Monsieur.'

'I am sorry for that. Since chance has thrown us side by side, I could have lent you, I could have shown you, an inestimable thing—this book which I hold in my hand.'

'What is it, pray?'

'It is a copy of my master, Schopenhauer, annotated with his own hand. All the margins, as you may see, are covered with his handwriting.'

I took the book from him reverently, and I gazed at these forms incomprehensible to me, but which revealed the immortal thoughts of the greatest shatterer of dreams who had ever dwelt on earth.

And Musset's verses arose in my memory:

'Hast thou found out, Voltaire, that it is bliss to die,
And does thy hideous smile over thy bleached bones fly?'

And involuntarily, I compared the childish sarcasm, the religious sarcasm of Voltaire with the irresistible irony of the German philosopher, whose influence is henceforth ineffaceable.

Let us protest and let us be angry, let us be indignant, or let us be enthusiastic, Schopenhauer has marked humanity with the seal of his disdain and of his disenchantment.

A disabused pleasure-seeker, he overthrew beliefs, hopes, poetic ideals and chimeras, destroyed the aspirations, ravaged the confidence of souls, killed love, dragged down the chivalrous worship of women, crushed the illusions of hearts, and accomplished the most gigantic task ever attempted by scepticism. He spared nothing with his mocking spirit, and exhausted everything. And even to-day those who execrate him seem to carry in their own souls particles of his thought.

'So, then, you were intimately acquainted with Schopenhauer?' I said to the German.

He smiled sadly.

'Up to the time of his death, Monsieur.'

And he spoke to me about the philosopher and told me about the almost supernatural impression this strange being made on all who came near him.

He gave me an account of the interview of the old iconoclast with a French politician, a doctrinaire Republican, who wanted to get a glimpse of this man, and found him in a noisy tavern, seated in the midst of his disciples, dry, wrinkled, laughing with an unforgettable laugh, attacking and tearing to pieces ideas and beliefs with a single word, as a dog tears with one bite of his teeth the tissues with which he plays.

He repeated for me the comment of this Frenchman as he went away, astonished and terrified: 'I thought I had spent an hour with the devil.'

Then he added:

'He had, indeed, Monsieur, a frightful smile, which terrified us even after his death. I can tell you an anecdote about it that is not generally known, if it would interest you.'

And he began, in a languid voice, interrupted by frequent fits of coughing.

'Schopenhauer had just died, and it was arranged that we should watch, in turn, two by two, till morning.

'He was lying in a large apartment, very simple, vast and gloomy. Two wax candles were burning on the stand by the bedside.

'It was midnight when I went on watch, together with one of our comrades. The two friends whom we replaced had left the apartment, and we came and sat down at the foot of the bed.

'The face was not changed. It was laughing. That pucker which we knew so well lingered still around the corners of the lips, and it seemed to us that he was about to open his eyes, to move and to speak. His thought, or rather his thoughts, enveloped us. We felt ourselves more than ever in the atmosphere of his genius, absorbed, possessed by him. His domination seemed to be even more sovereign now that he was dead. A feeling of mystery was blended with the power of this incomparable spirit.

'The bodies of these men disappear, but they themselves remain; and in the night which follows the cessation of their heart's pulsation I assure you, Monsieur, they are terrifying.

'And in hushed tones we talked about him, recalling to mind certain sayings, certain formulas of his, those startling maxims which are like jets of flame flung, in a few words, into the darkness of the Unknown Life.

'"It seems to me that he is going to speak," said my comrade. And we stared with uneasiness bordering on fear at the motionless face, with its eternal laugh. Gradually, we began to feel ill at ease, oppressed, to the point of fainting. I faltered:

'"I don't know what is the matter with me, but, I assure you I am not well."

'And at that moment we noticed that there was an unpleasant odour from the corpse.

'Then, my comrade suggested that we should go into the adjoining room, and leave the door open; and I assented to his proposal.

'I took one of the wax candles which burned on the stand, and I left the second behind. Then we went and sat down at the other end of the adjoining apartment, in such a position that we could see the bed and the corpse, clearly revealed by the light.

'But he still held possession of us. One would have said that his immaterial essence, liberated, free, all-powerful and dominating, was flitting around us. And sometimes, too, the dreadful odour of the decomposed body came toward us and penetrated us, sickening and indefinable.

'Suddenly a shiver passed through our bones: a sound, a slight sound, came from the death-chamber. Immediately we fixed our glances on him, and we saw, yes, Monsieur, we saw distinctly, both of us, something white pass across the bed, fall on the carpet, and vanish under an armchair.

'We were on our feet before we had time to think of anything, distracted by stupefying terror, ready to run away. Then we stared at each other. We were horribly pale. Our hearts throbbed fiercely enough to have raised the clothing on our chests. I was the first to speak:

'"Did you see?"

'"Yes, I saw."

"'Can it be that he is not dead?'"

"'Why, when the body is putrefying?'"

"'What are we to do?'"

'My companion said in a hesitating tone:

"'We must go and look.'"

'I took our wax candle and entered first, glancing into all the dark corners in the large apartment. Nothing was moving now, and I approached the bed. But I stood transfixed with stupor and fright:

'Schopenhauer was no longer laughing! He was grinning in a horrible fashion, with his lips pressed together and deep hollows in his cheeks. I stammered out:

"'He is not dead!'"

'But the terrible odour ascended to my nose and stifled me. And I no longer moved, but kept staring fixedly at him, terrified as if in the presence of an apparition.

'Then my companion, having seized the other wax candle, bent forward. Next, he touched my arm without uttering a word. I followed his glance, and saw on the ground, under the armchair by the side of the bed, standing out white on the dark carpet, and open as if to bite, Schopenhauer's set of artificial teeth.

'The work of decomposition, loosening the jaws, had made it jump out of the mouth.

'I was really frightened that day, Monsieur.'

And as the sun was sinking toward the glittering sea, the consumptive German rose from his seat, gave me a parting bow, and retired into the hotel.

THE DOOR

Guy de Maupassant

'Bah!' exclaimed Karl Massouligny, 'the question of complaisant husbands is a difficult one. I have seen many kinds, and yet, I am unable to give an opinion about any of them. I have often tried to determine whether they are blind, weak or clairvoyant. I believe that there are some which belong to each of these categories.

'Let us quickly pass over the blind ones. They cannot rightly be called complaisant, since they do not know, but they are good creatures who cannot see farther than their nose. It is a curious and interesting thing to notice the ease with which men and women can be deceived. We are taken in by the slightest trick of those who surround us, by our children, our friends, our servants, our tradespeople. Humanity is credulous, and in order to discover deceit in others, we do not display one-tenth the shrewdness which we use when we, in turn, wish to deceive someone else.

'Clairvoyant husbands may be divided into three classes: Those who have some interest, pecuniary, ambitious or otherwise, in their wives' having love affairs. These ask only to safeguard appearances as much as possible, and they are satisfied.

'Next come those who get angry. What a beautiful novel one could write about them!

'Finally the weak ones! Those who are afraid of scandal.

'There are also those who are powerless, or, rather, tired, who flee from the duties of matrimony through fear of ataxia or apoplexy, who are satisfied to see a friend run these risks.

'But I once met a husband of a rare species, who guarded against the common accident in a strange and witty manner.

'In Paris I had made the acquaintance of an elegant, fashionable couple. The woman, nervous, tall, slender, courted, was supposed to have had many love adventures. She pleased me with her wit, and I believe that I pleased her also. I courted her, a trial courting, to which she answered with evident provocations. Soon we got to tender glances, hand pressures, all the little gallantries which precede the final attack.

'Nevertheless, I hesitated. I consider that, as a rule, the majority of society intrigues, however short they may be, are not worth the trouble which they give us and the difficulties which may arise. I therefore mentally compared the advantages and disadvantages which I might expect, and I thought I noticed that the husband suspected me.

'One evening, at a ball, as I was saying tender things to the young woman in a little parlour leading from the big hall where the dancing was going on, I noticed in a mirror the reflection of someone who was watching me. It was him. Our looks met and then I saw him turn his head and walk away.

'I murmured: "Your husband is spying on us."

'She seemed dumbfounded and asked: "My husband?"

'"Yes, he has been watching us for some time."

'"Nonsense! Are you sure?"

'"Very sure."

'"How strange! He is usually extraordinarily pleasant to all my friends."

'"Perhaps he guessed that I love you!"

'"Nonsense! You are not the first one to pay attention to me. Every woman who is a little in view drags behind her a herd of admirers."

'"Yes. But I love you deeply."

'"Admitting that that is true, does a husband ever guess those things?"

'"Then he is not jealous?"

'"No-no!"

'She thought for an instant and then continued: "No. I do not think that I ever noticed any jealousy on his part."

'"Has he never watched you?"

'"No. As I said, he is always agreeable to my friends."

'From that day my courting became much more assiduous. The woman did not please me any more than before, but the probable jealousy of her husband tempted me greatly.

'As for her, I judged her coolly and clearly. She had a certain worldly charm, due to a quick, gay, amiable and superficial mind, but no real, deep attraction. She was, as I have already said, an excitable little being, all on the surface, with rather a showy elegance. How can I explain myself? She was an ornament, not a home.

'One day, after taking dinner with her, her husband said to me, just as I was leaving: "My dear friend" (he now called me "friend"), "we soon leave for the country. It is a great pleasure to my wife and myself to entertain people whom we like. We would be very pleased to have you spend a month with us. It would be very nice of you to do so."

'I was dumbfounded, but I accepted.

'A month later I arrived at their estate of Vertcresson, in Touraine. They were waiting for me at the station, five miles from the château. There were three of them, she, the husband and a gentleman unknown to me, the Comte de Morterade, to whom I was introduced. He appeared to be delighted to make my acquaintance, and the strangest ideas passed through my mind while we trotted along the beautiful road between two hedges. I was saying to myself: "Let's see, what can this mean? Here is a husband who cannot doubt that his wife and I are on more than friendly terms, and yet he invites me to his house, receives me like an old friend and seems to say: 'Go ahead, my friend, the road is clear!'"

'Then I am introduced to a very pleasant gentleman, who seems already to have settled down in the house, and—and who is perhaps trying to get out of it, and who seems as pleased at my arrival as the husband himself.

'Is it some former admirer who wishes to retire? One might think so. But, then, would these two men tacitly have come to one of these infamous little agreements so common in society? And it is proposed to me that I should quietly enter into the pact and carry it out. All hands and arms are held out to me. All doors and hearts are open to me.

'And what about her? An enigma. She cannot be ignorant of everything. However—however—Well, I cannot understand it.

'The dinner was very gay and cordial. On leaving the table, the husband and his friend began to play cards, while I went out on the porch to look at the moonlight with madame. She seemed to be greatly affected by nature, and I judged that the moment for my happiness was near. That evening she was really delightful. The country had seemed to make her more tender. Her long, slender waist looked pretty on this stone porch beside a great vase in which grew some flowers. I felt like dragging her out under the trees, throwing myself at her feet and speaking to her words of love.

'Her husband's voice called "Louise!"

'"Yes, dear."

'"You are forgetting the tea."

'"I'll go and see about it, my friend."

'We returned to the house, and she gave us some tea. When the two men had finished playing cards, they were visibly tired. I had to go to my room. I did not get to sleep till late, and then I slept badly.

'An excursion was decided upon for the following afternoon, and we went in an open carriage to visit some ruins. She and I were in the back of the vehicle and they were opposite us, riding backward. The conversation was sympathetic and agreeable. I am an orphan, and it seemed to me as though I had just found my family, I felt so at home with them.

'Suddenly, as she had stretched out her foot between her

husband's legs, he murmured reproachfully: 'Louise, please don't wear out your old shoes yourself. There is no reason for being neater in Paris than in the country.'

'I lowered my eyes. She was indeed wearing worn-out shoes, and I noticed that her stockings were not pulled up tight.

'She had blushed and hidden her foot under her dress. The friend was looking out in the distance with an indifferent and unconcerned look.

'The husband offered me a cigar, which I accepted. For a few days it was impossible for me to be alone with her for two minutes; he was with us everywhere. He was delightful to me, however.

'One morning he came to get me to take a walk before breakfast, and the conversation happened to turn on marriage. I spoke a little about solitude and about how charming life can be made by the affection of a woman. Suddenly he interrupted me, saying: "My friend, don't talk about things you know nothing about. A woman who has no other reason for loving you will not love you long. All the little coquetries, which make them so exquisite when they do not definitely belong to us, cease as soon as they become ours. And then—the respectable women—that is to say our wives—are—are not—in fact do not understand their profession of wife. Do you understand?"

'He said no more, and I could not guess his thoughts.

'Two days after this conversation he called me to his room quite early, in order to show me a collection of engravings. I sat in an easy chair opposite the big door which separated his apartment from his wife's, and behind this door I heard someone walking and moving, and I was thinking very little of the engravings, although I kept exclaiming: "Oh, charming! delightful! exquisite!"

'He suddenly said: "Oh, I have a beautiful specimen in the next room. I'll go and get it."

'He ran to the door quickly, and both sides opened as though for theatrical effect.

'In a large room, all in disorder, in the midst of skirts, collars, waists lying around on the floor, stood a tall, dried-up creature. The lower part of her body was covered with an old, worn-out silk petticoat, which was hanging limply on her shapeless form, and she was standing in front of a mirror brushing some short, sparse blond hairs. Her arms formed two acute angles, and as she turned around in astonishment I saw under a common cotton chemise a regular cemetery of ribs, which were hidden from the public gaze by well-arranged pads.

'The husband uttered a natural exclamation and came back, closing the doors, and said: "Gracious! how stupid I am! Oh, how thoughtless! My wife will never forgive me for that!"

'I already felt like thanking him. I left three days later, after cordially shaking hands with the two men and kissing the lady's fingers. She bade me a cold good-bye.'

Karl Massouligny was silent. Someone asked: 'But what was the friend?'

'I don't know—however—however he looked greatly distressed to see me leaving so soon.'

THE MARQUIS DE FUMEROL

Guy de Maupassant

Roger de Tourneville was whiffing a cigar and blowing out small clouds of smoke every now and then, as he sat astride a chair amid a party of friends. He was talking.

'We were at dinner when a letter was brought in which my father opened. You know my father, who thinks that he is king of France ad interim. I call him Don Quixote, because for twelve years, he has been running a tilt against the windmill of the Republic, without quite knowing whether it was in the cause of the Bourbons or the Orléanists. At present, he is bearing the lance in the cause of the Orléanists alone, because there is no one else left. In any case, he thinks himself the first gentleman of France, the best known, the most influential, the head of the party; and as he is an irremovable senator, he thinks that the thrones of the neighbouring kings are very insecure.

'As for my mother, she is my father's soul, she is the soul of the kingdom and of religion, and the scourge of all evil-thinkers.

'Well, a letter was brought in while we were at dinner, and my father opened and read it, and then he said to Mother: "Your brother is dying." She grew very pale. My uncle was scarcely ever mentioned in the house, and I did not know him at all; all I knew from public talk was that he had led, and was still leading, a gay life. After having spent his fortune in fast living, he was now in small apartments in the Rue des Martyrs.

'An ancient peer of France and former colonel of cavalry, it was said that he believed in neither God nor devil. Not believing, therefore, in a future life he had abused the present life in every way, and had become a live wound in my mother's heart.

'"Give me that letter, Paul," she said, and when she read it, I asked for it in my turn. Here it is:

> 'Monsieur le Comte, I think I ought to let you know that your brother-in-law, the Comte Fumerol, is going to die. Perhaps you would like to make some arrangements, and do not forget I told you.
>
> Your servant,
> 'MÉLANIE.'

'"We must take counsel," papa murmured. "In my position, I ought to watch over your brother's last moments."

'Maman continued: "I will send for Abbé Poivron and ask his advice, and then I will go to my brother with the abbé and Roger. Remain here, Paul, for you must not compromise yourself; but a woman can, and ought to do these things. For a politician in your position, it is another matter. It would be a fine thing for one of your opponents to be able to bring one of your most laudable actions up against you." "You are right," my father said. "Do as you think best, my dear wife."

'A quarter of an hour later, the Abbé Poivron came into the drawing-room, and the situation was explained to him, analysed and discussed in all its bearings. If the Marquis de Fumerol, one of the greatest names in France, were to die without the ministrations of religion, it would assuredly be a terrible blow to the nobility in general, and to the Count de Tourneville in particular, and the freethinkers would be triumphant. The liberal newspapers would sing songs of victory for six months; my mother's name would be dragged through the mire and brought into the prose of Socialistic journals, and my father's name would be smirched. It was impossible that such a thing should be.

'A crusade was therefore immediately decided upon, which was to be led by the Abbé Poivron, a little, fat, clean priest with a faint perfume about him, a true vicar of a large church in a noble and rich quarter.

'The landau was ordered and we all three set out, my mother, the cure and I, to administer the last sacraments to my uncle.

'It had been decided first of all we should see Madame Mélanie, who had written the letter, and who was most likely the porter's wife, or my uncle's servant, and I dismounted, as an advance guard, in front of a seven-story house and went into a dark passage, where I had great difficulty in finding the porter's den. He looked at me distrustfully, and I said:

'"Madame Mélanie, if you please." "Don't know her!" "But I have received a letter from her." "That may be, but I don't know her. Are you asking for a lodger?" "No, a servant probably. She wrote to me about a place." "A servant?—a servant? Perhaps it is the marquis'. Go and see the fifth story on the left."

'As soon as he found I was not asking for a doubtful character, he became friendlier and came as far as the corridor with me. He was a tall, thin man with white whiskers, the manners of a beadle and majestic gestures.

'I climbed up a long spiral staircase, the railing of which I did not venture to touch, and I gave three discreet knocks at the left-hand door on the fifth story. It opened immediately, and an enormous dirty woman appeared before me. She barred the entrance with her extended arms which she placed against the two doorposts, and growled:

'"What do you want?" "Are you Madame Mélanie?" "Yes." "I am the Visconte de Tourneville." "Ah! Alright! Come in." "Well, the fact is, my mother is downstairs with a priest." "Oh! All right; go and bring them up; but be careful of the porter."

'I went downstairs and came up again with my mother, who was followed by the abbé, and I fancied that I heard other footsteps behind us. As soon as we were in the kitchen, Mélanie offered us chairs, and we all four sat down to deliberate.

'"Is he very ill?" my mother asked. "Oh! Yes, Madame; he will not be here long." "Does he seem disposed to receive a visit from a priest?" "Oh! I do not think so." "Can I see him?" "Well—yes, Madame—only—only—those young ladies are with him." "What young ladies?" "Why—why—his lady friends, of course." "Oh!" Maman had grown scarlet, and the Abbé Poivron had lowered his eyes.

'The affair began to amuse me, and I said: "Suppose I go in first? I shall see how he receives me, and perhaps I shall be able to prepare him to receive you."

'My mother, who did not suspect any trick, replied: "Yes, go, my dear." But a woman's voice cried out: "Mélanie!"

'The servant ran out and said: "What do you want, Mademoiselle Claire?" "The omelette; quickly." "In a minute, Mademoiselle." And coming back to us, she explained this summons.

'They had ordered a cheese omelette at two o'clock as a slight collation. And she, at once, began to break the eggs into a salad bowl, and to whip them vigorously, while I went out on the landing and pulled the bell, so as to formally announce my arrival. Mélanie opened the door to me, and made me sit down in an ante-room, while she went to tell my uncle that I had come; then she came back and asked me to go in, while the abbé hid behind the door, so that he might appear at the first signal.

'I was certainly very much surprised at the sight of my uncle, for he was very handsome, very solemn and very elegant, the old rake.

'Sitting, almost lying, in a large armchair, his legs wrapped in blankets, his hands, his long, white hands, over the arms of the chair, he was waiting for death with the dignity of a patriarch. His white beard fell on his chest, and his hair, which was also white, mingled with it on his cheeks.

'Standing behind his armchair, as if to defend him against me, were two young women, who looked at me with bold eyes. In their petticoats and morning wrappers, with bare arms, with coal black hair twisted in a knot on the nape of their neck, with embroidered, Oriental slippers, which showed their ankles and silk stockings, they looked like the figures in some symbolical painting, by the side of the dying man. Between the easy-chair and the bed, there was a table covered with a white cloth, on which two plates, two glasses, two forks and two knives, were waiting for the cheese omelette which had been ordered some time before of Mélanie.

'My uncle said in a weak, almost breathless, but clear voice:

'"Good-morning, my child; it is rather late in the day to come and see me; our acquaintanceship will not last long." I stammered out, "It was not my fault, uncle:" "No; I know that," he replied. "It is your father and mother's fault more than yours. How are they?" "Pretty well, thank you. When they heard that you were ill, they sent me to ask after you." "Ah! Why did they not come themselves?"

'I looked up at the two girls and said gently: "It is not their fault if they could not come, uncle. But it would be difficult for my father, and impossible for my mother to come in here." The old man did not reply, but raised his hand toward mine, and I took the pale, cold hand and held it in my own.

'The door opened, Mélanie came in with the omelette and put it on the table, and the two girls immediately sat down at the table, and began to eat without taking their eyes off me. Then I said: "Uncle, it would give great pleasure to my mother to embrace you." "I also," he murmured, "should like—" He said no more, and I could think of nothing to propose to him, and there was silence except for the noise of the plates and that vague sound of eating.

'Now, the abbé, who was listening behind the door, seeing our embarrassment, and thinking we had won the game, thought the time had come to interpose, and showed himself. My uncle was so stupefied at the sight of him that at first, he remained motionless; and then he opened his mouth as if he meant to swallow up the priest, and shouted to him in a strong, deep, furious voice: "What are you doing here?"

'The abbé, who was used to difficult situations, came forward into the room, murmuring: "I have come in your sister's name, Monsieur le Marquis; she has sent me. She would be happy, Monsieur—"

'But the marquis was not listening. Raising one hand, he pointed to the door with a proud, tragic gesture, and said angrily and breathing hard: "Leave this room—go out—robber of souls. Go out from here, you violator of consciences. Go out from here, you lock-picker of dying men's doors!"

'The abbé retreated, and I also went to the door, beating a retreat with the priest; the two young women, who had the best of it, got up, leaving their omelette only half eaten, and went and stood on either side of my uncle's easy-chair, putting their hands on his arms to calm him, and to protect him against the criminal enterprises of the Family, and of Religion.

'The abbé and I rejoined my mother in the kitchen, and Mélanie again offered us chairs. "I knew quite well that this method would not work; we must try some other means, otherwise he will escape us." And they began deliberating afresh, my mother being of one opinion and the abbé of another, while I held a third.

'We had been discussing the matter in a low voice for half an hour, perhaps, when a great noise of furniture being moved and of cries uttered by my uncle, more vehement and terrible even than the former had been, made us all four jump up.

'Through the doors and walls we could hear him shouting: "Go out—out—rascals—humbugs, get out, scoundrels—get out—get out!"

'Mélanie rushed in, but came back immediately to call me to help her, and I hastened in. Opposite to my uncle, who was terribly excited by anger, almost standing up and vociferating, stood two men, one behind the other, who seemed to be waiting till he should be dead with rage.

'By his ridiculous long coat, his long English shoes, his manners of a tutor out of a position, his high collar, white necktie and straight hair, his humble face of a false priest of a bastard religion,

I immediately recognized the first as a Protestant minister.

'The second was the porter of the house, who belonged to the reformed religion and had followed us, and having seen our defeat, had gone to fetch his own pastor, in hopes that he might meet a better reception. My uncle seemed mad with rage! If the sight of the Catholic priest, of the priest of his ancestors, had irritated the Marquis de Fumerol, who had become a freethinker, the sight of his porter's minister made him altogether beside himself. I therefore took the two men by the arm and threw them out of the room so roughly that they bumped against each other twice, between the two doors which led to the staircase; and then, I disappeared in my turn and returned to the kitchen, which was our headquarters, in order to take counsel with my mother and the abbé.

'But Mélanie came back in terror, sobbing out:

'"He is dying—he is dying—come immediately—he is dying."

'My mother rushed out. My uncle had fallen to the ground, and lay full length along the floor, without moving. I fancy he was already dead. My mother was superb at that moment! She went straight up to the two girls who were kneeling by the body and trying to raise it up, and pointing to the door with irresistible authority, dignity and majesty, she said: "Now it is time for you to leave the room."

'And they went out without a word of protest. I must add that I was getting ready to turn them out as unceremoniously as I had done the parson and the porter.

'Then the Abbé Poivron administered the last sacraments to my uncle with all the customary prayers, and remitted all his sins, while my mother sobbed as she knelt near her brother. Suddenly, however, she exclaimed: "He recognized me; he pressed my hand; I am sure he recognized me!!!—and that he thanked me! Oh, God, what happiness!"

'Poor Maman! If she had known or guessed for whom those thanks were intended!

'They laid my uncle on his bed; he was certainly dead this time.

'"Madame," Mélanie said, "we have no sheets to bury him in; all the linen belongs to these two young ladies," and when I looked at the omelette which they had not finished, I felt inclined to laugh and to cry at the same time. There are some humorous moments and some humorous situations in life, occasionally!

'We gave my uncle a magnificent funeral, with five speeches at the grave. Baron de Croiselles, the senator, showed in admirable terms that God always returns victorious into well-born souls which have temporarily been led into error. All the members of the Royalist and Catholic party followed the funeral procession with the enthusiasm of victors, as they spoke of that beautiful death after a somewhat troublesome life.'

Viscount Roger ceased speaking; his audience was laughing. Then somebody said: 'Bah! That is the story of all conversions in extremis.'

THE THIEF

Guy de Maupassant

While apparently thinking of something else, Dr. Sorbier had been listening quietly to those amazing accounts of burglaries and daring deeds that might have been taken from the trial of Cartouche. 'Assuredly,' he exclaimed, 'assuredly, I know of no viler fault nor any meaner action than to attack a girl's innocence, to corrupt her, to profit by a moment of unconscious weakness and of madness, when her heart is beating like that of a frightened fawn, and her pure lips seek those of her tempter; when she abandons herself without thinking of the irremediable stain, nor of her fall, nor of the morrow.

'The man who has brought this about slowly, viciously, who can tell with what science of evil, and who, in such a case, has not steadiness and self-restraint enough to quench that flame by some icy words, who has not sense enough for two, who cannot recover his self-possession and master the runaway brute within him, and who loses his head on the edge of the precipice over which she is going to fall, is as contemptible as any man who breaks open a lock, or as any rascal on the lookout for a house left defenceless and unprotected or for some easy and dishonest stroke of business, or as that thief whose various exploits you have just related to us.

'I, for my part, utterly refuse to absolve him, even when extenuating circumstances plead in his favour, even when he is carrying on a dangerous flirtation, in which a man tries in vain to keep his balance, not to exceed the limits of the game, any more than at lawn tennis; even when the parts are inverted and a man's adversary is some precocious, curious, seductive girl, who shows you immediately that she has nothing to learn and nothing to experience, except the last chapter of love, one of those girls from whom may fate always preserve our sons, and whom a psychological novel writer has christened "The Semi-Virgins."

'It is, of course, difficult and painful for that coarse and unfathomable vanity which is characteristic of every man, and which might be called "malism", not to stir such a charming fire, difficult to act the Joseph and the fool, to turn away his eyes, and, as it were, to put wax into his ears, like the companions of Ulysses when they were attracted by the divine, seductive songs of the Sirens, difficult only to touch that pretty table covered with a perfectly new cloth, at which you are invited to take a seat before anyone else, in such a suggestive voice, and are requested to quench your thirst and to taste that new wine, whose fresh and strange flavour you will never forget. But who would hesitate to exercise such self-restraint if, when he rapidly examines his conscience, in one of those instinctive returns to his sober self in which a man thinks clearly and recovers his head, he were to measure the gravity of his fault, consider it, think of its consequences, of the reprisals, of the uneasiness which he would always feel in the future, and which would destroy the repose and happiness of his life?

'You may guess that behind all these moral reflections, such as a greybeard like myself may indulge in, there is a story hidden, and, sad as it is, I am sure it will interest you on account of the strange heroism it shows.'

He was silent for a few moments, as if to classify his recollections, and, with his elbows resting on the arms of his easy-chair and his eyes looking into space, he continued in the slow voice of a hospital professor who is explaining a case to his class of medical students, at a bedside:

'He was one of those men who, as our grandfathers used to say, never met with a cruel woman, the type of the adventurous knight who was always foraging, who had something of the scamp about him, but who despised danger and was bold even to rashness.

He was ardent in the pursuit of pleasure, and had an irresistible charm about him, one of those men in whom we excuse the greatest excesses as the most natural things in the world. He had run through all his money at gambling and with pretty girls, and so became, as it were, a soldier of fortune. He amused himself whenever and however he could, and was at that time quartered at Versailles.

'I knew him to the very depths of his childlike heart, which was only too easily seen through and sounded, and I loved him as some old bachelor uncle loves a nephew who plays tricks on him, but who knows how to coax him. He had made me his confidant rather than his adviser, kept me informed of his slightest pranks, though he always pretended to be speaking about one of his friends, and not about himself; and I must confess that his youthful impetuosity, his careless gaiety, and his amorous ardour sometimes distracted my thoughts and made me envy the handsome, vigorous young fellow who was so happy at being alive, that I had not the courage to check him, to show him the right road, and to call out to him: "Take care!" as children do at blind man's buff.

'And one day, after one of those interminable cotillions, where the couples do not leave each other for hours, and can disappear together without anybody thinking of noticing them, the poor fellow at last discovered what love was, that real love which takes up its abode in the very centre of the heart and in the brain, and is proud of being there, and which rules like a sovereign and a tyrannous master, and he became desperately enamoured of a pretty but badly brought up girl, who was as disquieting and wayward as she was pretty.

'She loved him, however, or rather, she idolized him despotically, madly, with all her enraptured soul and all her being. Left to do as she pleased by imprudent and frivolous parents, suffering from neurosis, in consequence of the unwholesome friendships which she contracted at the convent school, instructed by what she saw and heard and knew was going on around her, in spite of her deceitful and artificial conduct, knowing that neither her father nor her mother, who were very proud of their race as well as avaricious, would ever agree to let her marry the man whom she had taken a liking to, that handsome fellow who had little besides vision, ideas and debts, and who belonged to the middle-class, she laid aside all scruples, thought of nothing but of becoming his, no matter what might be the cost.

'By degrees, the unfortunate man's strength gave way, his heart softened, and he allowed himself to be carried away by that current which buffeted him, surrounded him, and left him on the shore like a waif and a stray.

'They wrote letters full of madness to each other, and not a day passed without their meeting, either accidentally, as it seemed, or at parties and balls. She had yielded her lips to him in long, ardent caresses, which had sealed their compact of mutual passion.'

The doctor stopped, and his eyes suddenly filled with tears, as these former troubles came back to his mind; and then, in a hoarse voice, he went on, full of the horror of what he was going to relate:

'For months he scaled the garden wall, and, holding his breath and listening for the slightest noise, like a burglar who is going to break into a house, he went in by the servants' entrance, which she had left open, slunk barefoot down a long passage and up the broad staircase, which creaked occasionally, to the second story, where his sweetheart's room was, and stayed there for hours.

'One night, when it was darker than usual, and he was hurrying lest he should be later than the time agreed on, he knocked up against a piece of furniture in the anteroom and upset it. It so happened that the girl's mother had not gone to sleep, either because she had a sick headache, or else because she had sat up late over some novel, and, frightened at that unusual noise which disturbed the silence of the house, she jumped out of bed, opened the door, saw some one indistinctly running away and keeping close to the wall, and, immediately thinking that there were burglars in the house, she aroused her husband and the servants by her frantic screams. The unfortunate man understood the situation; and, seeing what a terrible fix he was in, and preferring to be taken for a common thief to dishonouring his adored one's name, he ran into the drawing-room, felt on the tables and what-nots, filled his pockets at random with valuable bric-a-brac, and then cowered down behind the grand piano, which barred the corner of a large room.

'The servants, who had run in with lighted candles, found him, and, overwhelming him with abuse, seized him by the collar and dragged him, panting and apparently half-dead with shame and terror, to the nearest police station. He defended himself with intentional awkwardness when he was brought up for trial, kept up his part with the most perfect self-possession and without any signs of the despair and anguish that he felt in his heart, and, condemned and degraded and made to suffer martyrdom in his honour as a man and a soldier—he was an officer—he did not protest, but went to prison as one of those criminals whom society gets rid of like noxious vermin.

'He died there of misery and of bitterness of spirit, with the name of the fair-haired idol, for whom he had sacrificed himself, on his lips, as if it had been an ecstatic prayer, and he intrusted his will to the priest who administered extreme unction to him, and requested him to give it to me. In it, without mentioning anybody, and without in the least lifting the veil, he at last explained the enigma, and cleared himself of those accusations, the terrible burden of which he had borne until his last breath.

'I have always thought to myself, though I do not know why, that the girl married and had several charming children, whom she brought up with the austere strictness and in the serious piety of former days!'

A VENDETTA

Guy de Maupassant

The widow of Paolo Saverini lived alone with her son in a poor little house on the outskirts of Bonifacio. The town, built on an outjutting part of the mountain, in places even overhanging the sea, looks across the straits, full of sandbanks, towards the southernmost coast of Sardinia. Beneath it, on the other side and almost surrounding it, is a cleft in the cliff like an immense corridor which serves as a harbour, and along it, the little Italian and Sardinian fishing boats come by a circuitous route between precipitous cliffs as far as the first houses, and every two weeks the old, wheezy steamer, which makes the trip to Ajaccio.

On the white mountain, the houses, massed together, make an even whiter spot. They look like the nests of wild birds, clinging to this peak, overlooking this terrible passage, where vessels rarely venture. The wind, which blows uninterruptedly, has swept bare the forbidding coast; it drives through the narrow straits and lays waste to both sides. The pale streaks of foam, clinging to the black rocks, whose countless peaks rise up out of the water, look like bits of rag floating and drifting on the surface of the sea.

The house of Widow Saverini, clinging to the very edge of the precipice, looks out, through its three windows, over this wild and desolate picture.

She lived there alone, with her son Antoine and their dog 'Semillante,' a big, thin beast, with a long rough coat, of the sheep-dog breed. The young man took her with him when out hunting.

One night, after some kind of a quarrel, Antoine Saverini was treacherously stabbed by Nicolas Ravolati, who escaped the same evening to Sardinia.

When the old mother received the body of her child, which the neighbours had brought back to her, she did not cry, but she stayed there for a long time motionless, watching him. Then, stretching her wrinkled hand over the body, she promised him a vendetta. She did not wish anybody near her, and she shut herself up beside the body with the dog, which howled continuously, standing at the foot of the bed, her head stretched towards her master and her tail between her legs. She did not move any more than did the mother, who, now leaning over the body with a blank stare, was weeping silently and watching it.

The young man, lying on his back, dressed in his jacket of coarse cloth, torn at the chest, seemed to be asleep. But he had blood all over him; on his shirt, which had been torn off in order to administer the first aid; on his vest, on his trousers, on his face, on his hands. Clots of blood had hardened in his beard and in his hair.

His old mother began to talk to him. At the sound of this voice the dog quieted down.

'Never fear, my boy, my little baby, you shall be avenged. Sleep, sleep; you shall be avenged. Do you hear? It's your mother's promise! And she always keeps her word, your mother does, you know she does.'

Slowly she leaned over him, pressing her cold lips to his dead ones.

Then Semillante began to howl again with a long, monotonous, penetrating, horrible howl.

The two of them, the woman and the dog, remained there until morning.

Antoine Saverini was buried the next day and soon his name ceased to be mentioned in Bonifacio.

He had neither brothers nor cousins. No man was there to carry on the vendetta. His mother, the old woman, alone pondered over it.

On the other side of the straits she saw, from morning until night, a little white speck on the coast. It was the little Sardinian village Longosardo, where Corsican criminals take refuge when they are too closely pursued. They compose almost the entire population of this hamlet, opposite their native island, awaiting the time to return, to go back to the 'maquis.' She knew that Nicolas Ravolati had sought refuge in this village.

All alone, all day long, seated at her window, she was looking over there and thinking of revenge. How could she do anything without help—she, an invalid and so near death? But she had promised, she had sworn on the body. She could not forget, she could not wait. What could she do? She no longer slept at night; she had neither rest nor peace of mind; she thought persistently. The dog, dozing at her feet, would sometimes lift her head and howl. Since her master's death, she often howled thus, as though she were calling him, as though her beast's soul, inconsolable too, had also retained a recollection that nothing could wipe out.

One night, as Semillante began to howl, the mother suddenly got hold of an idea, a savage, vindictive, fierce idea. She thought it over until morning. Then, having arisen at daybreak, she went to church. She prayed, prostrate on the floor, begging the Lord to help her, to support her, to give to her poor, broken-down body the strength which she needed in order to avenge her son.

She returned home. In her yard, she had an old barrel, which acted as a cistern. She turned it over, emptied it, made it fast to the ground with sticks and stones. Then she chained Semillante to this improvised kennel, and went into the house.

She walked ceaselessly now, her eyes always fixed on the distant coast of Sardinia. He was over there, the murderer.

All day and all night the dog howled. In the morning the old woman brought her some water in a bowl, but nothing more; no soup, no bread.

Another day went by. Semillante, exhausted, was sleeping. The following day her eyes were shining, her hair on end and she was pulling wildly at her chain.

All day the old woman gave her nothing to eat. The beast, furious, was barking hoarsely. Another night went by.

Then, at daybreak, Mother Saverini asked a neighbour for some straw. She took the old rags which had formerly been worn by her husband and stuffed them so as to make them look like a human body.

Having planted a stick in the ground, in front of Semillante's kennel, she tied to it this dummy, which seemed to be standing up. Then she made a head out of some old rags.

The dog, surprised, was watching this straw man, and was quiet, although famished. Then the old woman went to the store and bought a piece of black sausage. When she got home she started a fire in the yard, near the kennel, and cooked the sausage. Semillante, frantic, was jumping about, frothing at the mouth, her eyes fixed on the food, the odour of which went right to her stomach.

Then the mother made of the smoking sausage a necktie for the dummy. She tied it very tight around the neck with string, and when she had finished she untied the dog.

With one leap the beast jumped at the dummy's throat, and with her paws on its shoulders she began to tear at it. She would fall back with a piece of food in her mouth, then would jump again, sinking her fangs into the string, and snatching few pieces of meat, she would fall back again and once more spring forward. She was tearing up the face with her teeth and the whole neck was in tatters.

The old woman, motionless and silent, was watching eagerly. Then she chained the beast up again, made her fast for two more days and began this strange performance again.

For three months she accustomed her to this battle, to this meal conquered by a fight. She no longer chained her up, but just pointed to the dummy.

She had taught her to tear him up and to devour him without

even leaving any traces in her throat.

Then, as a reward, she would give her a piece of sausage.

As soon as she saw the man, Semillante would begin to tremble. Then she would look up to her mistress, who, lifting her finger, would cry, 'Go!' in a shrill tone.

When she thought that the proper time had come, the widow went to confession and, one Sunday morning, she partook of communion with an ecstatic fervour. Then, putting on men's clothes and looking like an old tramp, she struck a bargain with a Sardinian fisherman who carried her and her dog to the other side of the straits.

In a bag she had a large piece of sausage. Semillante had had nothing to eat for two days. The old woman kept letting her smell the food and whetting her appetite.

They got to Longosardo. The Corsican woman walked with a limp. She went to a baker's shop and asked for Nicolas Ravolati. He had taken up his old trade, that of carpentry. He was working alone at the back of his store.

The old woman opened the door and called:

'Hello, Nicolas!'

He turned around. Then releasing her dog, she cried:

'Go, go! Eat him up! eat him up!'

The maddened animal sprang for his throat. The man stretched out his arms, clasped the dog and rolled to the ground. For a few seconds he squirmed, beating the ground with his feet. Then he stopped moving, while Semillante dug her fangs into his throat and tore it to ribbons. Two neighbours, seated before their door, remembered perfectly having seen an old beggar come out with a thin, black dog which was eating something that its master was giving him.

At nightfall the old woman was at home again. She slept well that night.

LEGEND OF MONT ST. MICHEL

Guy de Maupassant

I had first seen it from Cancale, this fairy castle in the sea. I got an indistinct impression of it as of a grey shadow outlined against the misty sky. I saw it again from Avranches at sunset. The immense stretch of sand was red, the horizon was red, the whole boundless bay was red. The rocky castle rising out there in the distance like a weird, seignorial residence, like a dream palace, strange and beautiful—this alone remained black in the crimson light of the dying day.

The following morning at dawn, I went toward it across the sands, my eyes fastened on this gigantic jewel, as big as a mountain, cut like a cameo, and as dainty as lace. The nearer I approached, the greater my admiration grew, for nothing in the world could be more wonderful or more perfect.

As surprised as if I had discovered the habitation of a god, I wandered through those halls supported by frail or massive columns, raising my eyes in wonder to those spires which looked like rockets starting for the sky, and to that marvellous assemblage of towers, of gargoyles, of slender and charming ornaments, a regular fireworks of stone, granite lace, a masterpiece of colossal and delicate architecture.

As I was looking up in ecstasy, a Lower Normandy peasant came up to me, and told me the story of the great quarrel between Saint Michel and the devil.

A sceptical genius has said: 'God made man in his image and man has returned the compliment.'

This saying is an eternal truth, and it would be very curious to write the history of the local divinity of every continent as well as the history of the patron saints in each one of our provinces. The negro has his ferocious man-eating idols; the polygamous Mahometan fills his paradise with women; the Greeks, like a practical people, deified all the passions.

Every village in France is under the influence of some protecting saint, modelled according to the characteristics of the inhabitants.

Saint Michel watches over Lower Normandy, Saint Michel, the radiant and victorious angel, the sword-carrier, the hero of Heaven, the victorious, the conqueror of Satan.

But this is how the Lower Normandy peasant, cunning, deceitful and tricky, understands and tells of the struggle between the great saint and the devil.

To escape from the malice of his neighbour, the devil, Saint Michel built himself, in the open ocean, this habitation worthy of an archangel; and only such a saint could build a residence of such magnificence.

But as he still feared the approaches of the wicked one, he surrounded his domains by quicksands, more treacherous even than the sea.

The devil lived in a humble cottage on the hill, but he owned all the salt marshes, the rich lands where grow the finest crops, the wooded valleys and all the fertile hills of the country, while the saint ruled only over the sands. Therefore Satan was rich, whereas Saint Michel was as poor as a church mouse.

After a few years of fasting, the saint grew tired of this state of affairs and began to think of some compromise with the devil, but the matter was by no means easy, as Satan kept a good hold on his crops.

He thought the thing over for about six months; then one morning, he walked across to the shore. The demon was eating his soup in front of his door when he saw the saint. He immediately rushed toward him, kissed the hem of his sleeve, invited him in and offered him refreshments.

Saint Michel drank a bowl of milk and then began: 'I have come here to propose to you a good bargain.'

The devil, candid and trustful, answered: 'That will suit me.'

'Here it is. Give me all your lands.'

Satan, growing alarmed, wished to speak 'But—'

The saint continued: 'Listen first. Give me all your lands. I will take care of all the work, the ploughing, the sowing, the fertilizing, everything, and we will share the crops equally. How does that suit you?'

The devil, who was naturally lazy, accepted. He only demanded, in addition, a few of those delicious grey mullets which are caught around the solitary mount. Saint Michel promised the fish.

They grasped hands and spat on the ground to show that it was a bargain, and the saint continued: 'See here, so that you will have nothing to complain of, choose that part of the crops which you prefer: the part that grows above ground or the part that stays in the ground.' Satan cried out: 'I will take all that will be above ground.'

'It's a bargain!' said the saint. And he went away.

Six months later, all over the immense domain of the devil, one could see nothing but carrots, turnips, onions, salsify, all the plants whose juicy roots are good and savoury, and whose useless leaves are good for nothing but for feeding animals.

Satan wished to break the contract, calling Saint Michel a swindler.

But the saint, who had developed quite a taste for agriculture, went back to see the devil and said:

'Really, I hadn't thought of that at all; it was just an accident, no fault of mine. And to make things fair with you, this year I'll let you take everything that is under the ground.'

'Very well,' answered Satan.

The following spring all the evil spirit's lands were covered with golden wheat, oats as big as beans, flax, magnificent colza, red clover, peas, cabbage, artichokes, everything that develops into grains or fruit in the sunlight.

Once more Satan received nothing, and this time he completely lost his temper. He took back his fields and remained deaf to all the fresh propositions of his neighbour.

A whole year rolled by. From the top of his lonely manor, Saint Michel looked at the distant and fertile lands and watched the devil direct the work, take in his crops and thresh the wheat. And he grew angry, exasperated at his powerlessness.

As he was no longer able to deceive Satan, he decided to wreak vengeance on him, and he went out to invite him to dinner for the following Monday.

'You have been very unfortunate in your dealings with me,' he said; 'I know it, but I don't want any ill-feeling between us, and I expect you to dine with me. I'll give you some good things to eat.'

Satan, who was as greedy as he was lazy, accepted eagerly. On the day appointed, he donned his finest clothes and set out for the castle.

Saint Michel sat him down to a magnificent meal. First, there was a 'vol-au-vent', full of cocks' crests and kidneys, with meat-balls, then two big grey mullets with cream sauce, a turkey stuffed with chestnuts soaked in wine, some salt-marsh lamb as tender as cake, vegetables which melted in the mouth, and nice hot pancake which was brought on smoking and spreading a delicious odour of butter.

They drank new, sweet, sparkling cider and heady red wine, and after each course, they whetted their appetites with some old apple brandy.

The devil drank and ate to his heart's content; in fact, he took so much that he was very uncomfortable, and began to retch.

Then Saint Michel arose in anger and cried in a voice like thunder: 'What! before me, rascal! You dare—before me—'

Satan, terrified, ran away, and the saint, seizing a stick, pursued him. They ran through the halls, turning round the pillars, running up the staircases, galloping along the cornices, jumping from gargoyle to gargoyle. The poor devil, who was woefully ill, was running about madly and trying hard to escape. At last he found himself at the top of the last terrace, right at the top, from which could be seen the immense bay, with its distant towns, sands and pastures. He could no longer escape, and the saint came up behind him and gave him a furious kick, which shot him through space like a cannonball.

He shot through the air like a javelin and fell heavily before the town of Mortain. His horns and claws stuck deep into the rock, which keeps through eternity the traces of this fall of Satan.

He stood up again, limping, crippled until the end of time, and as he looked at this fatal castle in the distance, standing out against the setting sun, he understood well that he would always be vanquished in this unequal struggle, and he went away limping, heading for distant countries, leaving to his enemy his fields, his hills, his valleys and his marshes.

And this is how Saint Michel, the patron saint of Normandy, vanquished the devil.

Another people would have dreamed of this battle in an entirely different manner.

MY WIFE

Guy de Maupassant

It had been a stag dinner. These men still came together once in a while without their wives, as they had done when they were bachelors. They would eat for a long time, drink for a long time; they would talk of everything, stir up those old and joyful memories which bring a smile to the lip and a tremor to the heart. One of them was saying: 'Georges, do you remember our excursion to Saint-Germain with those two little girls from Montmartre?'

'I should say I do!'

And a little detail here or there would be remembered, and all these things brought joy to the hearts.

The conversation turned to marriage, and each one said with a sincere air: 'Oh, if it were to do over again!' Georges Duportin added: 'It's strange how easily one falls into it. You have fully decided never to marry; and then, in the springtime, you go to the country; the weather is warm; the summer is beautiful; the fields are full of flowers; you meet a young girl at some friend's house—crash! all is over. You return married!'

Pierre Letoile exclaimed: 'Correct! that is exactly my case, only there were some peculiar incidents—'

His friend interrupted him: 'As for you, you have no cause to complain. You have the most charming wife in the world, pretty, amiable, perfect! You are undoubtedly the happiest one of us all.'

The other one continued: 'It's not my fault.'

'How so?'

'It is true that I have a perfect wife, but I certainly married her much against my will.'

'Nonsense!'

'Yes—this is the adventure. I was thirty-five, and I had no more idea of marrying than I had of hanging myself. Young girls seemed to me to be inane, and I loved pleasure.

'During the month of May, I was invited to the wedding of my cousin, Simon d'Erabel, in Normandy. It was a regular Normandy wedding. We sat down at the table at five o'clock in the evening and at eleven o'clock we were still eating. I had been paired off, for the occasion, with a Mademoiselle Dumoulin, daughter of a retired colonel, a young, blonde, soldierly person, well-formed, frank and talkative. She took complete possession of me for the whole day, dragged me into the park, made me dance willy-nilly, bored me to death. I said to myself: "That's all very well for to-day, but tomorrow I'll get out. That's all there is to it!"

'Toward eleven o'clock at night, the women retired to their rooms; the men stayed, smoking while they drank or drinking while they smoked, whichever you will.

'Through the open window we could see the country folks dancing. Farmers and peasant girls were jumping about in a circle, yelling at the top of their lungs a dance air, which was feebly accompanied by two violins and a clarinet. The wild song of the peasants often completely drowned the sound of the instruments, and the weak music, interrupted by the unrestrained voices, seemed to come to us in little fragments of scattered notes. Two enormous casks, surrounded by flaming torches, contained drinks for the crowd. Two men were kept busy rinsing the glasses or bowls in a bucket and immediately holding them under the spigots, from which flowed the red stream of wine or the golden stream of pure cider; and the parched dancers, the old ones quietly, the girls panting, came up, stretched out their arms and grasped some receptacle, threw back their heads and poured down their throats the drink which they preferred. On a table were bread, butter, cheese and sausages. Each one would step up from time to time and swallow a mouthful, and under the starlit sky, this healthy and violent exercise was a pleasing sight, and made one also feel like drinking from these enormous casks and eating the crisp bread and butter with a raw onion.

'A mad desire seized me to take part in this merrymaking, and I left my companions. I must admit that I was probably a little tipsy, but I was soon entirely so.

'I grabbed the hand of a big, panting peasant woman and I jumped her about until I was out of breath.

'Then I drank some wine and reached for another girl. In order to refresh myself afterward, I swallowed a bowlful of cider, and I began to bounce around as if possessed.

'I was very light on my feet. The boys, delighted, were watching me and trying to imitate me; the girls all wished to dance with me, and jumped about heavily with the grace of cows.

'After each dance I drank a glass of wine or a glass of cider, and toward two o'clock in the morning I was so drunk that I could hardly stand up.

'I realised my condition and tried to reach my room. Everybody was asleep and the house was silent and dark.

'I had no matches and everybody was in bed. As soon as I reached the vestibule, I began to feel dizzy. I had a lot of trouble finding the bannister. At last, by accident, my hand came in contact with it, and I sat down on the first step of the stairs in order to try to gather my scattered wits.

'My room was on the second floor; it was the third door to the left. Fortunately I had not forgotten that. Armed with this knowledge, I arose, not without difficulty, and I began to ascend, step by step. In my hands I firmly gripped the iron railing in order not to fall, and took great pains to make no noise.

'Only three or four times did my foot miss the steps, and I went down on my knees; but thanks to the energy of my arms and the strength of my will, I avoided falling completely.

'At last I reached the second floor, and I set out on my journey along the hall, feeling my way by the walls. I felt one door; I counted: "One"; but a sudden dizziness made me lose my hold on the wall, make a strange turn and fall up against the other wall. I wished to turn in a straight line: The crossing was long and full of hardships. At last I reached the shore, and, prudently, I began to travel along again until I met another door. In order to be sure to make no mistake, I again counted out loud: "Two." I started out on my walk again. At last I found the third door. I said: "Three, that's my room," and I turned the knob. The door opened. Notwithstanding my befuddled state, I thought: "Since the door opens, this must be home." After softly closing the door, I stepped out in the darkness. I bumped against something soft: my easy-chair. I immediately stretched myself out on it.

'In my condition it would not have been wise to look for my bureau, my candles, my matches. It would have taken me at least two hours. It would probably have taken me that long also to undress; and even then I might not have succeeded. I gave it up.

'I only took my shoes off; I unbuttoned my waistcoat, which was choking me, I loosened my trousers and went to sleep.

'This undoubtedly lasted for a long time. I was suddenly awakened by a deep voice which was saying: "What, you lazy girl, still in bed? It's ten o'clock!"

'A woman's voice answered: "Already! I was so tired yesterday."

'In bewilderment I wondered what this dialogue meant. Where was I? What had I done? My mind was wandering, still surrounded by a heavy fog. The first voice continued: "I'm going to raise your curtains."

'I heard steps approaching me. Completely at a loss as to what to do, I sat up. Then a hand was placed on my head. I started. The voice asked: "Who is there?" I took good care not to answer. A furious grasp seized me. I in turn seized him, and a terrific struggle ensued. We were rolling around, knocking over the furniture and crashing against the walls. A woman's voice was shrieking: "Help! help!"

'Servants, neighbours, frightened women crowded around us.

The blinds were open and the shades drawn. I was struggling with Colonel Dumoulin.

'I had slept beside his daughter's bed!

'When we were separated, I escaped to my room, dumbfounded. I locked myself in and sat down with my feet on a chair, for my shoes had been left in the young girl's room.

'I heard a great noise through the whole house, doors being opened and closed, whisperings and rapid steps.

'After half an hour, someone knocked on my door. I cried: "Who is there?" It was my uncle, the bridegroom's father. I opened the door:

'He was pale and furious, and he treated me harshly: "You have behaved like a scoundrel in my house, do you hear?" Then he added more gently, "But, you young fool, why the devil did you let yourself get caught at ten o'clock in the morning? You go to sleep like a log in that room, instead of leaving immediately—immediately after."

'I exclaimed: "But, uncle, I assure you that nothing occurred. I was drunk and got into the wrong room."

'He shrugged his shoulders! "Don't talk nonsense." I raised my hand, exclaiming: "I swear to you on my honour." My uncle continued: "Yes, that's all right. It's your duty to say that."

'I in turn grew angry and told him the whole unfortunate occurrence. He looked at me with a bewildered expression, not knowing what to believe. Then he went out to confer with the colonel.

'I heard that a kind of jury of the mothers had been formed, to which were submitted the different phases of the situation.

'He came back an hour later, sat down with the dignity of a judge and began: "No matter what may be the situation, I can see only one way out of it for you; it is to marry Mademoiselle Dumoulin."

'I bounded out of the chair, crying: "Never! never!"

'Gravely, he asked: "Well, what do you expect to do?"

'I answered simply: "Why—leave as soon as my shoes are returned to me."

'My uncle continued: "Please do not jest. The colonel has decided to blow your brains out as soon as he sees you. And you may be sure that he does not threaten idly. I spoke of a duel and he answered: 'No, I tell you that I will blow his brains out.'"

'"Let us now examine the question from another point of view. Either you have misbehaved yourself—and then so much the worse for you, my boy; one should not go near a young girl—or else, being drunk, as you say, you made a mistake in the room. In this case, it's even worse for you. You shouldn't get yourself into such foolish situations. Whatever you may say, the poor girl's reputation is lost, for a drunkard's excuses are never believed. The only real victim in the matter is the girl. Think it over."

'He went away, while I cried after him: "Say what you will, I'll not marry her!"

'I stayed alone for another hour. Then my aunt came. She was crying. She used every argument. No one believed my story. They could not imagine that this young girl could have forgotten to lock her door in a house full of company. The colonel had struck her. She had been crying the whole morning. It was a terrible and unforgettable scandal. And my good aunt added: "Ask for her hand, anyhow. We may, perhaps, find some way out of it when we are drawing up the papers."

'This prospect relieved me. And I agreed to write my proposal. An hour later I left for Paris. The following day I was informed that I had been accepted.

'Then, in three weeks, before I had been able to find any excuse, the banns were published, the announcement sent out, the contract signed, and one Monday morning I found myself in a church, beside a weeping young girl, after telling the magistrate that I consented to take her as my companion—for better, for worse.

'I had not seen her since my adventure, and I glanced at her out of the corner of my eye with a certain malevolent surprise. However, she was not ugly—far from it. I said to myself: "There is someone who won't laugh every day."

'She did not look at me once until the evening, and she did not say a single word.

'Toward the middle of the night I entered the bridal chamber with the full intention of letting her know my resolutions, for I was now master. I found her sitting in an armchair, fully dressed, pale and with red eyes. As soon as I entered, she rose and came slowly toward me saying: "Monsieur, I am ready to do whatever you may command. I will kill myself if you so desire."

'The colonel's daughter was as pretty as she could be in this heroic role. I kissed her; it was my privilege.

'I soon saw that I had not got a bad bargain. I have now been married for five years. I do not regret it in the least.'

Pierre Letoile was silent. His companions were laughing. One of them said: 'Marriage is indeed a lottery; you must never choose your numbers. The haphazard ones are the best.'

Another added by way of conclusion: 'Yes, but do not forget that the god of drunkards chose for Pierre.'

CLOCHETTE

Guy de Maupassant

How strange those old recollections are which haunt us, without our being able to get rid of them.

This one is so very old that I cannot understand how it has clung so vividly and tenaciously to my memory. Since then I have seen so many sinister things, which were either affecting or terrible, that I am astonished at not being able to pass a single day without the face of Mother Bellflower recurring to my mind's eye, just as I knew her formerly, now so long ago, when I was ten or twelve years old.

She was an old seamstress who came to my parents' house once a week, every Thursday, to mend the linen. My parents lived in one of those country houses called châteaux, which are merely old houses with gable roofs, to which are attached three or four farms lying around them.

The village, a large village, almost a market town, was a few hundred yards away, closely circling the church, a red brick church, black with age.

Well, every Thursday Mother Clochette came between half-past six and seven in the morning, and went immediately into the linen-room and began to work. She was a tall, thin, bearded or rather hairy woman, for she had a beard all over her face, a surprising, an unexpected beard, growing in improbable tufts, in curly bunches which looked as if they had been sown by a madman over that great face of a gendarme in petticoats. She had them on her nose, under her nose, round her nose, on her chin, on her cheeks; and her eyebrows, which were extraordinarily thick and long, and quite grey, bushy and bristling, looked exactly like a pair of moustaches stuck on there by mistake.

She limped, not as lame people generally do, but like a ship at anchor. When she planted her great, bony, swerving body on her sound leg, she seemed to be preparing to mount some enormous wave, and then suddenly, she dipped as if to disappear in an abyss, and buried herself in the ground. Her walk reminded one of a storm, as she swayed about, and her head, which was always covered with an enormous white cap, whose ribbons fluttered down her back, seemed to traverse the horizon from north to south and from south to north, at each step.

I adored Mother Clochette. As soon as I was up, I went into the linen-room where I found her installed at work, with a foot-warmer under her feet. As soon as I arrived, she made me take the foot-warmer and sit upon it, so that I might not catch a cold in that large, chilly room under the roof.

'That draws the blood from your throat,' she said to me.

She told me stories, whilst mending the linen with her long crooked nimble fingers; her eyes behind her magnifying spectacles, for age had impaired her sight, appeared enormous to me, strangely profound, double.

She had, as far as I can remember the things which she told me and by which my childish heart was moved, the large heart of a poor woman. She told me what had happened in the village, how a cow had escaped from the cow-house and had been found the next morning in front of Prosper Malet's windmill, looking at the sails turning, or about a hen's egg which had been found in the church belfry without anyone being able to understand what creature had been there to lay it, or the story of Jean-Jean Pila's dog, who had been ten leagues to bring back his master's breeches which a tramp had stolen whilst they were hanging up to dry out of doors, after he had been in the rain. She told me these simple adventures in such a manner, that in my mind they assumed the proportions of never-to-be-forgotten dramas, of grand and mysterious poems; and the ingenious stories invented by the poets which my mother told me in the evening, had none of the flavour, none of the breadth or vigour of the peasant woman's narratives.

Well, one Tuesday, when I had spent all the morning in listening to Mother Clochette, I wanted to go upstairs to her again during the day after picking hazelnuts with the manservant in the woods behind the farm. I remember it all as clearly as what happened only yesterday.

On opening the door of the linen-room, I saw the old seamstress lying on the ground by the side of her chair, with her face to the ground and her arms stretched out, but still holding her needle in one hand and one of my shirts in the other. One of her legs in a blue stocking, the longer one, no doubt, was extended under her chair, and her spectacles glistened against the wall, as they had rolled away from her.

I ran away uttering shrill cries. They all came running, and in a few minutes I was told that Mother Clochette was dead.

I cannot describe the profound, poignant, terrible emotion which stirred my childish heart. I went slowly down into the drawing-room and hid myself in a dark corner, in the depths of an immense old armchair, where I knelt down and wept. I remained there a long time, no doubt, for night came. Suddenly somebody came in with a lamp, without seeing me, however, and I heard my father and mother talking with the medical man, whose voice I recognized.

He had been sent for immediately, and he was explaining the causes of the accident, of which I understood nothing, however. Then he sat down and had a glass of liqueur and a biscuit.

He went on talking, and what he then said will remain engraved on my mind until I die! I think that I can give the exact words which he used.

'Ah!' said he, 'the poor woman! She broke her leg the day of my arrival here, and I had not even had time to wash my hands after getting off the diligence before I was sent for in all haste, for it was a bad case, very bad.

'She was seventeen, and a pretty girl, very pretty! Would anyone believe it? I have never told her story before, and nobody except myself and one other person who is no longer living in this part of the country ever knew it. Now that she is dead, I may be less discreet.

'Just then a young assistant-teacher came to live in the village; he was a handsome, well-made fellow, and looked like a non-commissioned officer. All the girls ran after him, but he paid no attention to them, partly because he was very much afraid of his superior, the schoolmaster, old Grabu, who occasionally got out of bed the wrong foot first.

'Old Grabu already employed pretty Hortense who has just died here, and who was afterwards nicknamed Clochette. The assistant master singled out the pretty young girl, who was, no doubt, flattered at being chosen by this impregnable conqueror; at any rate, she fell in love with him, and he succeeded in persuading her to give him a first meeting in the hay-loft behind the school, at night, after she had done her day's sewing.

'She pretended to go home, but instead of going downstairs when she left the Grabus' she went upstairs and hid among the hay, to wait for her lover. He soon joined her, and was beginning to say pretty things to her, when the door of the hay-loft opened and the schoolmaster appeared, and asked, "What are you doing up there, Sigisbert?" Feeling sure that he would be caught, the young schoolmaster lost his presence of mind and replied stupidly: "I came up here to rest a little amongst the bundles of hay, Monsieur Grabu."

'The loft was very large and absolutely dark, and Sigisbert pushed the frightened girl to the further end and said: "Go over there and hide yourself. I shall lose my position, so get away and hide yourself."

'When the schoolmaster heard the whispering, he continued: "Why, you are not by yourself?" "Yes, I am, Monsieur Grabu!" "But you are not, for you are talking." "I swear I am, Monsieur

Grabu." "I will soon find out," the old man replied, and double locking the door, he went down to get a light.

'Then the young man, who was a coward such as one frequently meets, lost his head, and becoming furious all of a sudden, he repeated: "Hide yourself, so that he may not find you. You will keep me from making a living for the rest of my life; you will ruin my whole career. Do hide yourself!" They could hear the key turning in the lock again, and Hortense ran to the window which looked out on the street, opened it quickly, and then said in a low and determined voice: "You will come and pick me up when he is gone," and she jumped out.

'Old Grabu found nobody, and went down again in great surprise, and a quarter of an hour later, Monsieur Sigisbert came to me and related his adventure. The girl had remained at the foot of the wall unable to get up, as she had fallen from the second story, and I went with him to fetch her. It was raining in torrents, and I brought the unfortunate girl home with me, for the right leg was broken in three places, and the bones had come through the flesh. She did not complain, and merely said, with admirable resignation: "I am punished, well punished!"

'I sent for assistance and for the work-girl's relatives, I told them a made-up story of a runaway carriage which had knocked her down and lamed her outside my door. They believed me, and the gendarmes for a whole month tried in vain to find the author of this accident.

'That is all! And I say that this woman was a heroine and belonged to the race of those who accomplish the grandest deeds of history.

'That was her only love affair, and she died a virgin. She was a martyr, a noble soul, a sublimely devoted woman! And if I did not absolutely admire her, I should not have told you this story, which I would never tell anyone during her life; you understand why.'

The doctor ceased. Maman cried and papa said some words which I did not catch; then they left the room and I remained on my knees in the armchair and sobbed, whilst I heard a strange noise of heavy footsteps and something knocking against the side of the staircase.

They were carrying away Clochette's body.

THE BEGGAR

Guy de Maupassant

He had seen better days, despite his present misery and infirmities.

At the age of fifteen, both his legs had been crushed by a carriage on the Varville highway. From that time forth he begged, dragging himself along the roads and through the farmyards, supported by crutches which forced his shoulders up to his ears. His head looked as if it were squeezed in between two mountains.

A foundling; picked up out of a ditch by the priest of Les Billettes on the eve of All Saints' Day and baptized, for that reason, Nicholas Toussaint; reared by charity; utterly without education; crippled in consequence of having drunk several glasses of brandy given him by the baker (such a funny story!) and a vagabond all his life afterward—the only thing he knew how to do was to hold out his hand for alms.

At one time the Baroness d'Avary allowed him to sleep in a kind of recess spread with straw, close to the poultry yard in the farm adjoining the château, and if he was in great need, he was sure of getting a glass of cider and a crust of bread in the kitchen. Moreover, the old lady often threw him a few pennies from her window. But she was dead now.

In the villages people gave him scarcely anything—he was too well known. Everybody had grown tired of seeing him, day after day for forty years, dragging his deformed and tattered person from door to door on his wooden crutches. But he could not make up his mind to go elsewhere, because he knew no place on earth but this particular corner of the country, these three or four villages where he had spent the whole of his miserable existence. He had limited his begging operations and would not for worlds have passed his accustomed bounds.

He did not even know whether the world extended for any distance beyond the trees which had always bounded his vision. He did not ask himself the question. And when the peasants, tired of constantly meeting him in their fields or along their lanes, exclaimed, 'Why don't you go to other villages instead of always limping about here?' he did not answer, but slunk away, possessed with a vague dread of the unknown—the dread of a poor wretch who fears confusedly a thousand things—new faces, taunts, insults, the suspicious glances of people who do not know him and the policemen walking in couples on the roads. These last he always instinctively avoided, taking refuge in the bushes or behind heaps of stones when he saw them coming.

When he perceived them in the distance, with uniforms gleaming in the sun, he was suddenly possessed with unwonted agility—the agility of a wild animal seeking its lair. He threw aside his crutches, fell to the ground like a limp rag, made himself as small as possible and crouched like a hare under cover, his tattered vestments blending in hue with the earth on which he cowered.

He had never had any trouble with the police, but the instinct to avoid them was in his blood. He seemed to have inherited it from the parents he had never known.

He had no refuge, no roof for his head, no shelter of any kind. In summer he slept out of doors and in winter he showed remarkable skill in slipping unperceived into barns and stables. He always decamped before his presence could be discovered. He knew all the holes through which one could creep into farm buildings, and, the handling of his crutches having made his arms surprisingly muscular, he often hauled himself up through sheer strength of wrist into hay-lofts, where he sometimes remained for four or five days at a time, provided he had collected a sufficient store of food beforehand.

He lived like the beasts of the field. He was in the midst of men, yet knew no one, loved no one, exciting in the breasts of the peasants only a sort of careless contempt and smouldering hostility. They nicknamed him 'Bell,' because he hung between his two crutches like a church bell between its supports.

For two days he had eaten nothing. No one gave him anything now. Everyone's patience was exhausted. Women shouted at him from their doorsteps when they saw him coming: 'Be off with you, you good-for-nothing vagabond! Why, I gave you a piece of bread only three days ago!'

And he turned on his crutches to the next house, where he was received in the same fashion.

The women declared to one another as they stood at their doors:

'We can't feed that lazy brute all year round!'

And yet the 'lazy brute' needed food every day.

He had exhausted Saint-Hilaire, Varville and Les Billettes without getting a single copper or so much as a dry crust. His only hope was in Tournolles, but to reach this place he would have to walk five miles along the highroad, and he felt so weary that he could hardly drag himself another yard. His stomach and his pocket were equally empty, but he started on his way.

It was December, and a cold wind blew over the fields and whistled through the bare branches of the trees; the clouds careered madly across the black, threatening sky. The cripple dragged himself slowly along, raising one crutch after the other with a painful effort, propping himself on the one distorted leg which remained to him.

Now and then he sat down beside a ditch for a few moments' rest. Hunger was gnawing his vitals, and in his confused, slow-working mind he had only one idea—to eat—but how this was to be accomplished, he did not know. For three hours he continued his painful journey. Then at last, the sight of the trees of the village inspired him with new energy.

The first peasant he met, and of whom he asked alms, replied:

'So it's you again, is it, you old scamp? Shall I never be rid of you?'

And 'Bell' went on his way. At every door he got nothing but hard words. He made rounds of the whole village, but received not a halfpenny for his pains.

Then he visited the neighbouring farms, toiling through the muddy land, so exhausted that he could hardly raise his crutches from the ground. He met with the same reception everywhere. It was one of those cold, bleak days, when the heart is frozen and the temper irritable, and hands do not open either to give money or food.

When he had visited all the houses he knew, 'Bell' sank down in the corner of a ditch running across Chiquet's farmyard. Letting his crutches slip to the ground, he remained motionless, tortured by hunger, but hardly intelligent enough to realize to the full his unutterable misery.

He awaited he knew not what, possessed with that vague hope which persists in the human heart in spite of everything. He awaited in the corner of the farmyard in the biting December wind, some mysterious aid from Heaven or from men, without the least idea whence it was to arrive. A number of black hens ran hither and thither, seeking their food in the earth which supports all living things. Every now and then, they snapped up in their beaks a grain of corn or a tiny insect; then they continued their slow, sure search for nutriment.

'Bell' watched them at first without thinking of anything. Then a thought occurred, rather, to his stomach than to his mind—the thought that one of those fowls would be good to eat if it were cooked over a fire of dead wood.

He did not reflect that he was going to commit a theft. He took up a stone which lay within reach, and, being of skillful aim, killed at the first shot the fowl nearest to him. The bird fell on its side, flapping its wings. The others fled wildly hither and thither, and 'Bell,' picking up his crutches, limped across to where his victim lay.

Just as he reached the little black body with its crimsoned head, he received a violent blow in his back, which made him let go of his crutches and sent him flying ten paces distant. And Farmer Chiquet, beside himself with rage, cuffed and kicked the marauder with all the fury of a plundered peasant as 'Bell' lay defenceless before him.

The farm hands came up also and joined their master in cuffing the lame beggar. Then when they were tired of beating him they carried him off and shut him up in the woodshed, while they went to fetch the police.

'Bell,' half dead, bleeding and perishing with hunger, lay on the floor. Evening came—then night—then dawn. And still he had not eaten.

About midday, the police arrived. They opened the door of the woodshed with the utmost precaution, fearing resistance on the beggar's part, for Farmer Chiquet asserted that he had been attacked by him and had had great difficulty in defending himself.

The sergeant cried:

'Come, get up!'

But 'Bell' could not move. He did his best to raise himself on his crutches, but without success. The police, thinking his weakness was feigned, pulled him up by main force and set him between the crutches.

Fear seized him—his native fear of a uniform, the fear of the game in presence of the sportsman, the fear of a mouse for a cat—and by the exercise of almost superhuman effort, he succeeded in remaining upright.

'Forward!' said the sergeant. He walked. All the inmates of the farm watched his departure. The women shook their fists at him. The men scoffed at and insulted him. He was taken at last! Good riddance! He went off between his two guards. He mustered sufficient energy—the energy of despair—to drag himself along until the evening, too dazed to know what was happening to him, too frightened to understand.

People whom he met on the road stopped to watch him go by and peasants muttered:

'It's some thief or other.'

Toward evening, he reached the country town. He had never been so far before. He did not realize in the least what he was there for or what was to become of him. All the terrible and unexpected events of the last two days, all these unfamiliar faces and houses struck dismay into his heart.

He said not a word, having nothing to say because he understood nothing. Besides, he had spoken to no one for so many years past that he had almost lost the use of his tongue, and his thoughts were too indeterminate to be put into words.

He was shut up in the town jail. It did not occur to the police that he might need food, and he was left alone until the following day. But when in the early morning they came to examine him, he was found dead on the floor. Such an astonishing thing!

IN THE WOODS

Guy de Maupassant

As the mayor was about to sit down to breakfast, word was brought to him that the rural policeman, with two prisoners, was awaiting him at the Hôtel de Ville. He went there at once and found old Hochedur standing guard before a middle-class couple, whom he was regarding with a severe expression on his face.

The man, a fat old fellow with a red nose and white hair, seemed utterly dejected; while the woman, a little roundabout individual with shining cheeks, looked at the official who had arrested them, with defiant eyes.

'What is it? What is it, Hochedur?'

The rural policeman made his deposition: he had gone out that morning at his usual time, in order to patrol his beat from the forest of Champioux till as far as the boundaries of Argenteuil. He had not noticed anything unusual in the country except that it was a fine day, and that the wheat was doing well, when the son of old Bredel, who was going over his vines, called out to him, 'Here, Daddy Hochedur, go and have a look at the outskirts of the wood. In the first thicket you will find a pair of pigeons who must be a hundred and thirty years old between them!'

He went in the direction indicated, entered the thicket, and there he heard words which made him suspect a flagrant breach of morality. Advancing, therefore, on his hands and knees as if to surprise a poacher, he had arrested the couple whom he found there.

The mayor looked at the culprits in astonishment, for the man was certainly sixty, and the woman fifty-five at least, and he began to question them, beginning with the man, who replied in such a weak voice that he could scarcely be heard.

'What is your name?'

'Nicholas Beaurain.'

'Your occupation?'

'Haberdasher, in the Rue des Martyrs, in Paris.'

'What were you doing in the woods?'

The haberdasher remained silent, with his eyes on his fat paunch, and his hands hanging at his sides, and the mayor continued, 'Do you deny what the officer of the municipal authorities states?'

'No, Monsieur.'

'So you confess it?'

'Yes, Monsieur.'

'What do you have to say in your defence?'

'Nothing, Monsieur.'

'Where did you meet the partner in your misdemeanour?'

'She is my wife, Monsieur.'

'Your wife?'

'Yes, Monsieur.'

'Then—then—you do not live together-in Paris?'

'I beg your pardon, Monsieur, but we are living together!'

'But in that case—you must be mad, altogether mad, my dear sir, to get caught playing lovers in the country at ten o'clock in the morning.'

The haberdasher seemed ready to cry with shame, and he muttered, 'It was she who enticed me! I told her it was very stupid, but when a woman once gets a thing into her head—you know—you cannot get it out.'

The mayor, who liked a joke, smiled and replied, 'In your case, the contrary ought to have happened. You would not be here, if she had had the idea only in her head.'

Then Monsieur Beaurain was seized with rage and, turning to his wife, he said, 'Do you see to what you have brought us with your poetry? And now we shall have to go before the courts at our age, for a breach of morals! And we shall have to shut up the shop, sell our good will, and go to some other neighbourhood! That's what it has come to.'

Madame Beaurain got up, and without looking at her husband, she explained herself without embarrassment, without useless modesty, and almost without hesitation.

'Of course, Monsieur, I know that we have made ourselves ridiculous. Will you allow me to plead my cause like an advocate, or rather like a poor woman? And I hope that you will be kind enough to send us home, and to spare us the disgrace of a prosecution.

'Years ago, when I was young, I made Monsieur Beaurain's acquaintance one Sunday in this neighbourhood. He was employed in a draper's shop, and I was a saleswoman in a ready-made clothing establishment. I remember it as if it were yesterday. I used to come and spend Sundays here occasionally with a friend of mine, Rose Lévêque, with whom I lived in the Rue Pigalle, and Rose had a sweetheart, while I had none. He used to bring us here, and one Saturday he told me laughing that he should bring a friend with him the next day. I quite understood what he meant, but I replied that it would be no good; for I was virtuous, Monsieur.

'The next day we met Monsieur Beaurain at the railway station, and in those days he was good-looking, but I had made up my mind not to encourage him, and I did not. Well, we arrived at Bezons. It was a lovely day, the sort of day that touches your heart. When it is fine even now, just as it used to be formerly, I grow quite foolish, and when I am in the country I utterly lose my head. The green grass, the swallows flying so swiftly, the smell of the grass, the scarlet poppies, the daisies, all that makes me crazy. It is like champagne when one is not accustomed to it!

'Well, it was lovely weather, warm and bright, and it seemed to penetrate your body through your eyes when you looked and through your mouth when you breathed. Rose and Simon hugged and kissed each other every minute, and that gave me a queer feeling! Monsieur Beaurain and I walked behind them, without speaking much, for when people do not know each other, they do not find anything to talk about. He looked timid, and I liked to see his embarrassment. At last we got to the little wood; it was as cool as in a bath there, and we four sat down. Rose and her lover teased me because I looked rather stern, but you will understand that I could not be otherwise. And then they began to kiss and hug again, without putting any more restraint upon themselves than if we had not been there; and then they whispered together, and got up and went off among the trees, without saying a word. You may fancy what I looked like, alone with this young fellow whom I saw for the first time. I felt so confused at seeing them go that it gave me courage, and I began to talk. I asked him what his business was, and he said he was a linen draper's assistant, as I told you just now. We talked for a few minutes, and that made him bold, and he wanted to take liberties with me, but I told him sharply to keep his place. Is that not true, Monsieur Beaurain?'

Monsieur Beaurain, who was looking at his feet in confusion, did not reply, and she continued, 'Then he saw that I was virtuous, and he began to make love to me nicely, like an honourable man, and from that time he came every Sunday, for he was very much in love with me. I was very fond of him also, very fond of him! He was a good-looking fellow, formerly, and in short he married me the next September, and we started in business in the Rue des Martyrs.

'It was a hard struggle for some years, Monsieur. Business did not prosper, and we could not afford many country excursions, and, besides, we had got out of the way of them. One has other things in one's head, and thinks more of the cash box than of pretty speeches, when one is in business. We were growing old by degrees without perceiving it, like quiet people who do not think much about love. One does not regret anything as long as one does not notice what one has lost.

'And then, Monsieur, business became better, and we were tranquil as to the future! Then, you see, I do not exactly know what went on in my mind, no, I really do not know, but I began to dream like a little boarding-school girl. The sight of the little carts full of flowers which are drawn about the streets made me cry; the smell of violets sought me out in my easy-chair, behind my cash box, and made my heart beat! Then I would get up and go out on the doorstep to look at the blue sky between the roofs. When one looks up at the sky from the street, it looks like a river which is descending on Paris, winding as it flows, and the swallows pass to and fro in it like fish. These ideas are very stupid at my age! But how can one help it, Monsieur, when one has worked all one's life? A moment comes in which one perceives that one could have done something else, and that one regrets, oh! yes, one feels intense regret! Just think, for twenty years I might have gone and had kisses in the woods, like other women. I used to think how delightful it would be to lie under the trees and be in love with someone! And I thought of it every day and every night! I dreamed of the moonlight on the water, until I felt inclined to drown myself.

'I did not venture to speak to Monsieur Beaurain about this at first. I knew that he would make fun of me, and send me back to sell my needles and cotton! And then, to speak the truth, Monsieur Beaurain never said much to me, but when I looked in the glass, I also understood quite well that I no longer appealed to anyone!

'Well, I made up my mind, and I proposed to him an excursion into the country, to the place where we had first become acquainted. He agreed without mistrusting anything, and we arrived here this morning, about nine o'clock.

'I felt quite young again when I got among the wheat, for a woman's heart never grows old! And really, I no longer saw my husband as he is at present, but just as he was formerly! That I will swear to you, Monsieur. As true as I am standing here I was crazy. I began to kiss him, and he was more surprised than if I had tried to murder him. He kept saying to me, "Why, you must be mad! You are mad this morning! What is the matter with you?" I did not listen to him, I only listened to my own heart, and I made him come into the woods with me. That is all. I have spoken the truth, Monsieur le Maire, the whole truth.'

The mayor was a sensible man. He rose from his chair, smiled, and said, 'Go in peace, Madame, and when you again visit our forests, be more discreet.'

MOONLIGHT

Guy de Maupassant

Madame Julie Roubere was expecting her elder sister, Madame Henriette Letore, who had just returned from a trip to Switzerland.

The Letore household had left nearly five weeks before. Madame Henriette had allowed her husband to return alone to their estate in Calvados, where some business required his attention, and had come to spend a few days in Paris with her sister. Night came on. In the quiet parlour, Madame Roubere was reading in the twilight in an absent-minded way, raising her eyes whenever she heard a sound.

At last, she heard a ring at the door, and her sister appeared, wrapped in a travelling cloak. And without any formal greeting, they clasped each other in an affectionate embrace, only desisting for a moment to give each other another hug. Then they talked about their health, about their respective families and a thousand other things, gossiping, jerking out hurried, broken sentences as they followed each other about, while Madame Henriette was removing her hat and veil.

It was now quite dark. Madame Roubere rang for a lamp, and as soon as it was brought in, she scanned her sister's face, and was on the point of embracing her once more. But she held back, scared and astonished at the other's appearance.

On her temples Madame Letore had two large locks of white hair. All the rest of her hair was of a glossy, raven-black hue; but there alone, at each side of her head, ran, as it were, two silvery streams which were immediately lost in the black mass surrounding them. She was, nevertheless, only twenty-four years old, and this change had come on suddenly since her departure for Switzerland.

Without moving, Madame Roubere gazed at her in amazement, tears rising to her eyes, as she thought that some mysterious and terrible calamity must have befallen her sister. She asked:

'What is the matter with you, Henriette?'

Smiling with a sad face, the smile of one who is heartsick, the other replied:

'Why, nothing, I assure you. Were you noticing my white hair?'

But Madame Roubere impetuously seized her by the shoulders, and with a searching glance at her, repeated:

'What is the matter with you? Tell me what is the matter with you. And if you tell me a falsehood, I'll soon find out.'

They remained face to face, and Madame Henriette, who looked as if she were about to faint, had two pearly tears in the corners of her drooping eyes.

Her sister continued:

'What has happened to you? What is the matter with you? Answer me!'

Then, in a subdued voice, the other murmured:

'I have—I have a lover.'

And, hiding her forehead on the shoulder of her younger sister, she sobbed.

Then, when she had grown a little calmer, when the heaving of her breast had subsided, she commenced to unbosom herself, as if to cast forth this secret from herself, to empty this sorrow of hers into a sympathetic heart.

Thereupon, holding each other's hands tightly clasped, the two women went over to a sofa in a dark corner of the room, into which they sank, and the younger sister, passing her arm over the elder one's neck, and drawing her close to her heart, listened.

'Oh! I know that there was no excuse for me; I do not understand myself, and since that day, I feel as if I were mad. Be careful, my child, about yourself—be careful! If you only knew how weak we are, how quickly we yield, and fall. It takes so little, so little, so little, a moment of tenderness, one of those sudden fits of melancholy which come over you, one of those longings to open your arms, to love, to cherish something, which we all have at certain moments.

'You know my husband, and you know how fond I am of him; but he is mature and sensible, and cannot even comprehend the tender vibrations of a woman's heart. He is always the same, always good, always smiling, always kind, always perfect. Oh! how I sometimes have wished that he would clasp me roughly in his arms, that he would embrace me with those slow, sweet kisses which make two beings intermingle, which are like mute confidences! How I have wished that he were foolish, even weak, so that he should have need of me, of my caresses, of my tears!

'This all seems very silly; but we women are made like that. How can we help it?

'And yet the thought of deceiving him never entered my mind. Now it has happened, without love, without reason, without anything, simply because the moon shone one night on the Lake of Lucerne.

'During the month when we were travelling together, my husband, with his calm indifference, paralysed my enthusiasm, extinguished my poetic ardour. When we were descending the mountain paths at sunrise, when as the four horses galloped along with the diligence, we saw, in the transparent morning haze, valleys, woods, streams, and villages, I clasped my hands with delight, and said to him, "How beautiful it is, dear! Give me a kiss! Kiss me now!" He only answered, with a smile of chilling kindliness: "There is no reason why we should kiss each other because you like the landscape."

'And his words froze me to the heart. It seems to me that when people love each other, they ought to feel more moved by love than ever, in the presence of beautiful scenes.

'In fact, I was brimming over with poetry which he kept me

from expressing. I was almost like a boiler filled with steam and hermetically sealed.

'One evening (we had, for four days, been staying in a hotel at Flüelen) Robert, having one of his sick headaches, went to bed immediately after dinner, and I went to take a walk all alone along the edge of the lake.

'It was a night such as one reads of in fairy tales. The full moon showed itself in the middle of the sky; the tall mountains, with their snowy crests, seemed to wear silver crowns; the waters of the lake glittered with tiny shining ripples. The air was mild, with that kind of penetrating warmth which enervates us till we are ready to faint, to be deeply affected without any apparent cause. But how sensitive, how vibrating the heart is at such moments! how quickly it beats, and how intense is its emotion!

'I sat down on the grass, and gazed at that vast, melancholy, and fascinating lake, and a strange feeling arose in me; I was seized with an insatiable need of love, a revolt against the gloomy dullness of my life. What! would it never be my fate to wander, arm in arm, with a man I loved, along a moon-kissed bank like this? Was I never to feel on my lips those kisses so deep, delicious, and intoxicating which lovers exchange on nights that seem to have been made by God for tenderness? Was I never to know ardent, feverish love in the moonlit shadows of a summer's night?

'And I burst out weeping like a crazy woman. I heard something stirring behind me. A man stood there, gazing at me. When I turned my head round, he recognized me, and, advancing, said, "You are weeping, Madame?"

'It was a young barrister who was travelling with his mother, and whom we had often met. His eyes had frequently followed me.

'I was so confused that I did not know what answer to give or what to think of the situation. I told him I felt ill.

'He walked by my side in a natural and respectful manner, and began talking to me about what we had seen during our trip. All that I had felt he translated into words; everything that made me thrilled he understood perfectly, better than I did myself. And all of a sudden he repeated some verses of Alfred de Musset. I felt myself choking, seized with indescribable emotion. It seemed to me that the mountains themselves, the lake, the moonlight, were singing to me about things ineffably sweet.

'And it happened, I don't know how, I don't know why, in a sort of hallucination.

'As for him, I did not see him again till the morning of his departure.

'He gave me his card!'

And, sinking into her sister's arms, Madame Letore broke into groans—almost into shrieks.

Then, Madame Roubere, with a self-contained and serious air, said very gently:

'You see, sister, very often it is not a man that we love, but love itself. And your real lover that night was the moonlight.'

THE LOVE OF LONG AGO

Guy de Maupassant

The old-fashioned château was built on a wooded knoll in the midst of tall trees with dark-green foliage; the park extended to a great distance, in one direction to the edge of the forest, in another to the distant country. A few yards from the front of the house was a huge stone basin with marble ladies taking a bath; other basins were seen at intervals down to the foot of the slope, and a stream of water fell in cascades from one basin to another.

From the manor house, which preserved the grace of a superannuated coquette, down to the grottos incrusted with shell-work, where slumbered the loves of a bygone age, everything in this antique demesne had retained the physiognomy of former days. Everything seemed to speak still of ancient customs, of the manners of long ago, of former gallantries, and of the elegant trivialities so dear to our grandmothers.

In a parlour in the style of Louis XV, whose walls were covered with shepherds paying court to shepherdesses, beautiful ladies in hoop-skirts, and gallant gentlemen in wigs, a very old woman, who seemed dead as soon as she ceased to move, was almost lying down in a large easy-chair, at each side of which hung a thin, mummy-like hand.

Her dim eyes were gazing dreamily toward the distant horizon as if they sought to follow through the park the visions of her youth. Through the open window every now and then came a breath of air laden with the odour of grass and the perfume of flowers. It made her white locks flutter around her wrinkled forehead and old memories float through her brain.

Beside her, on a tapestried stool, a young girl, with long fair hair hanging in braids down her back, was embroidering an altar-cloth. There was a pensive expression in her eyes, and it was easy to see that she was dreaming, while her agile fingers flew over her work.

But the old lady turned round her head, and said:

'Berthe, read me something out of the newspapers, that I may still know sometimes what is going on in the world.'

The young girl took up a newspaper, and cast a rapid glance over it.

'There is a great deal about politics, Grand-maman; shall I pass that over?'

'Yes, yes, darling. Are there no love stories? Is gallantry, then, dead in France, that they no longer talk about abductions or adventures as they did formerly?'

The girl made a long search through the columns of the newspaper.

'Here is one,' she said. 'It is entitled "A Love Drama!"'

The old woman smiled through her wrinkles. 'Read that for me,' she said.

And Berthe commenced. It was a case of vitriol throwing. A wife, in order to avenge herself on her husband's mistress, had burned her face and eyes. She had left the Court of Assizes acquitted, declared to be innocent, amid the applause of the crowd.

The grandmother moved about excitedly in her chair, and exclaimed,

'This is horrible—why, it is perfectly horrible!

'See whether you can find anything else to read to me, darling.'

Berthe again made a search; and farther down among the reports of criminal cases, she read,

'"Gloomy Drama. A shop girl, no longer young, allowed herself to be led astray by a young man. Then, to avenge herself on her lover, whose heart proved fickle, she shot him with a revolver. The unhappy man is maimed for life. The jury, all men of moral character, condoning the illicit love of the murderess, honourably acquitted her.'"

This time the old grandmother appeared quite shocked, and, in a trembling voice, she said,

'Why, you people are mad nowadays. You are mad! The good God has given you love, the only enchantment in life. Man has added to this gallantry the only distraction of our dull hours, and here you are mixing up with vitriol and revolvers, as if one were to put mud into a flagon of Spanish wine.'

Berthe did not seem to understand her grandmother's indignation.

'But, Grand-maman, this woman avenged herself. Remember she was married, and her husband deceived her.'

The grandmother gave a start.

'What ideas have they been filling your head with, you young girls of today?'

Berthe replied:

'But marriage is sacred, Grand-maman.'

The grandmother's heart, which had its birth in the great age of gallantry, gave a sudden leap.

'It is love that is sacred,' she said. 'Listen, child, to an old woman who has seen three generations, and who has had a long, long experience of men and women. Marriage and love have nothing in common. We marry to found a family, and we form families in order to constitute society. Society cannot dispense with marriage. If society is a chain, each family is a link in that chain. In order to weld those links, we always seek metals of the same order. When we marry, we must bring together suitable conditions; we must combine fortunes, unite similar races and aim at the common interest, which is riches and children. We marry only once, my child, because the world requires us to do so, but we may love twenty times in one lifetime because nature has made us like this. Marriage, you see, is law, and love is an instinct which impels us, sometimes along a straight path, and sometimes along a devious path. The world has made laws to combat our instincts—it was necessary to make them; but our instincts are always stronger, and we ought not to resist them too much, because they come from God; while the laws only come from men. If we did not perfume life with love, as much love as possible, darling, as we put sugar into drugs for children, nobody would care to take it just as it is.'

Berthe opened her eyes wide in astonishment. She murmured:

'Oh! Grand-maman, we can only love once.'

The grandmother raised her trembling hands toward Heaven, as if again to invoke the defunct god of gallantries. She exclaimed indignantly:

'You have become a race of serfs, a race of common people. Since the Revolution, it is impossible any longer to recognize society. You have attached big words to every action, and wearisome duties to every corner of existence; you believe in equality and eternal passion. People have written poetry telling you that people have died of love. In my time poetry was written to teach men to love every woman. And we! when we liked a gentleman, my child, we sent him a page. And when a fresh caprice came into our hearts, we were not slow in getting rid of the last Lover—unless we kept both of them.'

The old woman smiled a keen smile, and a gleam of roguery twinkled in her grey eye, the intellectual, sceptical roguery of those people who did not believe that they were made of the same clay as the rest, and who lived as masters for whom common beliefs were not intended.

The young girl, turning very pale, faltered out:

'So, then, women have no honour?'

The grandmother ceased to smile. If she had kept in her soul some of Voltaire's irony, she had also a little of Jean Jacques's glowing philosophy, 'No honour! because we loved, and dared to say so, and even boasted of it? But, my child, if one of us, among the greatest ladies in France, had lived without a lover, she would have had the entire court laughing at her. Those who wished to live differently had only to enter a convent. And you imagine, perhaps, that your husbands will love but you alone, all their lives. As if, indeed, this could be the case. I tell you that marriage is a thing necessary in order that society should exist, but it is not in the nature of our race, do you understand? There is only one good thing in life, and that is love. And how you misunderstand it! how you spoil it! You treat it as something solemn like a sacrament, or something to be bought, like a dress.'

The young girl caught the old woman's trembling hands in her own.

'Hold your tongue, I beg of you, Grand-maman!'

And, on her knees, with tears in her eyes, she prayed to Heaven to bestow on her a great passion, one sole, eternal passion in accordance with the dream of modern poets, while the grandmother, kissing her on the forehead, quite imbued still with that charming, healthy reason with which gallant philosophers tinctured the thought of the eighteenth century, murmured:

'Take care, my poor darling! If you believe in such folly as that, you will be very unhappy.'

FRIEND JOSEPH

Guy de Maupassant

They had been great friends all winter in Paris. As is always the case, they had lost sight of each other after leaving school, and had met again when they were old and grey-haired. One of them had married, but the other had remained in single blessedness.

M. de Meroul lived for six months in Paris and for the other six months in his little château at Tourbeville. Having married the daughter of a neighbouring squire, he had lived a good and peaceful life in the indolence of a man who has nothing to do. Of a calm and quiet disposition, and not over-intelligent, he used to spend his time quietly regretting the past, grieving over the customs and institutions of the day and continually repeating to his wife, who would lift her eyes, and sometimes her hands, to heaven, as a sign of energetic assent, 'Good gracious! What a government!'

Madame de Meroul resembled her husband intellectually as though she had been his sister. She knew, by tradition, that one should above all respect the Pope and the King!

And she loved and respected them from the bottom of her heart, without knowing them, with a poetic fervour, with an hereditary devotion, with the tenderness of a wellborn woman. She was good to the marrow of her bones. She had had no children, and never ceased mourning the fact.

On meeting his old friend, Joseph Mouradour, at a ball, M. de Meroul was filled with a deep and simple joy, for in their youth they had been intimate friends.

After the first exclamations of surprise at the changes which time had wrought in their bodies and countenances, they told each other about their lives since they had last met.

Joseph Mouradour, who was from the south of France, had become a government official. His manner was frank; he spoke rapidly and without restraint, giving his opinions without any tact. He was a Republican, one of those good fellows who do not believe in standing in ceremony, and who exercise an almost brutal freedom of speech.

He came to his friend's house and was immediately liked for his easy cordiality, in spite of his radical ideas. Madame de Meroul would exclaim:

'What a shame! Such a charming man!'

Monsieur de Meroul would say to his friend in a serious and confidential tone of voice; 'You have no idea the harm that you are doing to your country.' He loved him all the same, for nothing is stronger than the ties of childhood taken up again at a riper age. Joseph Mouradour bantered the wife and the husband, calling them 'my amiable snails,' and sometimes he would solemnly declaim against people who were behind the times, against old prejudices and traditions.

When he was once started on his democratic eloquence, the couple, somewhat ill at ease, would keep silent out of politeness and good-breeding; then the husband would try to turn the conversation into some other channel in order to avoid a clash. Joseph Mouradour was only seen in the intimacy of the family.

Summer came. The Merouls had no greater pleasure than to receive their friends at their country home at Tourbeville. It was a good, healthy pleasure, the enjoyments of good people and of country proprietors. They would meet their friends at the neighbouring railroad station and would bring them back in their carriage, always on the lookout for compliments on the country, on its natural features, on the condition of the roads, on the cleanliness of the farm-houses, on the size of the cattle grazing in the fields, on everything within sight.

They would call attention to the remarkable speed with which their horse trotted, surprising for an animal that did heavy work of the year behind a plough; and they would anxiously await the opinion of the newcomer on their family domain, sensitive to the least word, and thankful for the slightest good intention.

Joseph Mouradour was invited, and he accepted the invitation.

The husband and wife had come to the train, delighted to welcome him to their home. As soon as he saw them, Joseph Mouradour jumped from the train with a briskness which increased their satisfaction. He shook their hands, congratulated them and overwhelmed them with compliments.

All the way home he was charming, remarking on the height of the trees, the goodness of the crops and the speed of the horse.

When he stepped on the porch of the house, Monsieur de Meroul said, with a certain friendly solemnity, 'Consider yourself at home now.'

Joseph Mouradour answered, 'Thanks, my friend; I expected as much. Anyhow, I never stand on ceremony with my friends. That's how I understand hospitality.'

Then he went upstairs to dress as a farmer, he said, and he came back all togged out in blue linen, with a little straw hat and yellow shoes, a regular Parisian dressed for an outing. He also seemed to become more vulgar, more jovial, more familiar; having put on with his country clothes a free and easy manner which he judged suitable to the surroundings. His new manners shocked Monsieur and Madame de Meroul a little, for they always remained serious and dignified, even in the country, as though compelled by the two letters preceding their name to keep up a certain formality even in the closest intimacy.

After lunch they all went out to visit the farms, and the Parisian astounded the respectful peasants by his tone of comradeship.

In the evening the priest came to dinner, an old, fat priest, accustomed to dining there on Sundays, but who had been especially invited this day in honour of the new guest.

Joseph, on seeing him, made a wry face. Then he observed

him with surprise, as though he were a creature of some peculiar race, which he had never been able to observe at close quarters. During the meal he told some rather free stories, allowable in the intimacy of the family, but which seemed to the Merouls a little out of place in the presence of a minister of the Church. He did not say, 'Monsieur l'abbé', but simply, 'Monsieur.' He embarrassed the priest greatly by philosophical discussions about diverse superstitions current all over the world. He said, 'Your God, Monsieur, is of those who should be respected, but also one of those who should be discussed. Mine is called Reason; he has always been the enemy of yours.'

The Merouls, distressed, tried to turn the trend of the conversation. The priest left very early.

Then the husband said, very quietly:

'Perhaps you went a little bit too far with the priest.'

But Joseph immediately exclaimed:

'Well, that's pretty good! As if I would be on my guard with a shaveling! And say, do me the pleasure of not imposing him on me any more at meals. You can both make use of him as much as you wish, but don't serve him up to your friends, hang it!'

'But, my friend, think of his holy—'

Joseph Mouradour interrupted him:

'Yes, I know; they have to be treated like "rosières." But let them respect my convictions, and I will respect theirs!'

That was all for that day.

As soon as Madame de Meroul entered the parlour, the next morning, she noticed in the middle of the table three newspapers which made her start—the *Voltaire*, the *Republique-Française* and the *Justice*. Immediately Joseph Mouradour, still in blue, appeared on the threshold, attentively reading the *Intransigeant*. He cried,

'There's a great article in this by Rochefort. That fellow is a wonder!'

He read it aloud, emphasizing the parts which especially pleased him, so carried away by enthusiasm that he did not notice his friend's entrance. Monsieur de Meroul was holding in his hand the *Gaulois* for himself, the *Clarion* for his wife.

The fiery prose of the master writer who overthrew the empire, spouted with violence, sung in the southern accent, rang throughout the peaceful parsons seemed to spatter the walls and century-old furniture with a hail of bold, ironical and destructive words.

The man and the woman, one standing, the other sitting, were listening with astonishment, so shocked that they could not move.

In a burst of eloquence Mouradour finished the last paragraph, then exclaimed triumphantly:

'Well! that's pretty strong!'

Then, suddenly, he noticed the two sheets which his friend was carrying, and he, in turn, stood speechless from surprise. Quickly walking toward him he demanded angrily:

'What are you doing with those papers?'

Monsieur de Meroul answered hesitatingly:

'Why—those—those are my papers!'

'Your papers! What are you doing—making fun of me? You will do me the pleasure of reading mine; they will limber up your ideas, and as for yours—there! that's what I do with them.'

And before his astonished host could stop him, he had seized the two newspapers and thrown them out of the window. Then he solemnly handed the *Justice* to Madame de Meroul, the *Voltaire* to her husband, while he sank down into an arm-chair to finish reading the *Intransigeant*.

The couple, through delicacy, made a pretence of reading a little, they then handed him back the Republican sheets, which they handled gingerly, as though they might be poisoned.

He laughed and declared:

'One week of this regime and I will have you converted to my ideas.'

In truth, at the end of a week, he ruled the house. He had closed the door against the priest, whom Madame de Meroul had to visit secretly; he had forbidden the *Gaulois* and the *Clarion* to be brought into the house, so that a servant had to go mysteriously to the post-office to get them, and as soon as he entered they would be hidden under sofa cushions; he arranged everything to suit himself—always charming, always good-natured, a jovial and all-powerful tyrant.

Other friends were expected, pious and conservative friends. The unhappy couple saw the impossibility of having them there then, and, not knowing what to do, one evening they announced to Joseph Mouradour that they would be obliged to absent themselves for a few days, on business, and they begged him to stay on alone. He did not appear disturbed, and answered,

'Very well, I don't mind! I will wait here as long as you wish. I have already said that there should be no formality between friends. You are perfectly right—go ahead and attend to your business. It will not offend me in the least; quite the contrary, it will make me feel much more completely one of the family. Go ahead, my friends, I will wait for you!'

Monsieur and Madame de Meroul left the following day.

He is still waiting for them.

THE EFFEMINATES

Guy de Maupassant

How often we hear people say, 'He is charming, that man, but he is a girl, a regular girl.' They are alluding to the effeminates, the bane of our land.

For we are all girl-like men in France—that is, fickle, fanciful, innocently treacherous, without consistency in our convictions or our will, violent and weak as women are.

But the most irritating of girl-men is assuredly the Parisian and the boulevardier, in whom the appearance of intelligence is more marked and who combines in himself all the attractions and all the faults of those charming creatures to an exaggerated degree, in virtue of his masculine temperament.

Our Chamber of Deputies is full of girl-men. They form the greater number of the amiable opportunists whom one might call 'The Charmers.' These are they who control by soft words and deceitful promises, who know how to shake hands in such a manner as to win hearts, how to say 'My dear friend' in a certain tactful way to people he knows the least, to change his mind without suspecting it, to be carried away by each new idea, to be sincere in their weathercock convictions, to let themselves be deceived as they deceive others, to forget the next morning what he affirmed the day before.

The newspapers are full of these effeminate men. That is probably where one finds the most, but it is also where they are most needed. The *Journal des Débats* and the *Gazette de France* are exceptions.

Assuredly, every good journalist must be somewhat

effeminate—that is, at the command of the public, supple in following unconsciously the shades of public opinion, wavering and varying, sceptical and credulous, wicked and devout, a braggart and a true man, enthusiastic and ironical, and always convinced while believing in nothing.

Foreigners, our anti-types, as Mme. Abel called them, the stubborn English and the heavy Germans, regard us with a certain amazement mingled with contempt, and will continue to so regard us till the end of time. They consider us frivolous. It is not that, it is that we are girls. And that is why people love us in spite of our faults, why they come back to us despite the evil spoken of us; these are lovers' quarrels! The effeminate man, as one meets him in this world, is so charming that he captivates you after five minutes' chat. His smile seems made for you; one cannot believe that his voice does not assume specially tender intonations on their account. When he leaves you it seems as if one had known him for twenty years. One is quite ready to lend him money if he asks for it. He has enchanted you, like a woman.

If he commits any breach of manners towards you, you cannot bear any malice, he is so pleasant when you next meet him. If he asks your pardon you long to ask pardon of him. Does he tell lies? You cannot believe it. Does he put you off indefinitely with promises that he does not keep? One lays as much store by his promises as though he had moved heaven and earth to render them a service.

When he admires anything he goes into such raptures that he convinces you. He once adored Victor Hugo, whom he now treats as a back number. He would have fought for Zola, whom he has abandoned for Barbey and d'Aurevilly. And when he admires, he permits no limitation, he would slap your face for a word. But when he becomes scornful, his contempt is unbounded and allows no protest.

In fact, he understands nothing.

Listen to two girls talking.

'Then you are angry with Julia?' 'I slapped her face.' 'What had she done?' 'She told Pauline that I had no money thirteen months out of twelve, and Pauline told Gontran—you understand.' 'You were living together in the Rue Clauzel?' 'We lived together for four years in the Rue Bréda; we quarrelled about a pair of stockings that she said I had worn—it wasn't true—silk stockings that she had bought at Mother Martin's. Then I gave her a pounding and she left me at once. I met her six months ago and she asked me to come and live with her, as she has rented a flat that is twice too large.'

One goes on one's way and hears no more. But on the following Sunday, as one is on the way to Saint Germain, two young women get into the same railway carriage. One recognizes one of them at once; it is Julia's enemy. The other is Julia!

And there are endearments, caresses, plans. 'Say, Julia—listen, Julia,' etc.

The girl-man has his friendships of this kind. For three months he cannot bear to leave his old Jack, his dear Jack. There is no one but Jack in the world. He is the only one who has any intelligence, any sense, any talent. He alone amounts to anything in Paris. One meets them everywhere together, they dine together, walk about in company, and every evening walk home with each other back and forth without being able to part with one another.

Three months later, if Jack is mentioned,

'There is a drinker, a sorry fellow, a scoundrel for you. I know him well, you may be sure. And he is not even honest, and ill-bred,' etc., etc.

Three months later, and they are living together.

But one morning one hears that they have fought a duel, then embraced each other, amid tears, on the duelling ground.

Just now they are the dearest friends in the world, furious with each other half the year, abusing and loving each other by turns, squeezing each other's hands till they almost crush the bones, and ready to run each other through the body for a misunderstanding.

For the relations of these effeminate men are uncertain. Their temper is by fits and starts, their delight unexpected, their affection turn-about-face, their enthusiasm subject to eclipse. One day they love you, the next day they will hardly look at you, for they have in fact a girl's nature, a girl's charm, a girl's temperament, and all their sentiments are like the affections of girls.

They treat their friends as women treat their pet dogs.

It is the dear little Toutou whom they hug, feed with sugar, allow to sleep on the pillow, but whom they would be just as likely to throw out of a window in a moment of impatience, whom they turn round like a sling, holding it by the tail, squeeze in their arms till they almost strangle it, and plunge, without any reason, in a pail of cold water.

Then, what a strange thing it is when one of these beings falls in love with a real girl! He beats her, she scratches him, they execrate each other, cannot bear the sight of each other and yet cannot part, linked together by no one knows what mysterious psychic bonds. She deceives him, he knows it, sobs and forgives her. He despises and adores her without seeing that she would be justified in despising him. They are both atrociously unhappy and yet cannot separate. They cast invectives, reproaches and abominable accusations at each other from morning till night, and when they have reached the climax and are vibrating with rage and hatred, they fall into each other's arms and kiss each other ardently.

The girl-man is brave and a coward at the same time. He has, more than another, the exalted sentiment of honour, but is lacking in the sense of simple honesty, and, circumstances favouring him, would defalcate and commit infamies which do not trouble his conscience, for he obeys without questioning the oscillations of his ideas, which are always impulsive.

To him it seems permissible and almost right to cheat a haberdasher. He considers it honourable not to pay his debts, unless they are gambling debts—that is, somewhat shady. He dupes people whenever the laws of society admit of his doing so. When he is short of money, he borrows in all ways, not always being scrupulous as to tricking the lenders, but he would, with sincere indignation, run his sword through anyone who should suspect him of only lacking in politeness.

ROSALIE PRUDENT

Guy de Maupassant

There was a real mystery in this affair which neither the jury, nor the president, nor the public prosecutor himself could understand.

The girl Prudent (Rosalie), servant at the Varambots', of Nantes, having become enceinte without the knowledge of her masters, had, during the night, killed and buried her child in the garden.

It was the usual story of the infanticides committed by servant girls. But there was one inexplicable circumstance about this one. When the police searched the girl Prudent's room, they discovered a complete infant's outfit, made by Rosalie herself, who had spent her nights for the last three months in cutting and sewing it. The grocer from whom she had bought her candles, out of her own wages, for this long piece of work had come to testify. It came out, moreover, that the sage-femme of the district, informed by Rosalie of her condition, had given her all necessary instructions and counsel in case the event should happen at a time when it might not be possible to get help. She had also procured a place at Poissy for the girl Prudent, who foresaw that her present employers would discharge her, for the Varambot couple did not trifle with morality.

There were present at the trial both the man and the woman, a middle-class pair from the provinces, living on their income. They were so exasperated against this girl, who had sullied their house, that they would have liked to see her guillotined on the spot without a trial. The spiteful depositions they made against her became accusations in their mouths.

The defendant, a large, handsome girl of Lower Normandy, well educated for her station in life, wept continuously and would not answer to anything.

The court and the spectators were forced to the opinion that she had committed this barbarous act in a moment of despair and madness, since there was every indication that she had expected to keep and bring up her child.

The president tried for the last time to make her speak, to get some confession, and, having urged her with much gentleness, he finally made her understand that all these men gathered here to pass judgement upon her were not anxious for her death and might even have pity on her.

Then she made up her mind to speak.

'Come, now, tell us, first, who is the father of this child?' he asked.

Until then she had obstinately refused to give his name.

But she replied suddenly, looking at her masters who had so cruelly calumniated her:

'It is Monsieur Joseph, Monsieur Varambot's nephew.'

The couple started in their seats and cried with one voice— 'That's not true! She lies! This is infamous!'

The president had them silenced and continued, 'Go on, please, and tell us how it all happened.'

Then she suddenly began to talk freely, relieving her pent-up heart, that poor, solitary, crushed heart—laying bare her sorrow, her whole sorrow, before those severe men whom she had until now taken for enemies and inflexible judges.

'Yes, it was Monsieur Joseph Varambot, when he came on leave last year.'

'What does Mr. Joseph Varambot do?'

'He is a non-commissioned officer in the artillery, Monsieur. Well, he stayed two months at the house, two months of the summer. I thought nothing about it when he began to look at me, and then flatter me, and make love to me all day long. And

I let myself be taken in, Monsieur. He kept saying to me that I was a handsome girl, that I was good company, that I just suited him—and I, I liked him well enough. What could I do? One listens to these things when one is alone—all alone—as I was. I am alone in the world, Monsieur. I have no one to talk to—no one to tell my troubles to. I have no father, no mother, no brother, no sister, nobody. And when he began to talk to me it was as if I had a brother who had come back. And then he asked me to go with him to the river one evening, so that we might talk without disturbing anyone. I went—I don't know—I don't know how it happened. He had his arm around me. Really I didn't want to—no—no—I could not—I felt like crying, the air was so soft—the moon was shining. No, I swear to you—I could not—he did what he wanted. That went on for three weeks, as long as he stayed. I could have followed him to the ends of the world. He went away. I did not know that I was enceinte. I did not know it until the month after—'

She began to cry so bitterly that they had to give her time to collect herself.

Then the president resumed with the tone of a priest at the confessional, 'Come, now, go on.'

She began to talk again, 'When I realized my condition I went to see Madame Boudin, who is there to tell you, and I asked her how it would be, in case it should come if she were not there. Then I made the outfit, sewing night after night, every evening until one o'clock in the morning; and then I looked for another place, for I knew very well that I should be sent away, but I wanted to stay in the house until the very last, so as to save my pennies, for I have not got very much and I should need my money for the little one.'

'Then you did not intend to kill him?'

'Oh, certainly not, Monsieur!'

'Why did you kill him, then?'

'It happened this way. It came sooner than I expected. It came upon me in the kitchen, while I was doing the dishes. Monsieur and Madame Varambot were already asleep, so I went up, not without difficulty, dragging myself up by the bannister, and I lay down on the bare floor. It lasted perhaps one hour, or two, or three; I don't know, I had such pain; and then I pushed him out with all my strength. I felt that he came out and I picked him up.

'Ah! but I was glad, I assure you! I did all that Madame Boudin told me to do. And then I laid him on my bed. And then such a pain griped me again that I thought I should die. If you knew what it meant, you there, you would not do so much of this. I fell on my knees, and then toppled over backward on the floor; and it griped me again, perhaps one hour, perhaps two. I lay there all alone—and then another one comes—another little one—two, yes, two, like this. I took him up as I did the first one, and then I put him on the bed, the two side by side. Is it possible, tell me, two children, and I who get only twenty francs a month? Say, is it possible? One, yes, that can be managed by going without things, but not two. That turned my head. What do I know about it? Had I any choice, tell me?

'What could I do? I felt as if my last hour had come. I put the pillow over them, without knowing why. I could not keep them both; and then I threw myself down, and I lay there, rolling over and over and crying until I saw the daylight come into the window. Both of them were quite dead under the pillow. Then I took them under my arms and went down the stairs out in the vegetable garden. I took the gardener's spade and I buried them under the earth, digging as deep a hole as I could, one here and the other one there, not together, so that they might not talk of their mother if these little dead bodies can talk. What do I know about it?

'And then, back in my bed, I felt so sick that I could not get up. They sent for the doctor and he understood it all. I'm telling you the truth, Your Honor. Do what you like with me; I'm ready.'

Half of the jury were blowing their noses violently to keep from crying. The women in the courtroom were sobbing.

The president asked her, 'Where did you bury the other one?'

'The one that you have?' she asked.

'Why, this one—this one was in the artichokes.'

'Oh, then the other one is among the strawberries, by the well.'

And she began to sob so piteously that no one could hear her unmoved.

The girl Rosalie Prudent was acquitted.

THE GRAVE

Guy de Maupassant

The seventeenth of July, one thousand eight hundred and eighty-three, at half-past two in the morning, the watchman in the cemetery of Béziers, who lived in a small cottage on the edge of this field of the dead, was awakened by the barking of his dog, which was shut up in the kitchen.

Going down quickly, he saw the animal sniffing at the crack of the door and barking furiously, as if some tramp had been sneaking about the house. The keeper, Vincent, therefore took his gun and went out.

His dog, preceding him, at once ran in the direction of the Avenue Général Bonnet, stopping short at the monument of Madame Tomoiseau.

The keeper, advancing cautiously, soon saw a faint light on the side of the Avenue Malenvers, and stealing in among the graves, he came upon a horrible act of profanation.

A man had dug up the coffin of a young woman who had been buried the evening before and was dragging the corpse out of it.

A small dark lantern, standing on a pile of earth, lighted up this hideous scene.

Vincent sprang upon the wretch, threw him to the ground, bound his hands and took him to the police station.

It was a young, wealthy and respected lawyer in town, named Courbataille.

He was brought into court. The public prosecutor opened the case by referring to the monstrous deeds of Sergeant Bertrand.

A wave of indignation swept over the courtroom. When the

magistrate sat down, the crowd assembled cried, 'Death! death!' With difficulty the presiding judge established silence.

Then he said gravely, 'Defendant, what have you to say in your defence?'

Courbataille, who had refused counsel, rose. He was a handsome fellow, tall, brown, with a frank face, energetic manner and a fearless eye.

Paying no attention to the whistlings in the room, he began to speak in a voice that was low and veiled at first, but that grew more firm as he proceeded.

'Monsieur le Président, gentlemen of the jury: I have very little to say. The woman whose grave I violated was my sweetheart. I loved her.

'I loved her, not with a sensual love and not with mere tenderness of heart and soul, but with an absolute, complete love, with an overpowering passion.

'Hear me:

'When I met her for the first time I felt a strange sensation. It was not astonishment or admiration, nor yet that which is called love at first sight, but a feeling of delicious well-being, as if I had been plunged into a warm bath. Her gestures seduced me, her voice enchanted me, and it was with infinite pleasure that I looked upon her person. It seemed to me as if I had seen her before and as if I had known her a long time. She had within her something of my spirit.

'She seemed to me like an answer to a cry uttered by my soul, to that vague and unceasing cry with which we call upon Hope during our whole life.

'When I knew her a little better, the mere thought of seeing her again filled me with exquisite and profound uneasiness; the touch of her hand in mine was more delightful to me than anything that I had imagined; her smile filled me with a mad joy, with the desire to run, to dance, to fling myself upon the ground.

'So we became lovers.

'Yes, more than that: she was my very life. I looked for nothing further on earth, and had no further desires. I longed for nothing further.

'One evening, when we had gone on a somewhat long walk by the river, we were overtaken by the rain, and she caught a cold. It developed into pneumonia the next day, and a week later she was dead.

'During the hours of her suffering, astonishment and consternation prevented my understanding and reflecting upon it, but when she was dead I was so overwhelmed by blank despair that I had no thoughts left. I wept.

'During all the horrible details of the interment, my keen and wild grief was like madness, a kind of sensual, physical grief.

'Then when she was gone, when she was under the earth, my mind at once found itself again, and I passed through a series of moral sufferings so terrible that even the love she had vouchsafed to me was dear at that price.

'Then the fixed idea came to me: I shall not see her again.

'When one dwells on this thought for a whole day, one feels as if he were going mad. Just think of it! There is a woman whom you adore, a unique woman, for in the whole universe there is not a second one like her. This woman has given herself to you and has created with you the mysterious union that is called Love. Her eye seems to you more vast than space, more charming than the world, that clear eye smiling with her tenderness. This woman loves you. When she speaks to you her voice floods you with joy.

'And suddenly she disappears! Think of it! She disappears, not only for you, but forever. She is dead. Do you understand what that means? Never, never, never, not anywhere will she exist any more. Nevermore will that eye look upon anything again; nevermore will that voice, nor any voice like it, utter a word in the same way as she uttered it.

'Nevermore will a face be born that is like hers. Never, never! The moulds of statues are kept; casts are kept by which one can make objects with the same outlines and forms. But that one body and that one face will never more be born again upon the earth. And yet millions and millions of creatures will be born, and more than that, and this one woman will not reappear among all the women of the future. Is it possible? It drives one mad to think of it.

'She lived for twenty years, not more, and she has disappeared forever, forever, forever! She thought, she smiled, she loved me. And now nothing! The flies that die in the autumn are as many as we are in this world. And now nothing! And I thought that her body, her fresh body, so warm, so sweet, so white, so lovely, would rot down there in that box under the earth. And her soul, her thought, her love—where is it?

'Not to see her again! The idea of this decomposing body, that I might yet recognize, haunted me. I wanted to look at it once more.

'I went out with a spade, a lantern and a hammer; I jumped over the cemetery wall and I found the grave, which had not yet been closed entirely; I uncovered the coffin and took up a board. An abominable odour, the stench of putrefaction, greeted my nostrils. Oh, her bed perfumed with orris!

'Yet I opened the coffin, and, holding my lighted lantern down into it, I saw her. Her face was blue, swollen, frightful. A black liquid had oozed out of her mouth.

'She! That was her! Horror seized me. But I stretched out my arm to draw this monstrous face toward me. And then I was caught.

'All night I have retained the foul odour of this putrid body, the odour of my well beloved, as one retains the perfume of a woman after a love embrace.

'Do with me what you will.'

A strange silence seemed to oppress the room. They seemed to be waiting for something more. The jury retired to deliberate.

When they came back a few minutes later the accused showed no fear and did not even seem to think.

The president announced with the usual formalities that his judges declared him to be not guilty.

He did not move and the room applauded.

THE ENGLISHMAN OF ÉTRETAT

Guy de Maupassant

A great English poet has just crossed over to France in order to greet Victor Hugo. All the newspapers are full of his name and he is the great topic of conversation in all drawing-rooms. Fifteen years ago I had the occasion to meet Algernon Charles Swinburne several times. I will attempt to show him just as I saw him and to give an idea of the strange impression he made on me, which will remain with me throughout time.

I believe it was in 1867 or in 1868 that an unknown young Englishman came to Étretat and bought a little hut hidden under great trees. It was said that he lived there, always alone, in a strange manner; and he aroused the inimical surprise of the natives, for the inhabitants were sullen and foolishly malicious, as they always are in little towns.

They declared that this whimsical Englishman ate nothing but boiled, roasted or stewed monkey; that he would see no one; that he talked to himself hours at a time and many other surprising things that made people think that he was different from other men. They were surprised that he should live alone with a monkey. Had it been a cat or a dog they would have said nothing. But a monkey! Was that not frightful? What savage tastes the man must have!

I knew this young man only from seeing him in the streets. He was short, plump, without being fat, mild-looking, and he wore a little blond moustache, which was almost invisible.

Chance brought us together. This savage had amiable and pleasing manners, but he was one of those strange Englishmen that one meets here and there throughout the world.

Endowed with remarkable intelligence, he seemed to live in a fantastic dream, as Edgar Poe must have lived. He had translated into English a volume of strange Icelandic legends, which I ardently desired to see translated into French. He loved the supernatural, the dismal and grewsome, but he spoke of the most marvellous things with a calmness that was typically English, to which his gentle and quiet voice gave a semblance of reality that was maddening.

Full of a haughty disdain for the world, with its conventions, prejudices and code of morality, he had nailed to his house a name that was boldly impudent. The keeper of a lonely inn who should write on his door, 'Travellers murdered here!' could not make a more sinister jest. I never had entered his dwelling, when one day I received an invitation to luncheon, following an accident that had occurred to one of his friends, who had almost drowned and whom I had attempted to rescue.

Although I was unable to reach the man until he had already been rescued, I received the hearty thanks of the two Englishmen, and the following day I called upon them.

The friend was a man about thirty years old. He bore an enormous head on a child's body—a body without chest or shoulders. An immense forehead, which seemed to have engulfed the rest of the man, expanded like a dome above a thin face which ended in a little pointed beard. Two sharp eyes and a peculiar mouth gave one the impression of the head of a reptile, while the magnificent brow suggested a genius.

A nervous twitching shook this peculiar being, who walked, moved, acted by jerks like a broken spring.

This was Algernon Charles Swinburne, son of an English admiral and grandson, on the maternal side, of the Earl of Ashburnham.

His strange countenance was transfigured when he spoke. I have seldom seen a man more impressive, more eloquent, incisive or charming in conversation. His rapid, clear, piercing and fantastic imagination seemed to creep into his voice and to lend life to his words. His brusque gestures enlivened his speech, which penetrated one like a dagger, and he had bursts of thought, just as lighthouses throw out flashes of fire, great, genial lights that seemed to illuminate a whole world of ideas.

The home of the two friends was pretty and by no means commonplace. Everywhere were paintings, some superb, some strange, representing different conceptions of insanity. Unless I am mistaken, there was a water-colour which represented the head of a dead man floating in a rose-coloured shell on a boundless ocean, under a moon with a human face.

Here and there I came across bones. I clearly remember a flayed hand on which was hanging some dried skin and black muscles, and on the snow-white bones could be seen the traces of dried blood.

The food was a riddle which I could not solve. Was it good? Was it bad? I could not say. Some roast monkey took away all desire to make a steady diet of this animal, and the great monkey who roamed about among us at large and playfully pushed his head into my glass when I wished to drink cured me of any desire I might have to take one of his brothers as a companion for the rest of my days.

As for the two men, they gave me the impression of two strange, original, remarkable minds, belonging to that peculiar race of talented madmen from among whom have arisen Poe, Hoffmann and many others.

If genius is, as is commonly believed, a sort of aberration of great minds, then Algernon Charles Swinburne is undoubtedly a genius.

Great minds that are healthy are never considered geniuses, while this sublime qualification is lavished on brains that are often inferior but are slightly touched by madness.

At any rate, this poet remains one of the first of his time, through his originality and polished form. He is an exalted lyrical singer who seldom bothers about the good and humble truth, which French poets are now seeking so persistently and patiently. He strives to set down dreams, subtle thoughts, sometimes great, sometimes visibly forced, but sometimes magnificent.

Two years later I found the house closed and its tenants gone. The furniture was being sold. In memory of them, I bought the hideous flayed hand. On the grass, an enormous square block of granite bore this simple word: 'Nip.' Above this a hollow stone offered water to the birds. It was the grave of the monkey, who had been hanged by a young, vindictive black servant. It was said that this violent domestic had been forced to flee at the point of his exasperated master's revolver. After wandering about without home or food for several days, he returned and began to peddle barley-sugar in the streets. He was expelled from the country after he had almost strangled a displeased customer.

The world would be gayer if one could often meet homes like that.

AN UNCOMFORTABLE BED

Guy de Maupassant

One autumn, I went to spend the hunting season with some friends in a château in Picardy.

My friends were fond of practical jokes. I do not care to know people who are not.

When I arrived, they gave me a princely reception, which at once awakened suspicion in my mind. They fired off rifles, embraced me, made much of me, as if they expected to have great fun at my expense.

I said to myself,

'Look out, old ferret! They have something in store for you.'

During the dinner, the mirth was excessive, exaggerated, in fact. I thought, 'Here are people who have more than their share of amusement, and apparently without reason. They must have planned some good joke. Assuredly I am to be the victim of the joke. Attention!'

During the entire evening everyone laughed in an exaggerated fashion. I scented a practical joke in the air, as a dog scents game. But what was it? I was watchful, restless. I did not let a word, or a meaning, or a gesture escape me. Every one seemed to me an object of suspicion, and I even looked distrustfully at the faces of the servants.

The hour struck for retiring; and the whole household came to escort me to my room. Why?

They called to me, 'Good-night.' I entered the apartment, shut the door, and remained standing, without moving a single step, holding the wax candle in my hand.

I heard laughter and whispering in the corridor. Without doubt they were spying on me. I cast a glance round the walls, the furniture, the ceiling, the hangings, the floor. I saw nothing to justify suspicion. I heard people moving about outside my door. I had no doubt they were looking through the keyhole.

An idea came into my head, 'My candle may suddenly go out and leave me in darkness.'

Then I went across to the mantelpiece and lit all the wax candles that were on it. After that I cast another glance around me without discovering anything. I advanced with short steps, carefully examining the apartment. Nothing. I inspected every article, one after the other. Still nothing. I went over to the window. The shutters, large wooden shutters, were open. I shut them with great care, and then drew the curtains, enormous velvet curtains, and placed a chair in front of them, so as to have nothing to fear from outside.

Then I cautiously sat down. The armchair was solid. I did not venture to get into the bed. However, the night was advancing; and I ended by coming to the conclusion that I was foolish. If they were spying on me, as I supposed, they must, while waiting for the success of the joke they had been preparing for me, have been laughing immoderately at my terror. So I made up my mind to go to bed. But the bed was particularly suspicious-looking. I pulled at the curtains. They seemed to be secure.

All the same, there was danger. I was going perhaps to receive a cold shower both from overhead, or perhaps, the moment I stretched myself out, to find myself sinking to the floor with my mattress. I searched in my memory for all the practical jokes of which I ever had experience. And I did not want to be caught. Ah! certainly not! certainly not! Then I suddenly thought of a precaution which I considered insured safety. I caught hold of the side of the mattress gingerly, and very slowly drew it toward me. It came away, followed by the sheet and the rest of the bedclothes. I dragged all these objects into the very middle of the room, facing the entrance door. I made my bed over again as best I could at some distance from the suspected bedstead and the corner which had filled me with such anxiety. Then I extinguished all the candles, and, groping my way, I slipped under the bed clothes.

For at least another hour I remained awake, starting at the slightest sound. Everything seemed quiet in the château. I fell asleep.

I must have been in a deep sleep for a long time, but all of a sudden, I was awakened with a start by the fall of a heavy body tumbling right on top of my own, and, at the same time, I received on my face, on my neck, and on my chest a burning liquid which made me utter a howl of pain. And a dreadful noise, as if a sideboard laden with plates and dishes had fallen down, almost deafened me.

I was smothering beneath the weight that was crushing me and preventing me from moving. I stretched out my hand to find out what was the nature of this object. I felt a face, a nose, and whiskers. Then, with all my strength, I launched out a blow at this face. But I immediately received a hail of cuffings which made me jump straight out of the soaked sheets, and rush in my nightshirt into the corridor, the door of which I found open.

Oh, heavens! it was broad daylight. The noise brought my friends hurrying into my apartment, and we found, sprawling over my improvised bed, the dismayed valet, who, while bringing me my morning cup of tea, had tripped over this obstacle in the middle of the floor and fallen on his stomach, spilling my breakfast over my face in spite of himself.

The precautions I had taken in closing the shutters and going to sleep in the middle of the room had only brought about the practical joke I had been trying to avoid.

Oh, how they all laughed that day!

A PORTRAIT

Guy de Maupassant

'Hello! there's Milial!' said somebody near me. I looked at the man, who had been pointed out, as I had been wishing for a long time to meet this Don Juan.

He was no longer young. His grey hair looked a little like those fur bonnets worn by certain Northern peoples, and his long beard, which fell down over his chest, had also somewhat the appearance of fur. He was talking to a lady, leaning toward her, speaking in a low voice and looking at her with an expression full of respect and tenderness.

I knew his life, or at least as much as was known of it. He had loved madly several times, and there had been certain tragedies with which his name had been connected. When I spoke to women who were the loudest in his praise, and asked them whence came this power, they always answered, after thinking for a while, 'I don't know—he has a certain charm about him.'

He was certainly not handsome. He had none of the elegance that we ascribe to conquerors of feminine hearts. I wondered what might be his hidden charm. Was it mental? I never had heard of a clever saying of his. In his glance? Perhaps. Or in his voice? The voices of some beings have a certain irresistible attraction, almost suggesting the flavour of things good to eat. One is hungry for them, and the sound of their words penetrates us like a dainty morsel. A friend was passing. I asked him, 'Do you know Monsieur Milial?'

'Yes.'

'Introduce us.'

A minute later we were shaking hands and talking in the doorway. What he said was correct, agreeable to hear; it contained no irritable thought. The voice was sweet, soft, caressing, musical; but I had heard others much more attractive, much more moving. One listened to him with pleasure, just as one would look at a pretty little brook. No tension of the mind was necessary in order to follow him, no hidden meaning aroused curiosity, no expectation awoke interest. His conversation was rather restful, but it did not awaken in one either a desire to answer, to contradict or to approve, and it was as easy to answer him as it was to listen to him. The response came to the lips of its own accord, as soon as he had finished talking, and phrases turned toward him as if he had naturally aroused them.

One thought soon struck me. I had known him for a quarter of an hour, and it seemed as if he were already one of my old friends, that I had known all about him for a long time; his face, his gestures, his voice, his ideas. Suddenly, after a few minutes of conversation, he seemed already to be installed in my intimacy. All constraint disappeared between us, and, had he so desired, I might have confided in him as one confides only in old friends.

Certainly there was some mystery about him. Those barriers that are closed between most people and that are lowered with time when sympathy, similar tastes, equal intellectual culture and constant intercourse remove constraint—those barriers seemed not to exist between him and me, and no doubt this was the case between him and all people, both men and women, whom fate threw in his path.

After half an hour we parted, promising to see each other often, and he gave me his address after inviting me to have luncheon with him in two days.

I forgot what hour he had stated, and I arrived too soon; he was not yet home. A correct and silent domestic showed me into a beautiful, quiet, softly lighted parlour. I felt comfortable there, at home. How often I have noticed the influence of apartments on the character and on the mind! There are some which make one feel foolish; in others, on the contrary, one always feels lively. Some make us sad, although well-lighted and decorated in light-coloured furniture; others cheer us up, although hung with sombre material. Our eye, like our heart, has its likes and dislikes, of which it does not inform us, and which it secretly imposes on our temperament. The harmony of furniture, walls, the style of an ensemble, act immediately on our mental state, just as the air from the woods, the sea or the mountains modifies our physical natures.

I sat down on a cushion-covered divan and felt myself suddenly carried and supported by these little silk bags of feathers, as if the outline of my body had been marked out beforehand on this couch.

Then I looked about. There was nothing striking about the room; everywhere were beautiful and modest things, simple and rare furniture, Oriental curtains which did not seem to come from a department store but from the interior of a harem; and exactly opposite me hung the portrait of a woman. It was a portrait of medium size, showing the head and the upper part of the body, and the hands, which were holding a book. She was young, bareheaded; ribbons were woven in her hair; she was smiling sadly. Was it because she was bareheaded, was it merely her natural expression? I never have seen a portrait of a lady which seemed so much in its place as that one in that dwelling. Of all those I knew I have seen nothing like that one. All those that I know are on exhibition, whether the lady be dressed in her gaudiest gown, with an attractive headdress and a look which shows that she is posing first of all before the artist and then before those who will look at her or whether they have taken a comfortable attitude in an ordinary gown. Some are standing majestically in all their beauty, which is not at all natural to them in life. All of them have something, a flower or, a jewel, a crease in the dress or a curve of the lip, which one feels to have been placed there for effect by the artist. Whether they wear a hat or merely their hair, one can immediately notice that they are not entirely natural. Why? One cannot say without knowing them, but the effect is there. They seem to be calling somewhere, on people whom they wish to please and to whom they wish to appear at their best advantage; and they have studied their attitudes, sometimes modest, sometimes haughty.

What could one say about this one? She was at home and alone. Yes, she was alone, for she was smiling as one smiles when thinking in solitude of something sad or sweet, and not as one smiles when one is being watched. She seemed so much alone and so much at home that she made the whole large apartment seem absolutely empty. She alone lived in it, filled it, gave it life. Many people might come in and converse, laugh, even sing; she would still be alone with a solitary smile, and she alone would give it life with her pictured gaze.

That look also was unique. It fell directly on me, fixed and caressing, without seeing me. All portraits know that they are being watched, and they answer with their eyes, which see, think, follow us without leaving us, from the very moment we enter the apartment they inhabit. This one did not see me; it saw nothing, although its look was fixed directly on me. I remembered the surprising verse of Baudelaire:

And your eyes, attractive as those of a portrait.

They did indeed attract me in an irresistible manner; those painted eyes which had lived, or which were perhaps still living, threw over me a strange, powerful spell. Oh, what an infinite and tender charm, like a passing breeze, like a dying sunset of lilac rose and blue, a little sad like the approaching night, which comes behind the sombre frame and out of those impenetrable eyes! Those eyes, created by a few strokes from a brush, hide behind them the mystery of that which seems to be and which does not exist, which can appear in the eyes of a woman, which can make love blossom within us.

The door opened and M. Milial entered. He excused himself for being late. I excused myself for being ahead of time. Then I said, 'Might I ask you who is this lady?'

He answered, 'That is my mother. She died very young.'

Then I understood whence came the inexplicable attraction of this man.

THE MAID OF THILOUSE

Honore de Balzac

The Lord of Valennes, a pleasant place, of which the castle is not far from the town of Thilouse, had taken a mean wife, who by reason of taste or antipathy, pleasure or displeasure, health or sickness, allowed her good husband to abstain from those pleasures stipulated for in all contracts of marriage. In order to be just, it should be stated that the above-mentioned lord was a dirty and ill-favoured person, always hunting wild animals and not the more entertaining than is a room full of smoke. And what is more, the said sportsman was all sixty years of age, on which subject, however, he was as silent as a hempen widow on the subject of rope. But nature, which the crooked, the bandy-legged, the blind, and the ugly abuse so unmercifully here below, and have no more esteem for her than the well-favoured—since, like workers of tapestry, they know not what they do—gives the same appetite to all and to all the same mouth for pudding. So every beast finds a mate, and from the same fact comes the proverb, 'There is no pot, however ugly, that does not one day find a cover.' Now, the Lord of Valennes searched everywhere for nice little pots to cover, and often, in addition to wild, he hunted tame animals; but this kind of game was scarce in the land, and it was an expensive affair to discover a maid. At length, however, by reason of much ferreting about and much enquiry, it happened that the Lord of Valennes was informed that in Thilouse was the widow of a weaver who had a real treasure in the person of a little damsel of sixteen years, whom she had never allowed to leave her apron strings, and whom, with great maternal forethought, she always accompanied when the calls of nature demanded her obedience; she had her to sleep with her in her own bed, watched over her, got her up in the morning, and put her to such a work that between the twain they gained about eight pennies a day. On fête days, she took her to the church, scarcely giving her a spare moment to exchange a merry word with the young people; above all, was she strict in keeping hands off the maiden.

But the times were just then so hard that the widow and her daughter had only bread enough to save them from dying of hunger, and as they lodged with one of their poor relations, they often wanted wood in winter and clothes in summer, owing enough rent to frighten sergeants of justice, men who are not easily frightened at the debts of others; in short, while the daughter was increasing in beauty, the mother was increasing in poverty, and ran into debt on account of her daughter's virginity, as an alchemist will for the crucible in which his all is cast. As soon as his plans were arranged and perfect, one rainy day, the said lord of Valennes, by a mere chance, came into the hovel of the two spinners, and in order to dry himself sent for some fagots to Plessis, close by. While waiting for them, he sat on a stool between the two poor women. By means of the grey shadows and half light of the cabin, he saw the sweet countenance of the maid of Thilouse; her arms were red and firm, her breasts hard as bastions, which kept the cold from her heart, her waist round as a young oak and all fresh and clean and pretty, like the first frost, green and tender as an April bud; in fact, she resembled all that is prettiest in the world. She had eyes of a modest and virtuous blue, with a look more coy than that of the Virgin, for she was less forward, never having had a child.

Had any one said to her, 'Come, let us make love,' she would have said, 'Love! What is that?' She was so innocent and so little open to the comprehensions of the thing.

The good old lord twisted about upon his stool, eyeing the maid and stretching his neck like a monkey trying to catch nuts, which the mother noticed, but said not a word, being in fear of the lord to whom the whole of the country belonged. When the fagot was put into the grate and flared up, the good hunter said to the old woman, 'Ah, ah! that warms one almost as much as your daughter's eyes.'

'But alas, my lord,' said she, 'we have nothing to cook on that fire.'

'Oh yes,' replied he.

'What?'

'Ah, my good woman, lend your daughter to my wife, who has need of a good handmaiden: we will give you two fagots every day.'

'Oh, my lord, what could I cook at such a good fire?'

'Why,' replied the old rascal, 'good broth, for I will give you a measure of corn in season.'

'Then,' replied the old hag, 'where shall I put it?'

'In your dish,' answered the purchaser of innocence.

'But I have neither dish nor flower-bin, nor anything.'

'Well, I will give you dishes and flower-bins, saucepans, flagons, a good bed with curtains, and everything.'

'Yes,' replied the good widow, 'but the rain would spoil them, I have no house.'

'You can see from here,' replied the lord, 'the house of La Tourbelliere, where lived my poor huntsmen Pillegrain, who was ripped up by a boar?'

'Yes,' said the old woman.

'Well, you can make yourself at home there for the rest of your days.'

'By my faith;' cried the mother, letting fall her distaff, 'do you mean what you say?'

'Yes.'

'Well, then, what will you give my daughter?'

'All that she is willing to gain in my service.'

'Oh! my lord, you are joking.'

'No,' said he.

'Yes,' said she.

'By St. Gatien, St. Eleuther, and by the thousand million saints who are in heaven, I swear that—'

'Ah! Well; if you are not jesting I should like those fagots to pass through the hands of the notary.'

'By the blood of Christ and the charms of your daughter, am I not a gentleman? Is not my word good enough?'

'Ah! well I don't say that it is not; but as true as I am a poor spinner, I love my child too much to leave her; she is too young and weak at present, she will break down in service. Yesterday, in his sermon, the vicar said that we should have to answer to God for our children.'

'There! There!' said the lord, 'go and find the notary.'

An old woodcutter ran to the scrivener, who came and drew up a contract, to which the lord of Valennes then put his cross, not knowing how to write, and when all was signed and sealed—

'Well, old lady,' said he, 'now you are no longer answerable to God for the virtue of your child.'

'Ah! my lord, the vicar said until the age of reason, and my child is quite reasonable.' Then turning towards her, she added, 'Marie Fiquet, that which is dearest to you is your honour, and there where you are going, everyone, without counting my lord, will try to rob you of it, but you see well what it is worth; for that reason, do not lose it; save willingly and in proper manner. Now in order not to contaminate your virtue before God and before man, except for a legitimate motive, take heed that your chance of marriage be not damaged beforehand, otherwise you will go to the bad.'

'Yes, dear mother,' replied the maid.

And thereupon she left the poor abode of her relation, and came to the château of Valennes, there to serve my lady, who found her both pretty and to her taste.

When the people of Valennes, Saché, Villaines, and other places, learned the high price given for the maid of Thilouse, the good housewives, recognizing the fact that nothing is more profitable than virtue, endeavoured to nourish and bring up their daughters virtuous, but the business was as risky as that of rearing silkworms, which are liable to perish, since innocence is like a medlar, and ripens quickly on the straw. There were, however, some girls noted for it in Touraine, who passed for virgins in the convents of the religious, but I cannot vouch for these, not having proceeded to verify them in the manner laid down by Verville, in order to make sure of the perfect virtue of women. However, Marie Fiquet followed the wise counsel of her mother, and would take no notice of the soft requests, honied words, or apish tricks of her master, unless they were flavoured with a promise of marriage.

When the old lord tried to kiss her, she would put her back up like a cat at the approach of a dog, crying out 'I will tell Madame!' In short at the end of six months he had not even recovered the price of a single fagot. From her labour, Marie Fiquet became harder and firmer. Sometimes she would reply to the gentle request of her master, 'When you have taken it from me will you give it to me back again?'

Another time she would say, 'If I were as full of holes as a sieve, not one should be for you, so ugly do I think you.'

The good old man took these village sayings for flowers of innocence, and ceased not make little signs to her, long harangues and a hundred vows and sermons, for by reason of seeing the fine breasts of the maid, her plump hips, which, at certain movements, came into prominent relief, and by reason of admiring other things capable of inflaming the mind of a saint, this dear man became enamoured of her with an old man's passion, which augments in geometrical proportions as opposed to the passions of young men, because the old men love with their weakness which grows greater, and the young with their strength which grows less. In order to leave this headstrong girl no loophole for refusal, the old lord took into his confidence the steward, whose age was seventy odd years, and made him understand that he ought to marry in order to keep his body warm, and that Marie Fiquet was the very girl to suit him. The old steward, who had gained three hundred pounds by different services about the house, desired to live quietly without opening the front door again; but his good master begged him to marry to please him, assuring him that he need not trouble about his wife. So the good steward wandered out of sheer good nature into this marriage. The day of the wedding, bereft of all her reasons, and not able to find objections to her pursuer, she made him give her a fat settlement and dowry as the price of her conquest, and then gave the old knave leave to wink at her as often as he could, promising him as many embraces as he had given grains of wheat to her mother. But at his age a bushel was sufficient.

The festivities over, the lord did not fail, as soon as his wife had retired, to wend his way towards the well-glazed, well-carpeted, and pretty room where he had lodged his lass, his money, his fagots, his house, his wheat, and his steward. To be brief, know that he found the maid of Thilouse the sweetest girl in the world, as pretty as anything, by the soft light of the fire which was gleaming in the chimney, snug between the sheets, and with a sweet odour about her, as a young maiden should have, and in fact he had no regret for the great price of this jewel. Not being able to restrain himself from hurrying over the first mouthfuls of this royal morsel, the lord treated her more as a past master than a young beginner. So the happy man by too much gluttony, managed badly, and in fact knew nothing of the sweet business of love. Finding which, the good wench said, after a minute or two, to her old cavalier, 'My lord, if you are there, as I think you are, give a little more swing to your bells.'

From this saying, which became spread about, I know not how Marie Fiquet became famous, and it is still said in our country, 'She is a maid of Thilouse,' in mockery of a bride, and to signify a 'fricquenelle.'

'Fricquenelle' is said of a girl I do not wish you to find in your arms on your wedding night, unless you have been brought up in the philosophy of Zeno, which puts up with anything, and there are many people obliged to be Stoics in this funny situation, which is often met with, for Nature turns, but changes not, and there are always good maids of Thilouse to be found in Touraine, and elsewhere. Now if you asked me in what consists, or where comes in, the moral of this tale? I am at liberty to reply to the ladies; that the Cent Contes Drolatiques are made more to teach the moral of pleasure than to procure the pleasure of pointing a moral. But if it were a used up old rascal who asked me, I should say to him with all the respect due to his yellow or grey locks; that God wishes to punish the lord of Valennes, for trying to purchase a jewel made to be given.

HOW THE PRETTY MAID OF PORTILLON CONVINCED HER JUDGE

Honore de Balzac

The Maid of Portillon, who became, as everyone knows, La Tascherette, was, before she became a dyer, a laundress at the said place of Portillon, from which she took her name. If any there be who do not know Tours, it may be as well to state that Portillon is down the Loire, on the same side as St. Cyr, about as far from the bridge which leads to the cathedral of Tours as said bridge is distant from Marmoustier, since the bridge is in the centre of the embankment between Portillon and Marmoustier. Do you thoroughly understand?

Yes? Good! Now the maid had there her washhouse, from which she ran to the Loire with her washing in a second and took the ferry-boat to get to St. Martin, which was on the other side of the river, for she had to deliver the greater part of her work in Châteauneuf and other places.

About Midsummer day, seven years before marrying old Taschereau, she had just reached the right age to be loved, without making a choice from any of the lads who pursued her with their intentions. Although there used to come to the bench under her window the son of Rabelais, who had seven boats on the Loire, Jehan's eldest, Marchandeau the tailor, and Peccard the ecclesiastical goldsmith, she made fun of them all, because she wished to be taken to church before burthening herself with a man, which proves that she was an honest woman until she was wheedled out of her virtue. She was one of those girls who take great care not to be contaminated, but who, if by chance they get deceived, let things take their course, thinking that for one stain or for fifty, a good polishing up is necessary. These characters demand our indulgence.

A young noble of the court perceived her one day when she was crossing the water in the glare of the noonday sun, which lit up her ample charms, and seeing her, asked who she was. An old man, who was working on the banks, told him she was called the Pretty Maid of Portillon, a laundress, celebrated for her merry ways and her virtue. This young lord, besides ruffles to starch, had many precious draperies and things; he resolved to give the custom of his house to this girl, whom he stopped on the road. He was thanked by her heartily, because he was the Sire du Fou, the king's chamberlain. This encounter made her so joyful that her mouth was full of his name. She talked about it a great deal to the people of St. Martin, and when she got back to the washhouse, was still full of it, and on the morrow at her work, her tongue went nineteen to the dozen, and all on the same subject, so that as much was said concerning my Lord du Fou in Portillon as of God in a sermon; that is, a great deal too much.

'If she works like that in cold water, what will she do in warm?' said an old washerwoman. 'She wants du Fou; he'll give her du Fou!'

The first time this giddy wench, with her head full of Monsieur du Fou, had to deliver the linen at his hotel, the chamberlain wished to see her, and was very profuse in praises and compliments concerning her charms, and wound up by telling her that she was not at all silly to be beautiful, and therefore he would give her more than she expected. The deed followed the word, for the moment his people were out of the room, he began to caress the maid, who thinking he was about to take out the money from his purse, dared not look at the purse, but said, like a girl ashamed to take her wages—

'It will be for the first time.'

'It will be soon,' said he.

Some people say that he had great difficulty in forcing her to accept what he offered her, and hardly forced her at all; others that he forced her badly, because she came out like an army flagging on the route, crying and groaning, and came to the judge. It happened that the judge was out. La Portillone awaited his return in his room, weeping and saying to the servant that she had been robbed, because Monseigneur du Fou had given her nothing but his mischief; whilst a canon of the Chapter used to give her large sums for that which M. du Fou wanted for nothing. If she loved a man she would think it wise to do things for him for nothing, because it would be a pleasure to her; but the chamberlain had treated her roughly, and not kindly and gently, as he should have done, and that therefore he owed her the thousand crowns of the canon. Then the judge came in, saw the wench, and wished to kiss her, but she put herself on guard, and said she had come to make a complaint. The judge replied that certainly she could have the offender hanged if she liked, because he was most anxious to serve her. The injured maiden replied that she did not wish the death of her man, but that he should pay her a thousand gold crowns, because she had been robbed against her will.

'Ha! ha!' said the judge, 'what he took was worth more than that.'

'For the thousand crowns I'll cry quits, because I shall be able to live without washing.'

'He who has robbed you, is he well off?'

'Oh yes.'

'Then he shall pay dearly for it. Who is it?'

'Monseigneur du Fou.'

'Oh, that alters the case,' said the judge.

'But justice?' said she.

'I said the case, not the justice of it,' replied the judge. 'I must know how the affair occurred.'

Then the girl related naively how she was arranging the young lord's ruffles in his wardrobe, when he began to play with her skirt, and she turned round saying—

'Go on with you!'

'You have no case,' said the judge, 'for by that speech he thought that you gave him leave to go on. Ha! ha!'

Then she declared that she had defended herself, weeping and crying out, and that that constitutes an assault.

'A wench's antics to incite him,' said the judge.

Finally, La Portillone declared that against her will she had been taken round the waist and thrown, although she had kicked and cried and struggled, but that seeing no help at hand, she had lost courage.

'Good! good!' said the judge. 'Did you take pleasure in the affair?'

'No,' said she. 'My anguish can only be paid for with a thousand crowns.'

'My dear,' said the judge, 'I cannot receive your complaint, because I believe no girl could be thus treated against her will.'

'Hi! hi! hi! Ask your servant,' said the little laundress, sobbing, 'and hear what she'll tell you.'

The servant affirmed that there were pleasant assaults and unpleasant ones; that if La Portillone had received neither amusement nor money, either one or the other was due to her. This wise counsel threw the judge into a state of great perplexity.

'Jacqueline,' said he, 'before I sup I'll get to the bottom of this. Now go and fetch my needle and the red thread that I sew the law paper bags with.'

Jacqueline came back with a big needle, pierced with a pretty little hole, and a big red thread, such as the judges use. Then she remained standing to see the question decided, very much disturbed, as was also the complainant at these mysterious preparations.

'My dear,' said the judge, 'I am going to hold the bodkin, of which the eye is sufficiently large, to put this thread into it without trouble. If you do put it in, I will take up your case, and will make Monseigneur offer you a compromise.'

'What's that?' said she. 'I will not allow it.'

'It is a word used in justice to signify an agreement.'

'A compromise is then agreeable with justice?' said La Portillone.

'My dear, this violence has also opened your mind. Are you ready?'

'Yes,' said she.

The waggish judge gave the poor nymph fair play, holding the eye steady for her; but when she wished to slip in the thread that she had twisted to make straight, he moved a little, and the thread went on the other side. She suspected the judge's argument, wetted the thread, stretched it, and came back again. The judge moved, twisted about, and wriggled like a bashful maiden; still this cursed thread would not enter. The girl kept trying at the eye, and the judge kept fidgeting. The marriage of the thread could not be consummated, the bodkin remained virgin, and the servant began to laugh, saying to La Portillone that she knew better how to endure than to perform. Then the roguish judge laughed too, and the fair Portillone cried for her golden crowns.

'If you don't keep still,' cried she, losing patience; 'if you keep moving about I shall never be able to put the thread in.'

'Then, my dear, if you had done the same, Monseigneur would have been unsuccessful too. Think, too, how easy is the one affair, and how difficult the other.'

The pretty wench, who declared she had been forced, remained thoughtful, and sought to find a means to convince the judge by showing how she had been compelled to yield, since the honour of all poor girls liable to violence was at stake.

'Monseigneur, in order that the bet made the fair, I must do exactly as the young lord did. If I had only had to move I should be moving still, but he went through other performances.'

'Let us hear them,' replied the judge.

Then La Portillone straightens the thread, and rubs it in the wax of the candle, to make it firm and straight; then she looked towards the eye of the bodkin, held by the judge, slipping always to the right or to the left. Then she began making endearing little speeches, such as, 'Ah, the pretty little bodkin! What a pretty mark to aim at! Never did I see such a little jewel! What a pretty little eye! Let me put this little thread into it! Ah, you will hurt my poor thread, my nice little thread! Keep still! Come, my love of a judge, judge of my love! Won't the thread go nicely into this iron gate, which makes good use of the thread, for it comes out very much out of order?' Then she burst out laughing, for she was better up in this game than the judge, who laughed too, so saucy and comical and arch was she, pushing the thread backwards and forwards. She kept the poor judge with the case in his hand until seven o'clock, keeping on fidgeting and moving about like a schoolboy let loose; but as La Portillone kept on trying to put the thread in, he could not help it. As, however, his joint was burning, and his wrist was tired, he was obliged to rest himself for a minute on the side of the table; then very dexterously the fair maid of Portillon slipped the thread in, saying—

'That's how the thing occurred.'

'But my joint was burning.'

'So was mine,' said she.

The judge, convinced, told La Portillone that he would speak to Monseigneur du Fou, and would himself carry the affair through, since it was certain the young lord had embraced her against her will, but that for valid reasons he would keep the affair dark. On the morrow, the judge went to the Court and saw Monseigneur du Fou, to whom he recounted the young woman's complaint, and how she had set forth her case. This complaint lodged in court, tickled the king immensely. Young du Fou having said that there was some truth in it, the king asked if he had had much difficulty, and as he replied, innocently, 'No,' the king declared the girl was quite worth a hundred gold crowns, and the chamberlain gave them to the judge, in order not to be taxed with stinginess, and said the starch would be a good income to La Portillone. The judge came back to La Portillone, and said, smiling, that he had raised a hundred gold crowns for her. But if she desired the balance of the thousand, there were at that moment in the king's apartments certain lords who, knowing the case, had offered to make up the sum for her, with her consent. The little hussy did not refuse this offer, saying that in order to do no more washing in the future she did not mind doing a little hard work now. She gratefully acknowledged the trouble the good judge had taken, and gained her thousand crowns in a month. From this came the falsehoods and jokes concerning her, because out of these ten lords jealousy made a hundred, whilst, differently from young men, La Portillone settled down to a virtuous life directly; she had her thousand crowns. Even a Duke, who would have counted out five hundred crowns, would have found this girl rebellious, which proves she was niggardly with her property. It is true that the king caused her to be sent for to his retreat of Rue Quinquangrogne, on the mall of Chardonneret, found her extremely pretty, exceedingly affectionate, enjoyed her society, and forbade the sergeants to interfere with her in any way whatsoever. Seeing she was so beautiful, Nicole Beaupertuys, the king's mistress, gave her a hundred gold crowns to go to Orléans, in order to see if the colour of the Loire was the same there as at Portillon. She went there, and the more willingly because she did not care very much for the king. When the good man came, who confessed the king in his last hours, and was afterwards canonised, La Portillone went to him to polish up her conscience, did penance, and founded a bed in the leper-house of St. Lazare-aux-Tours. Many ladies whom you know have been assaulted by more than two lords, and have found no other beds than those in their own houses. It is as well to relate this fact, in order to cleanse the reputation of this honest girl, who herself once washed dirty things, and who afterwards became famous for her clever tricks and her wit. She gave a proof of her merit in marrying Taschereau, who she cuckolded right merrily, as has been related in the story of 'The Reproach'. This proves to us most satisfactorily that with strength and patience justice itself can be violated.

ODD SAYINGS OF THREE PILGRIMS

Honore de Balzac

When the pope left his good town of Avignon to take up his residence in Rome, certain pilgrims were thrown out who had set out for this country, and would have to pass the high Alps, in order to gain this said town of Rome, where they were going to seek the remittimus of various sins. Then were to be seen on the roads, and the hostelries, those who wore the order of Cain, otherwise the flower of the penitents, all wicked fellows, burdened with leprous souls, which thirsted to bathe in the papal piscina, and all carrying with them gold or precious things to purchase absolution, pay for their beds, and present to the saints. You may be sure that those who drank water going, on their return, if the landlords gave them water, wished it to be the holy water of the cellar.

At this time the three pilgrims came to this said Avignon to their injury, seeing that it was widowed of the pope. While they were passing the Rhodane, to reach the Mediterranean coast, one of the three pilgrims, who had with him a son about ten years of age, parted company with the others, and near the town of Milan suddenly appeared again, but without the boy. Now in the evening, at supper, they had a hearty feast in order to celebrate the return of the pilgrim, who they thought had become disgusted with penitence through the pope not being in Avignon. Of these three roamers to Rome, one had come from the city of Paris, the other from Germany, and the third, who doubtless wished to instruct his son on the journey, had his home in the duchy of Burgundy, in which he had certain fiefs, and was a younger son of the house of

Villers-la-Faye (Villa in Fago), and was named La Vaugrenand. The German baron had met the citizen of Paris just past Lyons, and both had accosted the Sire de la Vaugrenand in sight of Avignon.

Now in this hostelry the three pilgrims loosened their tongues, and agreed to journey to Rome together, in order the better to resist the foot pads, the night-birds, and other malefactors, who made it their business to ease pilgrims of that which weighed upon their bodies before the pope eased them of that which weighed upon their consciences. After drinking, the three companions commenced to talk together, for the bottle is the key of conversation, and each made this confession—that the cause of his pilgrimage was a woman. The servant who watched their drinking, told them that of a hundred pilgrims who stopped in the locality, ninety-nine were travelling from the same thing. These three wise men then began to consider how pernicious is woman to man. The Baron showed the heavy gold chain that he had in his hauberk to present to Saint Peter, and said his crime was such that he would not get rid of with the value of two such chains. The Parisian took off his glove, and exposed a ring set with a white diamond, saying that he had a hundred like it for the pope. The Burgundian took off his hat, and exhibited two wonderful pearls, that were beautiful ear-pendants for Notre-Dame-de-Lorette, and candidly confessed that he would rather have left them round his wife's neck.

Thereupon the servant exclaimed that their sins must have been as great as those of Visconti.

Then the pilgrims replied that they were such that they had made a solemn vow in their minds never to go astray again during the remainder of their days, however beautiful the woman might be, and this in addition to the penance which the pope might impose upon them.

Then the servant expressed her astonishment that all had made the same vow. The Burgundian added, that this vow had been the cause of his lagging behind, because he had been in extreme fear that his son, in spite of his age, might go astray, and that he had made a vow to prevent people and beasts alike gratifying their passions in his house, or upon his estates. The baron having inquired the particulars of the adventure, the sire narrated the affair as follows:—

'You know that the good Countess Jeane d'Avignon made formerly a law for the harlots, who she compelled to live in the outskirts of the town in houses with window-shutters painted red and closed. Now passing in my company in this vile neighbourhood, my lad remarked these houses with closed window-shutters, painted red, and his curiosity being aroused—for these ten-year old little devils have eyes for everything—he pulled me by the sleeve and kept on pulling until he had learnt from me what these houses were. Then, to obtain peace, I told him that young lads had nothing to do with such places, and could only enter them at the peril of their lives, because it was a place where men and women were manufactured, and the danger was such for anyone unacquainted with the business that if a novice entered, flying chancres and other wild beasts would seize upon his face. Fear seized the lad, who then followed me to the hostelry in a state of agitation, and not daring to cast his eyes upon the said bordels. While I was in the stable, seeing to the putting up of the horses, my son went off like a robber, and the servant was unable to tell me what had become of him. Then I was in great fear of the wenches, but had confidence in the laws, which forbade them to admit such children. At supper-time the rascal came back to me looking no more ashamed of himself than did our divine Saviour in the temple among the doctors.

'"Whence comes you?" said I to him.

'"From the houses with the red shutters," he replied.

'"Little blackguard," said I, "I'll give you a taste of the whip."

'Then he began to moan and cry. I told him that if he would confess all that had happened to him I would let him off the beating.

'"Ha," said he, "I took care not to go in, because of the flying chancres and other wild beasts. I only looked through the chinks of the windows, in order to see how men were manufactured."

"'And what did you see?' I asked.

"'I saw,' said he, "a fine woman just being finished, because she only wanted one peg, which a young worker was fitting in with energy. Directly, she was finished, she turned round, spoke to, and kissed her manufacturer."

"'Have your supper,' said I; and the same night I returned to Burgundy, and left him with his mother, being sorely afraid that at the first town he might want to fit a peg into some girl.'

'These children often make these sort of answers,' said the Parisian. 'One of my neighbour's children revealed the cuckoldom of his father by a reply. One day I asked, to see if he was well instructed at school in religious matters, "What is hope?" "One of the king's big archers, who comes here when father goes out," said he. Indeed, the sergeant of the Archers was named Hope. My friend was dumbfounded at this, and, although to keep his countenance he looked in the mirror, he could not see his horns there.'

The baron observed that the boy's remark was good in this way: that Hope is a person who comes to bed with us when the realities of life are out of the way.

'Is a cuckold made in the image of God?' asked the Burgundian.

'No,' said the Parisian, 'because God was wise in this respect, that he took no wife; therefore is He happy through all eternity.'

'But,' said the maid-servant, 'cuckolds are made in the image of God before they are horned.'

Then the three pilgrims began to curse women, saying that they were the cause of all the evils in the world.

'Their heads are as empty as helmets,' said the Burgundian.

'Their hearts are as straight as bill-hooks,' said the Parisian.

'Why are there so many men pilgrims and so few women pilgrims?' said the German baron.

'Their cursed member never sins,' replied the Parisian; 'it knows neither father nor mother, the commandments of God, nor those of the Church, neither laws divine or human: their member knows no doctrine, understands no heresies, and cannot be blamed; it is innocent of all, and always on the laugh; its understanding is nil; and for this reason do I hold it in utter detestation.'

'I also,' said the Burgundian, 'and I begin to understand the different reading by a learned man of the verses of the Bible, in which the account of the creation is given. In this Commentary, which in my country we call a Noel, lies the reason of imperfection of this feature of women, of which, different to that of other females, no man can slake the thirst, such diabolical heat existing there. In this Noel, is stated that the Lord God, having turned his head to look at a donkey, who had brayed for the first time in his Paradise, while he was manufacturing Eve, the devil seized this moment to put his finger into this divine creature, and made a warm wound, which the Lord took care to close with a stitch, from which comes the maid. By means of this frenum, the woman should remain closed, and children be made in the same manner in which God made the angels, by a pleasure far above carnal pleasure as the heaven is above the earth. Observing this closing, the devil, wild at being done, pinched the Sieur Adam, who was asleep, by the skin, and stretched a portion of it out in imitation of his diabolical tail; but as the father of man was on his back this appendage came out in front. Thus these two productions of the devil had the desire to reunite themselves, following the law of similarities which God had laid down for the conduct of the world. From this came the first sin and the sorrows of the human race, because God, noticing the devil's work, determined to see what would come of it.'

The servant declared that they were quite correct in the statements, for that woman was a bad animal, and that she herself knew some who were better under the ground than on it. The pilgrims, noticing then how pretty the girl was, were afraid of breaking their vows, and went straight to bed. The girl went and told her mistress she was harbouring infidels, and told her what they had said about women.

'Ah!' said the landlady, 'what matters it to me the thoughts my customers have in their brains, so long as their purses are well filled.'

And when the servant had told of the jewels, she exclaimed—

'Ah, these are questions which concern all women. Let us go and reason with them. I'll take the nobles, you can have the citizen.'

The landlady, who was the most shameless inhabitant of the duchy of Milan, went into the chamber where the Sire de La Vaugrenand and the German baron were sleeping, and congratulated them upon their vows, saying that the women would not lose much by them; but to accomplish these said vows it was necessary they should endeavour to withstand the strongest temptations. Then she offered to lie down beside them, so anxious were she to see if she would be left unmolested, a thing which had never happened to her yet in the company of a man.

On the morrow, at breakfast, the servant had the ring on her finger, her mistress had the gold chain and the pearl earrings. The three pilgrims stayed in the town about a month, spending there all the money they had in their purses, and agreed that if they had spoken so severely of women it was because they had not known those of Milan.

On his return to Germany the Baron made this observation: that he was only guilty of one sin, that of being in his castle. The Citizen of Paris came back full of stories for his wife, and found her full of Hope. The Burgundian saw Madame de La Vaugrenand so troubled that he nearly died of the consolations he administered to her, in spite of his former opinions. This teaches us to hold our tongues in hostelries.

INNOCENCE

Honore de Balzac

By the double crest of my fowl, and by the rose lining of my sweetheart's slipper! By all the horns of well-beloved cuckolds, and by the virtue of their blessed wives! the finest work of man is neither poetry, nor painted pictures, nor music, nor castles, nor statues, be they carved never so well, nor rowing, nor sailing galleys, but children.

Understand me, children up to the age of ten years, for after that they become men or women, and cutting their wisdom teeth, are not worth what they cost; the worst are the best. Watch them playing, prettily and innocently, with slippers; above all, cancellated ones, with the household utensils, leaving that which displeases them, crying after that which pleases them, munching the sweets and confectionery in the house, nibbling at the stores, and always laughing as soon as their teeth are cut, and you will agree with me that they are in every way lovable; besides which they are flower and fruit—the fruit of love, the flower of life. Before their minds have been unsettled by the disturbances of life, there is nothing in this world more blessed or more pleasant than their sayings, which are naive beyond description. This is as true as the double chewing machine of a cow. Do not expect a man to be innocent after the manner of children, because there is an, I know not what, ingredient of reason in the naivety of a man, while the naivety of children is candid, immaculate, and has all the finesse of the mother, which is plainly proved in this tale.

Queen Catherine was at that time Dauphine, and to make herself welcome to the king, her father-in-law, who at that time was very ill indeed, presented him, from time to time, with Italian pictures, knowing that he liked them much, being a friend of the Sieur Raphaël d'Urbin and of the Sieurs Primatice and Leonardo da Vinci, to whom he sent large sums of money. She obtained from her family—who had the pick of these works, because at that time the Duke of the Medicis governed Tuscany—a precious picture, painted by a Venetian named Titian (artist to the Emperor Charles, and in very high flavour), in which there were portraits of Adam and Eve at the moment when God left them to wander about the terrestrial Paradise, and were painted their full height, in the costume of the period, in which it is difficult to make a mistake, because they were attired in their ignorance, and caparisoned with the divine grace which enveloped them—a difficult thing to execute on account of the colour, but one in which the said Sieur Titian excelled. The picture was put into the room of the poor king, who was then ill with the disease of which he eventually died. It had a great success at the Court of France, where everyone wished to see it; but no one was able to until after the king's death, since at his desire it was allowed to remain in his room as long as he lived.

One day Madame Catherine took with her to the king's room her son Francis and little Margot, who began to talk at random, as children will. Now here, now there, these children had heard this picture of Adam and Eve spoken about, and had tormented their mother to take them there. Since the two little ones at times amused the old king, Madame the Dauphine consented to their request.

'You wished to see Adam and Eve, who were our first parents; there they are,' said she.

Then she left them in great astonishment before Titian's picture, and seated herself by the bedside of the king, who delighted to watch the children.

'Which of the two is Adam?' said Francis, nudging his sister Margot's elbow.

'You silly!' replied she, 'to know that, they would have to be dressed!'

This reply, which delighted the poor king and the mother, was mentioned in a letter written in Florence by Queen Catherine.

No writer having brought it to light, it will remain, like a sweet flower, in a corner of these Tales, although it is no way droll, and there is no other moral to be drawn from it except that to hear these pretty speeches of infancy one must beget the children.

AMYCUS AND CÉLESTINE

Anatole France

Prone upon the threshold of his rude cavern, the hermit Célestine passed in prayer the eve of the Easter Festival, that unearthly night upon which the shuddering demons are hurled into the abyss. And whilst the shades still enveloped the earth, at the moment when the exterminating angel winged his flight across Egypt, Célestine shivered, for he was seized with anguish and unease. He heard from afar in the forest the cries of the wild cats and the shrill voices of the frogs. Immersed in the unholy darkness, he even doubted whether the glorious mystery could come to pass. But when he saw the first signals of the day, gladness entered into his heart together with the dawn; he realized that Christ was risen from the dead, and cried—

'Jesus is arisen from the grave. Love has conquered death. Alleluia! He is risen all glorious from the foot of the hill. Alleluia! The whole creation is restored and made anew. Darkness and evil are put to flight. Light and pardon encompass the world. Alleluia!'

A lark, awakened amidst the wheat, answered him with song.

'He is risen again. I have dreamed of nests and eggs—white eggs, flecked with brown. Alleluia! He is risen again.'

Then the hermit Célestine left his cavern to go to the neighbouring chapel and celebrate the holy Easter Feast.

As he passed through the forest, he saw, in the midst of a glade, a splendid beech, whose bursting buds already gave passage to tiny leaves of a tender green. Garlands of ivy and fillets of wool were hung upon its branches, which spread out groundwards. Votive tablets fastened to its gnarled trunk spoke of youth and love, and here and there some Eros, fashioned in clay, shorn of garments and with outspread wings, balanced himself lightly upon a branch. At this sight, the hermit Célestine knitted his whitened brows.

'It is the fairies' tree,' he said, 'and the country maidens, according to ancient custom, have laden it with offerings. My life has passed in struggling against these fairies, and no one could conceive the annoyance these tiny creatures cause me. They do not openly rebel against me. Each year, at harvest time, I exorcise the tree with the customary rites, and sing the Gospel of St. John to them.

'There is nothing better to be done. Holy water and the Gospel of St. John have power to put them to flight, and there is nothing more heard of the little damsels throughout the winter; but in the spring back they come once more, and each year one must begin all over again.

'And they are subtle; a single bush of hawthorn is large enough to shelter a whole swarm. And they cast their spells upon the young folks, both the youths and the maidens.

'As I have grown older, my sight has become dim and now I can scarcely perceive their presence. They make a mockery of me, sport under my nose and laugh in my beard. But when I was only twenty, I often saw them in the clearings dancing in circles beneath the light of the moon like garlands of flowers. Oh, Lord God, Thou who madest the heaven and the dew, praised be Thou in Thy works. But why didst Thou create unholy trees and fairy springs? Why hast Thou planted beneath the hazel the screaming mandrake? These things of nature seduce the young to sin, and are the cause of unnumbered labours to anchorites who, like myself, have undertaken the sanctification of Thy creatures. If only the Gospel of St. John still availed to put the demons to flight! But it is no longer enough, and I am perplexed to know what to do.'

And as the good hermit went sighing on his way, the tree—for it was a fairy tree—called to him with a fresh rustling.

'Célestine! Célestine! My buds are eggs—true Easter eggs. Alleluia! Alleluia!'

Célestine plunged into the wood without turning his head. He made his way with difficulty by a narrow path through the midst of thorns which tore his gown, when suddenly the road was barred to him by a young lad who came bounding out of a thicket. He was half-clothed in the skin of some beast, and was indeed rather a faun than a boy. His glance was penetrating, his nose flattened, his countenance laughing. His curly hair concealed the two little horns upon his stubborn forehead; his lips disclosed white pointed teeth; a fair forked beard descended from his chin. Upon his chest a golden down shone. He was agile and slender, and his cloven feet were hidden in the grass.

Célestine, who had made himself the possessor of all the wisdom to be won by meditation, saw at once with whom he had to do, and raised his arm to make the sign of the cross. But the faun, seizing his hand, prevented him from completing the mighty spell.

'Good hermit,' said he, 'do not exorcise me. For me, as for you, this day is a day of festival. You would be wanting in charity if you should plunge me in grief during the Easter Feast. If you are willing, we will stroll along together, and you will see that I am not malicious.'

By good fortune Célestine was well-versed in the sacred sciences. He recalled to himself in these circumstances that St. Jerome in the desert had had for fellow-travellers—both satyrs and centaurs who had confessed the Truth.

He said to the faun—

'Faun, raise a hymn to God. Declare: He is risen.'

'He is indeed arisen,' replied the faun. 'And behold me all gladness thereupon.'

Here the path widened, so that they walked side by side. The hermit became pensive, and reflected—

'He cannot be a demon since he has witnessed the Truth. It is well that I refrained from grieving him. The example of the great St. Jerome has not been lost upon me.'

Then, turning towards his goat-footed companion, he asked him—

'What is your name?'

'I am called Amycus,' replied the faun. 'I dwell in this wood, where I was born. I came to you, good father, because behind your long white beard, your countenance was kindly. It seems to me that hermits must be fauns borne down by the years. When I am grown old, I shall be like unto you.'

'He is risen,' said the hermit.

'He is indeed arisen,' said Amycus.

And thus conversing, they climbed the hill on which arose a chapel consecrated to the true God. It was small and of homely construction. Célestine had built it with his own hands with the fragments of a temple of Venus. Within, the table of the Lord stood forth shapeless and uncovered.

'Let us fall down,' said the hermit, 'and sing Alleluia, for He is arisen. And do you, mysterious being, remain kneeling whilst I offer the holy sacrifice.'

But the faun drew near to the hermit, and stroked his beard, and said—

'Venerable old man, you are wiser than I, and you can discern that which is invisible. But the woods and the springs are better known to me than to you. I will bring to God leafage and blossoms. I know the banks where the cress half opens its lilac clusters, the meadows where the cowslip blossoms in yellow bunches. I detect, by its faint odour, the mistletoe upon the wild apple tree. Already the blackthorn bushes are decked with a snowy crown of flowers. Wait for me, good father.'

With three goat-like leaps he was back in the woods, and when he returned, Célestine fancied he beheld a walking hawthorn tree. Amycus had disappeared beneath his odorous harvest. He hung garlands of flowers about the rustic altar; he sprinkled it with violets, and said solemnly—

'I dedicate these flowers to the God who gave them being.'

And whilst Célestine celebrated the sacrifice of the mass, the goat-footed one bowed his horned head down to the very ground and worshipped the sun, and said—

'The earth is a vast egg which thou, O Sun, most holy Sun, dost render fruitful.'

From that day forward Célestine and Amycus lived together in fellowship. The hermit never succeeded, despite all his endeavours, in making the half-human creature understand the ineffable mysteries; but as through the exertions of Amycus, the chapel of the true God was constantly hung with garlands, and more gaily decked than the fairies' tree, the holy priest said—

'The faun is himself a hymn to God.'

And it was for this reason that he bestowed on him the rite of holy baptism.

Upon the hill where Célestine once raised the meagre chapel which Amycus garlanded with flowers from the hills, the woods, and the streams, there stands, at the present day, a church the nave of which goes back to the eleventh century, whilst the porch dates from the period of Henry II, when it was rebuilt in the style of the Renaissance. It is a place of pilgrimage, and the faithful assemble there to hold in pious memory the saints Amycus and Célestine.

THE MASS OF SHADOWS

Anatole France

This tale the sacristan of the church of St. Eulalie at Neuville-d'Aumont told me, as we sat under the arbour of the White Horse, one fine summer evening, drinking a bottle of old wine to the health of the dead man, now very much at his ease, whom that very morning he had borne to the grave with full honours, beneath a pall powdered with smart silver tears.

'My poor father, who is dead' (it is the sacristan who is speaking), 'was in his lifetime a gravedigger. He was of an agreeable disposition, the result, no doubt, of the calling he followed, for it has often been pointed out that people who work in cemeteries are of a jovial turn. Death has no terrors for them: they never give it a thought. I, for instance, Monsieur, enter a cemetery at night as little perturbed as though it were the arbour of the White Horse. And if by chance I meet with a ghost, I don't disturb myself in the least about it, for I reflect that he may just as likely have business of his own to attend to as I. I know the habits of the dead, and I know their character. Indeed, so far as that goes, I know things of which the priests themselves are ignorant. If I were to tell you all I have seen, you would be astounded. But a still tongue makes a wise head, and my father, who, all the same, delighted in spinning a yarn, did not disclose a twentieth part of what he knew. To make up for this, he often repeated the same stories, and to my knowledge, he told the story of Catherine Fontaine at least a hundred times.

'Catherine Fontaine was an old maid whom he well remembered having seen when he was a mere child. I should not be surprised if there were still, perhaps, three old fellows in the district who could remember having heard folks speak of her, for she was very well known and of excellent reputation, although poor enough. She lived at the corner of the Rue aux Nonnes, in the turret which is still to be seen there, and which formed part of an old half-ruined mansion looking on to the garden of the Ursuline nuns. On that turret can still be traced certain figures and half-obliterated inscriptions. The late Curé of St. Eulalie, Monsieur Levasseur, asserted that there are the words in Latin, *Love is stronger than death*, "which is to be understood," so he would add, "of divine love."

'Catherine Fontaine lived by herself in this tiny apartment. She was a lacemaker. You know, of course, that the lace made in our part of the world was formerly held in high esteem. No one knew anything of her relatives or friends. It was reported that when she was eighteen years of age, she had loved the young Chevalier d'Aumont-Cléry, and been secretly affianced to him. But decent folk didn't believe a word of it, and said it was nothing but a tale which had been concocted because Catherine Fontaine's demeanour was that of a lady rather than of a working woman, and because, moreover, she possessed beneath her white locks the remains of great beauty. Her expression was sorrowful, and on one finger she wore one of those rings fashioned by the goldsmith into the semblance of two tiny hands clasped together. In former days folks were accustomed to exchange such rings at their betrothal ceremony. I am sure you know the sort of thing I mean.

'Catherine Fontaine lived a saintly life. She spent a great deal of time in the churches, and every morning, whatever might be the weather, she went to assist at the six o'clock Mass at St. Eulalie.

'Now one December night, whilst she was abed in her little chamber, she was awakened by the sound of bells, and nothing doubting that they were ringing for the first Mass, the pious woman dressed herself and came downstairs and out into the street. The night was so obscure that not even the walls of the houses were visible, and not a ray of light shone from the murky sky. And such was the silence amid this black darkness, that there was not even the sound of a distant dog barking, and a feeling of aloofness from every living creature was perceptible. But Catherine Fontaine knew well every single stone she stepped on, and as she could have found her way to the church with her eyes shut, she reached without difficulty the corner of the Rue aux Nonnes and the Rue de la Paroisse, where the timbered house stands with the tree of Jesse carved on one of its massive beams. When she reached this spot, she perceived that the church doors were open, and that a great light was streaming out from the wax tapers. She resumed her journey, and when she had passed through the porch, she found herself in the midst of a vast congregation which entirely filled the church. But she did not recognize any of the worshippers, and was surprised to observe that all these people were dressed in velvets and brocades, with feathers in their hats, and that they wore swords in the fashion of days gone by. Here were gentlemen who carried tall canes with gold knobs, and ladies with lace caps fastened with coronet-shaped combs. Chevaliers of the Order of St. Louis extended their hands to these ladies, who concealed behind their fans painted faces, of which only the powdered brow and the patch at the corner of the eye were visible! And all of them proceeded to take up their places without the slightest sound, and as they moved, neither the sound of their footsteps on the pavement nor the rustle of their garments could be heard. The lower places were filled with a crowd of young artisans in brown jackets, dimity breeches, and blue stockings, with their arms round the waists of very pretty blushing girls who lowered their eyes. Near the holy water stoups, peasant women, in scarlet petticoats and laced bodices, sat upon the ground as immovable as domestic animals, whilst young lads, standing up behind them, stared out from wide-open eyes and twirled their hats round and round on their fingers, and all these silent countenances seemed centred irremovably on one and the same thought, at once sweet and sorrowful. On her knees, in her accustomed place, Catherine Fontaine saw the priest advance towards the altar, preceded by two servers. She recognized neither priest nor clerks. The Mass began. It was a silent Mass, during which neither the sound of the moving lips nor the tinkle of the bell, vainly swung to and fro, was audible. Catherine Fontaine felt that she was under the observation and the influence also of her mysterious neighbour, and when, scarcely turning her head, she stole a glance at him, she recognized the young Chevalier d'Aumont-Cléry who had once loved her, and who had been dead for five-and-forty years. She recognized him by a small mark which he had over the left ear, and, above all, by the shadow which his long black eyelashes cast upon his cheeks. He was dressed in his hunting clothes, scarlet with gold lace, the very clothes he wore that day when he met her in St. Leonard's Wood, begged her for a drink and stole a kiss. He had preserved his youth and his good looks. When he smiled he still displayed magnificent teeth. Catherine said to him in an undertone—

"'Monseigneur, you, who were my friend, and to whom in days gone by I gave all that a girl holds most dear, may God keep you in His grace! O, that he would at length inspire me with regret for the sin I committed in yielding to you; for it is a fact that, though my hair is white and I approach my end, I have not yet repented of having loved you. But, dear dead friend and noble seigneur, tell me, who are these folk, habited after the antique fashion, who are here assisting at this silent Mass?"

'The Chevalier d'Aumont-Cléry replied in a voice feebler than a breath, but none the less crystal clear—

"'Catherine, these men and women are souls from purgatory, who have grieved God by sinning as we ourselves sinned through love of the creature, but who are not on that account cast off by God, inasmuch as their sin, like ours, was not deliberate.

"'Whilst, separated from those they loved upon earth, they are purified in the cleansing fires of purgatory, they suffer the pangs of absence, which is for them the most cruel of tortures. They are so unhappy that an angel from heaven takes pity upon their love-torment. By the permission of the Most High, for one hour in the night, he reunites, each year, lover to loved in their parish church, where they are permitted to assist at the Mass of Shadows, hand clasped in hand. These are the facts. If it has been granted to me to see thee here before thy death, Catherine, it is a boon which has been bestowed by God's special permission."

'And Catherine Fontaine answered him—

'"I would die gladly enough, dear, dead lord, if I might recover the beauty that was mine when I gave you to drink in the forest."

'Whilst they conversed thus under their breath, a very old canon was taking the collection and proffering to the worshippers a great copper dish, wherein they let fall, each in his turn, ancient coins which have long since ceased to pass current: écus of six livres, florins, ducats and ducatoons, jacobuses and rose-nobles, and the pieces fell silently into the dish. When at length it was placed before the Chevalier, he dropped into it a louis which made no more sound than had the other pieces of gold and silver.

'Then the old canon stopped before Catherine Fontaine, who fumbled in her pocket without being able to find a farthing. Then, being unwilling to allow the dish to pass without an offering from herself, she slipped from her finger the ring which the Chevalier had given her the day before his death, and cast it into the copper bowl. As the golden ring fell, a sound like the heavy clang of a bell rang out, and on the stroke of this reverberation, the Chevalier, the canon, the celebrant, the servers, the ladies and their cavaliers, the whole assembly vanished utterly; the candles guttered out, and Catherine Fontaine was left alone in the darkness.'

Having concluded his narrative after this fashion, the sacristan drank a long draught of wine, remained pensive a moment, and then resumed his talk in these words:—

'I have told you this tale exactly as my father has told it to me over and over again, and I believe that it is authentic, because it agrees in all respects with what I have myself observed of the manners and customs peculiar to those who have passed away. I have associated a good deal with the dead ever since my childhood, and I know that they are accustomed to return to what they have loved.

'It is on this account that the miserly dead wander at night in the neighbourhood of the treasures they concealed during their lifetime. They keep a strict watch over their gold; but the trouble they give themselves, far from being of service to them, turns to their disadvantage; and it is not at all a rare thing to come upon money buried in the ground on digging in a place haunted by a ghost. In the same way, deceased husbands come by night to harass their wives who have made a second matrimonial venture, and I could easily name several who have kept a better watch over their wives since death than ever they did while living.

'That sort of thing is blameworthy, for in all fairness, the dead have no business to stir up jealousies. Still I do but tell you what I have observed myself. It is a matter to take into account if one marries a widow. Besides, the tale I have told you is vouched for in the manner following:

'The morning after that extraordinary night, Catherine Fontaine was discovered dead in her chamber. And the beadle attached to St. Eulalie found in the copper bowl used for the collection a gold ring with two clasped hands. Besides, I'm not the kind of man to make jokes. Suppose we order another bottle of wine?...'

THE BOON OF DEATH BESTOWED

Anatole France

When he had, for a long while, tramped through the deserted streets, André at last went and sat down on the bank of the Seine and watched the water lapping the base of the hill where, in the vanished days of joy and hope, Lucie, his dear mistress, had her home.

For long enough, he had not felt so restful.

At eight o'clock, he took a bath. Then he strolled into a restaurant in the Palais-Royal, and glanced through the newspapers whilst his meal was preparing. In the Courier of Equality, he read the list of the condemned prisoners who had been executed on the Place de la Révolution on the 24th of Floréal.

He ate his breakfast heartily. Then he rose, looked in a glass to make sure that he was presentably dressed, and that his colour was not likely to betray him, and set out at an easy pace to the other side of the river, towards the low house at the corner of the Rue de Seine and the Rue Mazarine. Here were the quarters of Citizen Lardillon, deputy public prosecutor at the revolutionary tribunal, a man well disposed towards André, who had known him first as a capuchin at Angers, and later as a sans-culotte in Paris.

He rang, and after an interval of some few minutes, a figure appeared behind a grating commanding the entrance, and Citizen Lardillon, having prudently satisfied himself as to the appearance and name of his visitor, at length threw open the door. His face was broad, his colour high, his eyes glittering, his lips moist, and his ears red. He looked a jovial but worried man. He led André into his ante-chamber.

There, on a small round table, a meal for two was set out. There was chicken, a pie, a ham, a terrine of foie-gras and various cold meats in aspic. On the floor, six bottles were cooling in a pail. A pineapple, cheese of various kinds, and preserved fruits occupied the mantelpiece, and flasks of liqueurs were deposited on a desk littered with papers.

Through the half-open door of the adjoining room a large bed was visible, not yet made.

'Citizen Lardillon,' began André, 'I have come to beg a favour of you.'

'I am quite ready to grant it, citizen, provided it involves no risk to the security of the Republic.'

André smilingly replied—

'The service I ask you to do me is not in the least compromising to the safety of either the Republic or yourself.'

At a sign from Lardillon, André sat down. 'Citizen deputy,' he said, 'you are aware that for the last two years I have been conspiring against your friends, and that I am the author of the pamphlet entitled, "The Altars of Fear". You will not be doing me a favour in having me arrested. You will only be doing your duty. Moreover, that is not the service I ask at your hands. But listen: my mistress, to whom I am devoted, is in prison.'

Lardillon nodded his head to indicate that he approved of the devotion André confessed to.

'I am sure that you are not unfeeling, Citizen Lardillon. I beg you to procure my reunion with the woman I love, and to have me conveyed to Port Libre as speedily as may be.'

'Come, come,' said Lardillon, and a smile played upon his lips, which were both delicate and firm, 'it is a greater boon than life that you demand of me. You require me to bestow happiness on you, citizen!'

He stretched out the arm nearest to the bedroom, and called—

'Epicharis! Epicharis!'

A big, dark woman entered, her arms and throat still bare, for she had only got as far with her toilette as a chemise and petticoat, though a cockade was fastened in her hair.

'Nymph of mine,' said Lardillon as he drew her on to his knees, 'look upon the face of this citizen, and never forget it! Like us, Epicharis, he is tender-hearted; like us, he realizes that the greatest of ills is to be separated from the beloved one. He wishes to go to prison—ay, to the guillotine—with his mistress, Epicharis. Can I withhold this boon from him?'

'No!' answered the girl, as she tapped the cheeks of the carmagnole-clad monk.

'You are right, my goddess. We shall be earning the gratitude of two devoted lovers. Citizen Germain, give me your address, and this very night you shall sleep in the Bourbe.'

'That is agreed?' said André.

'That is agreed,' replied Lardillon as he offered him his hand. 'Go and find your fair friend, and tell her how you saw Epicharis in Lardillon's embrace. I trust that that recollection may stir your hearts to joyous measures.'

André replied that possibly they would be able to call up even more affecting memories, but that he was none the less grateful to Lardillon, and that he only regretted that it was not likely to be in his power to be of service to him in return.

'A humane action needs no recompense,' replied Lardillon.

Then he rose, and clasping Epicharis to his heart, said—

'Who knows when our own turn may come?'

Omnes eodem cogimur: omnium
Versatur urna; serius ocius
Sors exitura, et nos in æternum
Exilium impositura cymbæ.

[We all must tread the paths of Fate,
And ever shakes the mortal Urn,
Whose Lot embarks us, soon or late,
On Charon's Boat, ah! never to return.]

—Francis's *Horace*.

'In the meanwhile, let us drink! Citizen, will you join us at the table?'

Epicharis said it would only be polite of him, and made to seize him by the arm. But he tore himself away, relying on the promise the deputy public prosecutor had made.

THE LAST LESSON

Alphonse Daudet

This morning, I was very late in getting to school and I was afraid of being scolded because M. Hamel had said he would be quizzing us on the participles and I didn't know the first word. It occurred to me that I might skip class and run afield. The day was warm and bright, the blackbirds were whistling at the edge of the woods, and in the meadow behind the sawmill, the Prussians were practising. Everything seemed much nicer than the rule of participles; but I resisted the urge and hurried toward school.

Passing the town hall, I saw a group of people gathered in front of the notice board. For the past two years, that has been where we've gotten all the bad news, the battles lost, the demands, the commands; and I thought without stopping: 'What now?' Then as I ran by, the blacksmith Wachter, who was there with his apprentice reading the postings, called to me, 'Don't rush, boy; you have plenty of time to get to school!' I thought he was teasing me, and I was out of breath as I reached M. Hamel's.

Normally, when class starts, there is noise enough to be heard from the street as desks are opened and shut, students repeat lessons together and loudly with hands over ears to learn better, and the teacher's big ruler knocking on the tables, 'Let's have some quiet!' I was hoping to use the commotion to sneak into place unnoticed, but today all was silent, like a Sunday morning. Through the open window, I saw my classmates already in their seats and M. Hamel, who went back and forth with his terrible iron ruler under his arm. I had to open the door and enter amidst this great calm. You can imagine how flushed and fearful I was!

But no, M. Hamel looked at me evenly and said gently, 'Take your seat quickly, little Franz, we were starting without you.' I hopped the bench and sat at my desk right away. Only after I had settled in did I notice our teacher had on his fancy green coat, his ruffled shirt and the embroidered silk cap he only wore on inspection or award days. Also, the whole room seemed oddly solemn. But what surprised me most was at the back of the room where the benches were always empty now sat people of the village, quietly like us: the old Hauser with his tricorn, the former mayor, the former postmaster, and some others. Everyone looked sad; and Hauser had brought his old primer, worn at the edges, which he held open on his knees with his glasses resting on the pages.

While I was taking all this in, M. Hamel stood by his chair and in the same grave, gentle voice with which he had welcomed me told us, 'Children, this is the last time I will teach the class. Orders from Berlin require that only German be taught in the schools of Alsace and Lorraine... the new teacher arrives tomorrow. Today is your last French lesson. I ask for your best attention.' These words hit me hard. Ah! Those beasts, that's what they had posted at the town hall. My last French lesson...

Yet I hardly knew how to write! I had learned nothing! And I would learn no more! I wished now to have the lost time back, the classes missed as I hunted for eggs or went skating on the Saar! My books that I had always found so boring, so heavy to carry, my grammar text, my history of the saints—they seemed to me like old friends I couldn't bear to abandon. It was the same with M. Hamel. The idea that he was leaving made me forget his scolding and the thumps of his ruler. Poor man!

It was in honour of this final class that he had worn his best Sunday outfit, and now I understood why the old men from the village were gathered at the rear of the class. They were there to show that they too were sorry for neglecting to attend school more. It was also a way to thank our teacher of forty years for his fine service, and to show their respect for the country that was disappearing.

I was pondering these things when I heard my name called. It was my turn to recite. What wouldn't I have given to say that vaunted rule of participles loudly, clearly, flawlessly? Instead I tangled the first words and stood, hanging onto my desk, my heart pounding, unable to raise my head. I heard M. Hamel say, 'I won't scold you, my little Franz, you must already feel bad... That's how it is. We always say, "Bah! I have time. I'll learn 'tomorrow.'" And now you see it has come... Ah! It is Alsace's great trouble that she always puts off learning until tomorrow. Now people will be justified in saying to us, "How come you pretend to be French and yet don't know how to read or write your language!" You are not the most guilty of this, my poor Franz. We all have good reason to blame ourselves.

'Your parents did not press you to learn your lessons. They'd prefer to have you work in the fields or at the mill to earn some more money. Myself, I am not blameless. Haven't I sent you to water my garden instead of work? And when I wanted to go fishing, didn't I give you the day off?'

Then, from one thing to another, M. Hamel spoke of the French tongue, saying it was the most beautiful language in the world, the most clear, the most sensible. That we must keep it ourselves and never forget it, because when a people hold onto their language it is like holding the prison key...

Then he took a grammar text and read us our lesson. I was stunned to realize how well I understood it. Everything he said seemed so easy, easy! I believe also that I had never listened so well and that he had never explained to us so patiently. One might think that the poor man wished to give us all his knowledge, to fill our heads in a single try.

After grammar, we moved on to writing. For this day, M. Hamel had prepared new examples, written in beautiful, round script: France, Alsace, France, Alsace. They looked like little flags floating about the classroom, hung from the rods atop our desks. It was something to see everyone set to our work, and so silently! The only sound was the scratching of pens on paper. Once some beetles flew in but no one paid them any attention, not even the little ones who were assiduously tracing their figures with one heart, one mind, as if this also were French… On the roof the pigeons cooed softly. When I heard them I said to myself, 'Will they be forced to sing in German, too?' From time to time when I'd raise my eyes from my writing, I would see M. Hamel still in his chair, staring at the objects around him as if he wanted to memorize exactly how things were in the little schoolhouse.

Imagine! For forty years, he'd been in the same place with his yard before him and all the class likewise. The benches and desks were polished, worn with use; the walnut trees had grown, and the hops he'd planted himself now climbed around the windows to the roof. How heart-breaking it must be for the poor man to leave all these things, to hear his sister packing their things in the room above.

They would have to leave the country the next day, forever.

All the same, he bravely kept class to the very end. After writing, we had a history lesson, then the little ones sang together their BA BE BI BO BU. At the rear of the room, old Hauser put on his glasses and, holding his primer in both hands, chanted the letters with them. It was obviously a great effort for him; his voice trembled with emotion and it was so funny to hear him that we wanted to laugh and cry. Ah! I do remember that last class…

Suddenly the church clock struck noon. During the Angelus, we could hear the Prussians' trumpets beneath the windows as they returned from their exercises… M. Hamel rose, colourless, from his chair. Never had he appeared so large.

'My friends, say, my, I… I…' But something choked him. He couldn't say it.

He turned to the board, took a piece of chalk and, using all of his strength, he wrote as large as he could,

'VIVE LA FRANCE!'

He stayed there, his head resting on the wall, and wordlessly used his hand to motion to us: 'It's over... you may go.'